BLACKSTAR

BOMBER

THE AUTHOR

 T. C. Miller's twenty-four year Air Force career, combined with his study of Hakkoryu Jujitsu give him a unique perspective. It was during his assignment at Mather Air Force Base, California that he formulated the basic plot for his debut novel, *BlackStar Bomber.* His love of hiking and camping produced the locale information that inspired him to write his second book, *Black Star Bay.*

He is the founder of *Coffee With the Author,* a twice-weekly event in the center court of Shawnee Mall, Shawnee, OK that features local authors discussing and signing their books.

T.C. is a speaker at writing conferences He is also available for televideo, (Skype) calls to conferences and book clubs.

He is a member of the *Military Writers Society of America* (MWSA), the *Oklahoma Writers Federation Incorporated* (OWFI), and the *McLoud Writers Group.* T.C. welcomes comments and suggestions in the form of e-mails at:

tcmiller@blackstaropsgroup.com

BLACKSTAR BOMBER

BY

T. C. MILLER

Cover by Ken Farmer

ISBN-10: 0996248331
ISBN-13: 978-0-9962483-3-4

ISBN -13: 978-0-9962483-2-7   E
ISBN - 10 0996248323

Timber Creek Press
Imprint of Timber Creek Productions, LLC
312 N. Commerce St.
Gainesville, Texas

ACKNOWLEDGMENT

No book is written in a vacuum, or without the support of family and friends. Thank you to my wife of almost twenty five years, Jake, for her assistance and patience through the sometimes all-absorbing process. Ken Farmer and Buck Stienke of *Timber Creek Press* have provided invaluable assistance and advice. I can only hope they are as proud as I am of the result.

Other writers have also provided encouragement and support. Thank you, Doran Ingrham, Loree Lough, Joe McKinney and members of the McLoud Writers Group.

Contact Us:
Published by: Timber Creek Press
timbercreekpresss@yahoo.com
www.timbercreekpress.net
Twitter: @pagact
214-533-4964

Facebook Fan Page: T.C. Miller, Author
Website: www.blackstaropsgroup.com

DEDICATION

This book is dedicated to my smart and lovely wife, Jake.

First printing - 6/22/2015

PRAISE FOR *BLACKJACK BOMBER*

"This book is a must read - I couldn't put it down. It's full of suspense and surprises in each chapter that get you thinking... that was well thought out - could it really happen? I look forward to the next book!"
—Lauren, *Amazon.com*

"TC Miller has created a true page-turner…There are twists and turns in this story that will definitely hold the reader's attention. …guaranteed to keep you involved in the story so do not start your read late at night. I found myself staying up far too late just to see how things worked out, or as the case may be - didn't work out for the group. Great job, TC Miller, can't wait for your next book."
—Nancy Pendleton, *Examiner.com*

"Compelling drama, a page turner with multiple twists, couldn't read fast enough to reach the finale. Can hardly wait for the next book."
—Barbara Telford, *Amazon.com*

"A group of jaded middle-aged men who get together for their weekly card meetings ponder their dead end lives and try to find a way to break out of their doldrums. What happens next, in this riveting thriller is a story that could very well be taken from today's headlines. T.C. Miller delivers a powerful story that will keep you turning the pages until the exciting conclusion."
—Jeffrey Miller, Author of *War Remains*.

"This is a GREAT book for those who like suspense, mystery, apprehension, and things military…the attention to detail in this story is incredible. You can tell that Mr. Miller has Air Force experience. Being an Air Force veteran myself, I especially

enjoyed the incredibly accurate detail of how such an event
would be handled. It brings back memories of operational
excercises I used to do. I am looking forward to the next book.
And, it would be GREAT if a movie could be made based on
this book. Exciting stuff!!!"
—AirForceVet, *Amazon.com*

OTHER NOVELS FROM
TIMBER CREEK PRESS
www.timbercreekpress.net

MILITARY ACTION/TECHNO

BLACK EAGLE FORCE: Eye of the Storm (Revised)
by Buck Stienke and Ken Farmer

BLACK EAGLE FORCE: Sacred Mountain (Book #2)
by Buck Stienke and Ken Farmer
www.tinyurl.com/SacMtn2

RETURN of the STARFIGHTER (Book #3)
by Buck Stienke and Ken Farmer
www.tinyurl.com/StarF01

BLACK EAGLE FORCE: BLOOD IVORY (Book #4)
by Buck Stienke and Ken Farmer with Doran Ingrham
www.tinyurl.com/befivory

BLACK EAGLE FORCE: FOURTH REICH (Book #5)
By Buck Stienke and Ken Farmer
www.tinyurl.com/befreich

BLOOD BROTHERS - Doran Ingrham, Buck Stienke
and Ken Farmer
Www.tinyurl.com/bloodbrothers1

DARK SECRET - Doran Ingrham
Http://tinyurl.com/darksecret-2
BLACKSTAR BAY by T.C. Miller
Http://amzn.to/1oYSFO6

HISTORICAL FICTION WESTERN
THE NATIONS by Ken Farmer and Buck Stienke
Www.tinyurl.com/the-nations-Bass
Audio version: www.tinyurl.com/NationsAudio
HAUNTED FALLS by Ken Farmer and Buck Stienke
Www.tinyurl.com/haunted-falls-Bass
Audio version: www.tinyurl.com/HauntedFallsAudio
HELL HOLE by Ken Farmer
Www.tinyurl.com/hell-hole-Bass3

Audio version: www.tinyurl.com/HcllHoleAudio
ACROSS the RED by Ken Farmer & Buck Stienke
Www.tinyurl.com/AcrossRed

Audio version: www.tinyurl.com/AcrossRedAudio
DEVIL'S CANYON by Buck Stienke
Http://tinyurl.com/devils-canyon-B

SYFY
LEGEND OF AURORA by Ken Farmer & Buck
Stienke
www.tinyurl.com/LegendAurora-E
AURORA: INVASION by Ken Farmer & Buck Stienke
Www.tinyurl.com/AuroraInvasion

Coming Soon
MILITARY ACTION/TECHNO
BLACK EAGLE FORCE: ISIS by Buck Stienke and
Ken Farmer
BLACK STAR MOUNTAIN by T.C. Miller

HISTORICAL FICTION WESTERN
BASS and the LADY by Ken Farmer & Buck Stienke
Book five of the Bass Reeves Saga

GLOSSARY

Alert Pad	Facility on USAF bases where aircraft are kept for immediate response missions.
ABG	Air Base Group
APB	All Points Bulletin.
APU	Auxillary Power Unit-Electrical generator that supplies power when the aircraft engines are not running.
BDUs	Battle Dress Uniform-Sometimes referred to as fatigues. In 1988, they were the Woodland Camoflage Pattern, which consists of varying shades of green and black in a random pattern for concealment in forests.
BlackStar	Anti-terrorist destructive device carried on all US aircraft and vessels that carry nuclear weapons.
BSOG	BlackStar Operations Group - Special investigative section within the NSA.
BUFF	Big Ugly Freakin' Fellow-Nickname for B-52
IMA	Individual Mobilization Augmentee, Air Force Reserve Program for one day-a-month service with active duty units.
NSA	National Security Agency - Conducts electronic surveillance programs and cryptologic support for US government agencies.
NSC	National Security Council - Advises the President and Congress.
NRO	National Reconnaissance Office - Responsible for surveillance satellite operation and data analysis.
NEST	Nuclear Emergency Security Team-Specialized response units that recover nuclear materials after an incident and perform cleanup of radioactive material.
ORI	Operational Readiness Inspection

Para Cord	Parachute cord.
POTUS	President of the United States
POV	Privately owned vehicle.
SAFE-HAVEN	Coded directive for nuclear material transportation teams to report to the nearest secure facility for safeguarding, usually after an incident.
SAC	Strategic Air Command
SAC/CC	Commander, SAC
SORT	Special Operations Response Team
SPS	Security Police Squadron
SRT	Special Response Team
Suppressor	Mechanical device used to reduce the sound of the muzzle blast from a weapon. Sometimes referred to as a can, it is usually a machined piece that is attached to the barrel. Often referred to erroneously as a "silencer."

TIMBER CREEK PRESS

CHAPTER 1

COMMUNIST EAST BERLIN
JUNE, 1984

"Well, Tupelo, or whatever your real name is, guess we've come to the end of the line…Been nice working with you."

"Same here, Butte, but you sound like we're fixin' to die, or something…Mission's not quite finished."

Bart Winfield, the tall, rangy figure dressed all in black strode across the flat-roofed building toward a wide double chimney with Butte close behind. They carefully picked their way around short vent pipes that would have been easy to trip over in the moonless night.

"Wait, you're serious, aren't you? I mean, we're on the roof of a building surrounded by dozens of Soviet Spetsnaz troops and you still expect to finish the mission?"

"That's why the NSA sent us, isn't it?"

"Yes, and I suppose that little device is worth a couple of agents dying, but how're you going to get it back to our people?"

"Gonna hand it to 'em. Don't know about you, but I'm a little young to cash in my chips."

"Okay, I'll go along with your little fantasy, but unless you've got a helicopter hidden up here, I'd say it's pretty much over for us."

"No chopper, but the next best thing to it." He reached the ten-foot tall chimney and opened the door of a service compartment next to it. "Should be right here...Sure 'nough, our local contact didn't drop the ball. Help me haul these rigs to the center of the roof."

"Parachutes? What the hell good will it do to drop right into their waiting arms?" Butte said with a note of frustration.

"Because, pardner, we're not goin' down, we're goin' up."

"Now I know you're crazy...There's no wind at all, not even a breeze. Besides, there's no way we can float all the way over the wall...It's at least a mile away."

"Have faith, my friend...This is are our ticket home. Just put the harness on and stand back."

He looked at him with a puzzled expression and replied, "Whatever...You're the team leader."

He put the harness on and fastened it securely. Tupelo did the same and stepped back as he motioned to Butte. "Stay at least twenty feet away."

The sound of security agents pounding on the stairwell door indicated they had only a few minutes left before their capture. The interrogation that followed would undoubtedly lead to their death, since neither was inclined to divulge any details of the operation.

"Well, like I said earlier, it's been..."

Butte was interrupted by Bart, who pointed toward the western sky. "Looks like our ride's here."

The inkblot-like shadow of a C-130 cargo plane flying just over the rooftops was visible only because it blocked out the stars behind it. Bart watched it intently, silently counting out the seconds. "Pull your D-ring now!"

Butte hesitated until he saw Tupelo reach across and pull the parachute release on his rig. He did the same and was startled when a self-inflating balloon popped out of his backpack and quickly rose into the night sky. Both balloons shot up and tugged at the harnesses. He rose up on tiptoes and grasped the straps.

"Hang on, pardner...You're about to get the ride of your life," Bart yelled as the stairway door yielded to the pounding on the other side.

Spetsnaz troops with automatic weapons poured from the shattered door that now hung haphazardly from the top hinge only. It took a moment for their eyes to adjust to the darkness and even longer to locate the American spies.

Before they could react, however, the roar of the four-engine turboprop plane caused them to freeze in their tracks and stare up. A V-shaped prong mounted to the front of the plane snagged the support lines for the two balloons and dragged them to the tail of the aircraft where a winch began pulling the two attached men upward.

Tupelo felt like the sudden jerk might pull him apart and was glad he had tightly fastened the straps securely around him. He hoped the other man had done the same. The aircraft did the tightest turnabout it could while trailing the precious human cargo. It passed over a different set of border guards who stared cluelessly up into the night sky.

The stealth C-130 returned to its home base after the two men were winched aboard and the back ramp was raised to the closed position. They stood inside the cargo compartment while a couple of Special Ops loadmasters helped them remove the Fulton STARS Extraction System harnesses.

Butte stomped the slatted wooden cargo floor and shook himself all over like a wet dog coming in from the rain. "Wow! Man, you weren't kidding…That was the ride of my life…but, don't think I ever want to do it again!"

Tupelo grinned and replied, "For sure. You gotta love a job that takes you seconds from death and lets you have this much fun, to boot."

He patted the electronic device strapped securely to his chest and looked at one of the helmeted loadmasters. His reflection stared back at him from the shiny visor. "Hey, pard, any way a body could get a hot cup of Joe?"

MATHER AFB, CALIFORNIA
PRESENT DAY

The street was poorly lit and it was late. Jake Thomas knew he shouldn't be there alone. "Are you my partner?" The question was directed to a tall figure standing next to him in a long black coat who, although a stranger, seemed oddly familiar. It moved its head from side to side in a silent reply. "Then who is my partner?"

No movement this time. The figure tilted its head and stared at him, its facial features a murky blur.

Jake tried to remember his partner's name, but not a clue came to mind. *That's not the way it should be…They're the one you should always be able to rely on.* That was what the instructor of every law enforcement class he had ever taken drilled into him from the very first day.

He had trained in one martial art or another since childhood and been taught to rely on his abilities alone. On the other hand, Jake knew teamwork was essential in law enforcement. Sheer numbers were often necessary to cordon off an area or to defend against multiple attackers. His entire life had been spent preparing for combat and law enforcement. He felt like he should be working with a partner, so where were they?

Maybe I was injured. A blow to the head or a traumatic fall could have left him confused. He stood motionless for a while and tried to orient himself. Still, no answer came to mind. A haziness began swelling up inside of him and his heart pounded in his ears. *Calm down, dummy.*

The uneasiness inside him grew like tide rushing into a small bay. He glanced around and noticed he was standing in a vacant intersection. A strong urge to move away gripped him and he considered his options. A glance to the left showed only a ghostly image of meager traffic three blocks away on a cross street. An eight-foot construction fence around a demolition site blocked the path to his right.

Jake stared straight ahead and slowly focused on a narrow, dimly-lit street that was more like an alley. It looked deserted with only a pale yellow glow here and there in the windows of nondescript buildings.

He shuddered as he was drawn toward the end of the block. Foggy references to concealed threats and hidden foes came to him through the haze. Flashes of faceless bad guys and whispered threats lingered. False identities that concealed ulterior motives echoed through the darkness.

His feet felt like they were encased in concrete as he moved slowly toward whatever awaited him in the lonely darkness. The black-coated figure stood motionless as Jake moved away, offering not even so much as a good bye. The comforting glow of the solitary streetlight faded and each step drew him closer to the dim passage ahead. A sense of overwhelming dread settled on his shoulders as a heavy mist arose and swirled about him. The stink of moldy garbage, stale urine and vomit assaulted his nostrils.

Storefronts faded into the thickening fog and direction no longer had meaning. He was startled by faint whispers on both side of the street as shadows danced on the shiny pavement.

An ominous scraping noise behind him caused him to whirl around as a shadowy form retreated silently into the mist. He assumed a defensive stance and swept the area for attackers.

None appeared. Still, the foreboding sense of danger increased with each pounding heartbeat. His breathing quickened and he forced himself to control his respiration and heart rate.

Years of training came into play as the warrior within him prepared for battle. He flexed his muscles one-by-one and switched to stealthy movements that let him glide purposefully in any direction. Like a ballet dancer, each movement was measured in balance and timing. His sensitivity increased to the point he could feel fog settle on his skin.

A sinister shape rushed at him from the mist and he responded with calculated movements that shifted from one position to another. The hooded figure swung at him with an overhead blow from a heavy weapon. Jake slid to one side and deflected the attack with a strike to the elbow that paralyzed the attacker's arm.

A clanging sound as it hit the pavement confirmed it was a piece of pipe. He parried a strike from the attacker's other arm and followed through with a crunching blow to the throat. A gurgling gasp testified to his accuracy and the attacker sank to his knees. A snap kick to the side of the head gave merciful unconsciousness to the thug.

Jake swept the area again in time to meet a second attacker with a semicircular sweep. He delivered a shattering strike to the man's stationary knee and the figure rolled away into the darkening fog.

He paused to regain his fighting composure and his heightened senses told him there were numerous foes in close proximity. None moved toward him and he could not see them in the thickening pea soup. Instead, he heard brief movement and saw ghosts of shadows. An occasional whiff of unwashed bodies and the sound of muted voices teased him.

"Come out and face me," he challenged the invisible assailants."

The only response was the muffled murmur of the night breeze. Sweat trickled down the back of his neck and his entire body tingled with a prickly feeling. The coppery taste of adrenaline filled his sinuses.

He spun in place, hoping they didn't start throwing things at him from the haze and praying they didn't have guns. His pulse pounded, and his body ached with keen anticipation. His knees began to weaken and muscles became knotted like guy wires. He did his best to relax and keep blood flowing normally. Suddenly, a startled gasp jolted him awake.

Jake sat straight up in bed and took long and deep breaths. His T-shirt and the bed sheets were soaking wet. He slowly swung his feet over the edge of the bed and stumbled to the bathroom.

The flickering fluorescent tube above the mirror cast a greenish glow that highlighted the creases in his forehead and the fatigue in his eyes. He twisted the hot water tap and stared numbly at himself until the mirror was hazy with steam.

The eyes in the mirror were weary from the inner demons he

faced almost every night. The skin under them sagged in desperation. He held both hands under the faucet, and then splashed his face, rinsing away as much of the sweat and nightmare as he could. It was one more night spent running from his demons. One more night in an endless stream.

He plodded slowly back to his bed and lay there staring at the ceiling. The old-fashioned wind-up clock on the bedside table ticked off the minutes with military efficiency as the seconds marched by in a steady column.

He longed for the dawn that would bring a new day, when he could resume his duties in military law enforcement. He eagerly awaited the start of the day shift and the structured order of the day-to-day routine of an Air Force installation. He let out a long drawn-out sigh and eventually returned to a fitful sleep.

***

CHAPTER 2

JULY, 1988
MATHER AIR FORCE BASE, CALIFORNIA

Her head nodded closer and closer to her chest and her shoulders slumped as she leaned forward in the rickety, cast-off desk chair. Sitting in the doorway of the old wooden guard shack staring out at the empty road that led in from the county highway to a side gate of Mather Air Force Base, she stifled a yawn. The steady chirping sound of crickets humming on the night air lured her into a near catatonic state. The mildewy smell of the night air tickled her nose.

She reluctantly got to her feet and stepped outside. Stretching was awkward in the four-foot by six-foot shack that held a curtained toilet in the back and a bookshelf with half a dozen three-ring binders filled with regulations and procedures on the short counter in front.

Airman First Class Joanna Davies stretched her arms above her head and yawned just this side of violence. A delightful shiver ran the full length of her petite five-foot-four-inch frame.

She reached back into the shack, grabbed the wall-phone receiver and dialed 114 without looking.

"Desk Sergeant," was the greeting from Sergeant John Haverhill, one of her softball teammates.

"Hey, Big John, what's happenin'?"

"Same old, same old…Trying to stay awake, just like you. Can't believe how slow it's been. Whatchu doing?"

"Writing a letter to my fiancé…Maybe gonna get some studying done for the promotion exam. Mostly just trying to stay awake."

"Seems to be the norm tonight."

"Who ever came up with an eleven at night until seven in the morning shift, anyway? We should be sleeping," she noted.

"Exactly…Sunrise is when you get up, not go to bed."

"Guess somebody's gotta watch out for all those folks snoring away in their racks."

"Yeah, us…the few and the proud."

"Not sure, Dude, but I think that's the Marines."

"Oh, yeah…Hoo-rah!"

"That's Army…Should be Oorah," she offered.

"Right…I'll make a note."

She glanced down at her neat uniform and picked at a stray thread, known in the services as an Irish pennant. "Whoops, gotta go…Got company."

A distant pair of headlights interrupted the follow-up yawn forming in the back of her throat. She hung up the phone, rubbed her eyes and squinted out through the darkness. Whatever was coming up the road was moving way too fast, causing the headlights to sway and bounce erratically. "Oh, no," she mumbled, "Not another drunk."

A retired lieutenant colonel crashed this gate less than a month earlier a few minutes after 0300. Joanna glanced down at the digital chronograph her parents got her for Christmas two years ago—0256 glowed silently back at her.

The inebriated retiree had not even slowed down for the hapless security policeman who shouted, "Halt!" behind his raised hand. In fact, the dusty old Mercedes continued through the intersection, crossed ten yards of dusty scrub, struck a culvert and went airborne.

It gained enough altitude to clear the steel beams of an anti-vehicle barricade and came to rest with most of the front-end pushed through the twelve-foot high chain link fence that surrounded the alert pad. The colonel was so drunk he stumbled out of the car and passed out, which was probably better. Any resistance to security teams would have been met with deadly force.

The Special Response Team took a little more than two and a half minutes to locate and handcuff him with plastic zip-ties. The Alert Pad was too sensitive and crucial an area for anything less than an immediate and forceful response.

The B-52 bombers with their nuclear weapons and KC-135 in-air refueling tankers loaded with jet fuel were parked and ready to go with just a few minute's notice. They were some of the last remnants of the Cold War and were guarded with a zeal that approached fanaticism.

The incident was quietly settled the next day. Filing charges against the colonel could have resulted in the permanent withdrawal of his base privileges and possibly even jail time. Neither happened, but not because of his rank or any political pull. It was his first offense, although that was not the reason he escaped the wrath of the law.

A much larger concern for the base commander was the possible disclosure of a breach of security. The effectiveness of security for nuclear weapons depended on secrecy. The more information foreign agents could discover about breaches, the more likely they were to compromise security.

All security flights were briefed during guard-mount about the incident and steps were taken to prevent a recurrence, including the installation of a longer and stronger barrier at the end of the T-intersection.

Procedural changes were also made. The red Emergency Action Books, or EABs, now instructed security personnel to quickly react to potential threats and report them immediately.

Failure to follow procedures definitely affects promotion. She pulled the reg off the shelf and opened it to the section entitled *Challenging Unknowns*.

Step One dictated an attempt to identify the vehicle. Joanna stared out the window at two yellow dots of light bouncing around half a mile away. "So much for that one," she mumbled.

Step Two was revised after last month's incident and now directed her to report any nighttime encounter to the Operations NCO immediately. She grabbed the old-fashioned wall phone and dialed 114 again.

"Desk Sergeant," John Haverhill monotoned.

"Hey, Jack, Joanna…Got an unknown vehicle approaching my twenty that seems to be driving erratically."

"Noted…You want backup?"

"Don't know…Looks like he's stopped and turned off his headlights. Could be a couple looking for a place to make out. Maybe mixed up our road with the one that leads to the old mine tailings…Those three-story high piles of rock do offer privacy."

"Don't they ever? Been out there myself a few times to drink some beers and plink at cans," Jack declared. "Kinda hidden, though."

"Yeah…But you're right…They're a little hard to find, especially in the dark. Probably realize their mistake any minute, spin around and lay rubber…Especially after seeing the Federal Installation signs, or the gate and my guard shack. After all, they wouldn't wannna mess with a security policeman, right?"

"Uh huh, 'cause you know how much they fear us," he said sarcastically. "Most of 'em think we're nothing but glorified night watchmen."

"If they only knew about the weapons training and exercises…"

"Or that Excellent on our last ORI…"

"Put the fear of God into 'em," she proclaimed.

"Somehow, I doubt it."

"Me too…Say, Jack, on second thought, why don't you send the flight chief over? Might be a good idea to document what good troops we're being…You know, following procedures and all." Her slight southern drawl lent a deceptively casual air to the steel-edged request.

"Sure…If nothing else, might keep Sergeant Thomas awake."

"Yeah, like that's a problem…Wish I had half the experience that dude has," she said. "…Always running off on some classified TDY or another."

"Better than when he's here…Pretty tough on his troops."

"Roger that…Really drilled me on the regs when he was my FTO."

The radio on her hip crackled. "Uh, Ops One, this is Base…Request you assist Seven with an unknown at her location, over."

The reply was immediate, "Roger that, Base…Ops One on the way. Details?"

"Affirmative, One," Jack replied. "Seven reports subject vehicle has approached her post to approximately eight hundred meters and is stationary with headlights off, over."

"Seven, Ops One," Thomas addressed Joanna directly. "Can you identify subject vehicle or occupants?"

Joanna keyed the radio mike clipped to her shirt pocket. "Negative, One…Still way off base and outside my lights. It appears to be a truck or van though, over."

"Acknowledged, Seven. ETA is two minutes, out."

She switched back to the phone. "Thanks, Jack…Glad he's on the way…Nothing else, it might take the edge off the boredom. You know, seeing a live person and all."

"Know what you mean. Call me if you need anything… even just to talk. Sure ain't got nothin' goin' on here."

She smiled and hung up the phone. The smile faded as the headlights of the unidentified vehicle burst into life and started moving toward her.

She subconsciously reached for the M16 combat rifle in the rack below the window, unclipped it and pulled it to her side. *Might seem silly…But I'm alone in the middle of the night, a few hundred yards from the Alert Pad.*

The ten-acre compound held two KC-135, in-air-refueling tankers and five B-52 bombers with highly-classified weapons parked within its secure perimeter. Although, as the press releases put it, Mather Air Force Base would neither confirm, nor deny the existence of nuclear weapons on base, everybody assumed they were there.

The mere possession of just one of the nuclear devices would be a coup for any terrorist cell in one of two-dozen countries around the world. It was a tribute to the men and women of the security forces of the worldwide nuclear community that not one bomb, artillery shell or missile had ever been lost to the political maniacs and suicide bombers who hungered for them.

Joanna mentally went over the security procedures for the Alert Pad. Two three-man Special Response Teams constantly roamed the grounds in armored vehicles. A five-story high structure nicknamed The Tower overlooked the area and contained sophisticated alarm panels connected to hundreds of sensors. The two-person crew could tell you the weight of a jack rabbit passing near any one of the sensors scattered around inside the Alert Pad when everything worked right—in theory.

Unfortunately, the equipment didn't always function to design specifications. Aging electronics often fed miscues to the alarm panel. Each and every "hit" was investigated like the real thing, often with bored irritation by the SRT sent to respond. It was annoying to gear up to one hundred percent for a few misplaced electrons or a computer hiccup. It was their job, however, and they strove to be uniform in their response.

The security lights reflected off the windshield of the approaching vehicle, now within a quarter mile of the gate and moving very slowly into the pool of light that surrounded it. *An armored car?* Her anxiety level shot up like a rocket and she stabbed the mike button on the radio.

"Ops One, Seven. Unidentified vehicle appears to be an armored car."

"An Armored Personnel Carrier?"

"No, a bank armored car…You know, the kind that carries money. What's it doing out here at night?"

"Don't know, Seven, but I don't like it. Base, I'm declaring a situation. Request the Alert Pad get an SRT over near Seven

ASAP. I'm going Code Two." He switched on the red and blue flashing light bar on top of his patrol car and floored the accelerator. The plain-Jane, six-cylinder government vehicle lurched ahead and slowly began gathering speed. He could see Guard Post 7 a half-mile ahead around a flat curve. Everything should be under control in a few more minutes. *Hope the Alert Pad SRT is on their toes.*

Joanna turned her head slightly, saw the approaching red and blue lights of the patrol car and breathed a sigh of relief. She would feel a lot better when Sergeant Thomas was on scene. She started to move toward the chain-link gate to close it, but stopped when a motion drew her attention to the unknown vehicle.

It had stopped about a hundred feet from the gate and her post. The passenger door opened and two figures slunk out of the vehicle. They crouched next to it while unpacking something from a case. One of them rested a tubular-shaped object on the fender of the vehicle. Even in the dim light, Joanna could see a cylinder. She keyed her mike and yelled, "Sarge, RPG!"

The nose of the patrol car dipped as Jake slammed on the brakes. The driver's door flew open and he rolled smoothly out of the vehicle.

A flash of light from the attacker's weapon illuminated a puff of smoke and a ball of flame erupted on the passenger side of the patrol car. The explosion catapulted it over him and the other lane into the dry drainage ditch along the other side of the road.

Joanna knew Thomas' chances of escape were slim and began thinking of her own. She ran back to her post, hit the light switches and the guard booth and surrounding area began to blend into the darkness.

Crouching low with the M-16 firmly in her grasp, she ran for the cover of a nearby ditch, dropped into it and began belly-crawling as fast as possible. The fading amber glow from the sodium vapor security lights guided her.

She managed to tuck most of her body into a culvert before her senses were overwhelmed by an earsplitting roar. Burning pieces of the guard shack rained down on the ditch and started half a dozen small grass fires. The smell of wood smoke and explosives blossomed around her and hit her like a wall.

The shifting rattle of a diesel engine penetrated the fading roar of the explosion. She poked her head up in time to see the armored car slowly gather speed as it rolled past her post toward the Alert Pad.

The scene played out in slow motion and she felt like she was watching a movie. The vehicle stopped in the middle of the intersection and the driver's door flew open. The glow of the burning patrol car silhouetted a shadowy figure as it pointed the RPG toward the Alert Pad, fired and climbed back into the armored car.

The explosion cleared a hole in the barricade and the driver expertly shifted gears as the armored car lumbered awkwardly through the crumpled mass of steel. The chain link fence of the Alert Pad stretched like the mailed fist of a medieval knight and collapsed under the force of the forty-ton vehicle.

This is freaking unbelievable...They're in the Alert Pad! She looked around for the SRT and spotted it as it headed for a distant breach in the fence on the other side of the Alert Pad.

Powerful security lights inside the compound mounted on thirty-foot high towers cast a pool of light over the area that made it nearly as bright as day. They blinked and began to fade to an anemic yellow until emergency generators kicked on to rekindle them.

They were no sooner on the way to their usual brightness when they died once again and the scene was thrown into darkness in the moonless night. Only flames from the burning guard shack and the patrol car shed any light.

Lights around the base were also methodically winking out. She brought the mike as close to her mouth as she could and tried to sound calm. "Base, Seven...Base, come in, please."

"Seven, Base...What the hell's going on?"

"We're under attack, that's what!" Joanna's voice went up in pitch. "Ops One got hit by an RPG..."

"Say again, Seven?"

"I repeat, Ops One's hit by a grenade...It's toast and my post is gone. Armored car's in the Alert Pad on the east side...Other intruder's on the west side. Security lights are out...An SRT's engaging them in the dark...We need help out here, now!"

She looked up in time to see the tower erupt in a ball of

flame that shot fiery tendrils out thirty feet or more. It folded in half and collapsed.

"Control tower…gone."

"What about the crew?"

"No way to know."

"Hang in there, Jo. I'll get help to you ASAP."

"I don't believe this…They're in the freakin' Alert Pad! Never seen anything like this…Like a bad dream."

"I know…Not supposed to happen."

"But it's happening," she said. "I've heard rumors of them testing defenses…But why here…why now?"

"No idea…Whatever it is, though, it's bad news."

"And well-planned. Power to half of the base knocked out…Two sets of perps and they know the layout." A thought bubbled up inside her like a green hot dog. She felt nauseous and infuriated at the same time and fought to maintain her composure. "Gotta be an inside job."

"Could be…They've been real lucky…"

"Not luck…planning. Must have scoped us out…Maybe from the old mine tailings or that stand of cottonwoods over the east fence. Always seem to be civilians there, right off-base…Wait, footsteps coming…Be off the air for a bit."

"Roger that, Jo."

The steady crunching sounds reminded her of moving along in formation during training exercises. She slowly raised her head above the level of the road and used a cluster of cattails to disguise herself. Light from the burning guard shack cast a dancing orange glow on a short, bearded guy holding what looked like a machine pistol at waist height.

He was standing spread-legged about twenty feet from the remains of the shack. The telltale bulge of a suppressor sat at the end of the rifle. He raised it to chest height and half a dozen flashes spit out the end of the rifle, accompanied by muffled pops. Spurts of dust and gravel erupted around the remains of the guard shack. *Guess he thought I'd panic.*

A second figure was moving toward Sergeant Thomas's burning vehicle. The two were trying to clean up the area, but she could tell by the way they moved they had little military training. Too many Jean Claude Van Damme movies left them with the mistaken impression that swagger replaced training. They thought they knew how to operate like seasoned mercenaries.

She hoped to prove them wrong by using every ounce of her knowledge and training against them. She reached down and turned off the radio that had stayed securely clipped to her belt. There would be no stray transmissions or static to alert them. She knew the next few minutes would create a lot of questions later.

First, I need to get through this. The main force of intruders must not know she was still a threat. *Gotta take him out with no noise.* The M-16 by her side could be heard half a mile away. *No good.* Normally, the Mace on her leather equipment belt would subdue a rowdy suspect. *Not now...This guy wants me dead. God willing, I'll take him out first.*

The six-inch long Gerber knife slid noiselessly out of the ankle sheath. She held the knife with the blade facing toward her and waited patiently while the intruder moved past the culvert. Joanna stood and slipped up behind him.

He either heard her breathing or caught her scent and started to turn around. She grabbed a handful of his hair with her left hand and yanked his head back. The razor sharp knife slid across the width of his exposed throat.

Gurgling noises stifled any real cry for help. The move was successful. She hung on to him so he couldn't spin around and shoot her. A few spurts of gravel erupted around their feet as the intruder spasmodically jerked the trigger. His partners would think he located the guard at Post 7 and dispatched them. The clattering sound of the empty assault pistol as it dropped to the pavement let her know she was safe for the moment.

The intruder clawed ineffectively at Joanna's arm for a few more seconds as she felt his energy slipping away. He stopped struggling, dropped to his knees and jerked a few times before falling forward. *No need to cuff him.* She felt something sticky on her hand and wiped it off on the dead man's jacket.

A feeling of revulsion hit her like a blow to the stomach. She staggered back as a voice surged from deep inside her. *You killed him!* She picked up the intruder's weapon and moved back into the ditch.

Joanna crouched on rubbery knees and softly sobbed. Her hands shook and her whole body quivered. Her insides were colder than a walk-in freezer and she needed to throw up.

Time to man up or give up... She shivered one last time. A twist of a knob and the radio crackled with energy. It took her a few moments to clear her head and pick up the flow of urgent communications. Supervisors were taking a head count of their troops and actions were confirmed and recorded.

Senior base staff members were contacted and pyramid recall rosters activated to bring the base to full staffing. The fire department had already quelled a number of small fires and was ready to move in on others when the gunfire stopped.

She keyed the mike and spoke softly, "Base, Seven, over."

The quickness of the response startled her. "Seven, Base, what's your twenty?"

"Rather not say...They may be listening. Also, call me by name...They may know our post designations. Understood?"

"Roger that. What happened, Jo?"

"What happened?" She screeched into the radio. "It turned to crap, that's what!" She realized her voice was two octaves higher than normal. "Killed one and the other's headed toward Thomas...Need to get over there to help...You need to get us backup, ASAP."

"Acknowledged, Jo, but stay put 'til we figure out what's going on...Thomas can take care of himself...You could get caught in the crossfire. Right now, I gotta go...busy, over."

"You're not listening, Jack...He needs me...may be wounded or trapped."

"I heard you...Don't argue with me. Haven't heard from him...He may not even be alive. Look, gotta get back to work...Haven't gone through half the checklist."

"Screw the checklist, Jack...You're right, we don't know if he's dead or alive," she continued before he could interrupt her. "...Need to check it out. I'm not leaving him alone."

"Listen up, Airman, we need to regroup. Stay where you are…And that's an order. Besides, you still have an entry point to guard…could be more perps coming. Stay calm…Base, over and out."

Stay calm? Joanna played the phrase over in her mind and realized Jack was right. Whatever was going on called for calm, cool action and teamwork. She pressed the mike switch and said in the calmest voice she could muster, "Roger that…Davies standing by and clear."

Her gaze shifted from the incoming road to the burning guard shack and finally, to the burning patrol vehicle. She whispered a quick prayer for Thomas and hoped she could share a cup of coffee with him in the morning.

The rest of the shift was going to be one long grueling affair and she knew she had to remain as vigilant as possible. She pulled her emergency Snickers bar out of her pocket, peeled back the label and took a big bite. The peanuts and nougat tasted really good and would help stall shock.

A shiver ran down her spine and she shrank a little deeper into the cold damp ditch as she took a drink from her canteen. This could turn out to be one of the longest nights of her life.

EXACT LOCATION UNDISCLOSED
EUROPEAN CONTINENT

"You are confident this operative can accomplish his mission?" The man asking the question was a senior leader in a global clandestine intelligence organization called the Consortium. The words were spoken in an accent that hinted at an origin in Eastern Europe tempered with a diplomatic background. He was in a private meeting with one of his aides.

The executive office was paneled in dark wood with built-in shelves filled with musty old tomes and mementos from a lifetime in espionage work. Heavy dark drapes covered the nearly floor to ceiling windows.

He sat behind a massive desk made of the same wood as the shelves and puffed on a Cuban cigar. Wraithlike circles of dense smoke engulfed him as he leaned back in a leather chair that was once used by Joseph Stalin during his reign of terror in the old Soviet Union.

The aide swallowed hard before he answered, fearing the Commissioner was trying somehow to trap him. "I would not have brought him to your attention without some measure of trust in his abilities," the younger man replied. *Especially since my reputation and maybe my life are at stake.*

"Why have I not known of him before?" The senior man's tone made it less a question than a demand.

"We only recently were made aware of his existence…"

"By whom?"

"One our clients in the United States. He was assigned to the same deep-cover operation twenty years ago with this former spy. The client operates a smuggling ring in Northern California and uses our services quite often."

"For which he pays well," the older man commented.

"Indeed, sir. He and many of his associates trained under the old Soviet Union. As a matter of fact, the leader of the smuggling ring went through his initial training with this operative. He is conducting an operation we are supporting with classified information. The goal is to obtain nuclear material from a military base."

"The one in Sacramento?"

"Yes," the aide answered.

"I have never understood the Americans' propensity for locating military bases near major cities, especially one that is the capitol for a state. How foolish…Do they think other countries will hesitate to attack? I think not."

"Agreed, sir…The policy they refer to as Mutually Assured Destruction, assumes other countries fear annihilation if they do so."

"They may be correct, but now we are getting off subject…Back to this operative, what is his name?"

"His real name is Yuri Petrovich, but he has been using the cover Rick Eichner."

"Petrovich is a common name…Is he related to Yuri Petrovich the member of the inner council in the old Soviet government?"

"Yes, he is the son, which is how he was chosen for the intelligence field. His father pressured one old friend after another to assure the assignment for him."

"I do not understand. Why would he want to get his son into a job that would take him out of the mother country for so long? Was there animosity between them?"

"Sorry, sir, I do not have an answer. Shall I make further inquiries on your behalf?"

"No...It is irrelevant. Tell me, how is the operation progressing?"

"I have studied information from all of our sources and can only conclude it is going well...Although, to be sure, it is only at the midpoint of Eichner's plan."

"Midpoint?"

"Yes, sir, that is what I've been told...Shall I keep you informed?"

"Yes, daily...Unless something of significance occurs."

"The next phase of the plan is about to begin...However, it will take at least a day or two."

"Fine, now back to our friends in North Africa. Have arrangements been made for my trip next week?"

"They are nearly complete. Gaddafi and his Intelligence Minister are most anxious to meet with you. Do you require my attendance?"

"Would I go without one of my key assistants? I want you by my side when Moamar and I cement the plans for his nuclear program."

"As you wish. I will make the necessary reservations." *Key assistant? He has never referred to me as a key assistant.*

***

CHAPTER 3

ALERT PAD OBSERVATION TOWER
MATHER AFB, CALIFORNIA
PRESENT DAY

Airman First Class John Tomczak stared out the broad windows
of the observation tower at the Alert Pad five stories below. The
persimmon glow of the security lights gave the scene an almost
alien appearance that he was still getting used to after almost
three months. The wide expanse of concrete looked like a lake
and the airplanes he was monitoring resembled ships at anchor.

His eyes constantly swept back and forth across the console
in front of him. There was a monotonous routine to it that might
lull other people into a dazed slumber. He checked the alarm
panel and raised his sights to check the corresponding area of

the Alert Pad. It was a slow night by any measure. Even the usual hiccups were strangely absent and all lights were green.

He was about to stretch his lanky frame for the hundredth time when a knock came at the door. *Guess Landon forgot his keys.* Mike Landon was the sergeant who comprised the other half of the observation tower crew tonight. He had trekked downstairs to the base of the tower to grab their lunches from one of the Special Response Team drivers.

John usually performed the menial task of slogging down and back up the 148 steps, since he was the junior member. Tonight, Landon decided he needed the exercise. John hadn't argued with him, although he usually liked the break offered from the scopolamine-like trance of the blinking lights.

He walked over to the door. "Hey, Sarge, getting forgetful in your old age?"

The door banged into him as a heavyset figure in black wearing a balaclava mask over his face shoved his way into the room. "Hey, what the…"

The barrel of an automatic pistol was thrust under his chin. A steely voice growled, "No heroics, Junior, and you might just live to see the sunrise."

John glanced past the intruder to the rack beside the door that held his M-16 rifle.

"That's right, newbie…Should've challenged me with weapon in hand."

John stood stock-still like a recalcitrant schoolboy and tried to stammer a reply. A second intruder spun him around and duct-taped his hands behind his back.

Sergeant Landon was thrust roughly into the room, tripped and fell. John was shoved down on the floor next to him.

They seemed to know tower protocol as well as any crew member, which was confirmed when intruder one sat down at the alarm panel and began deactivating the automatic communications links. He was isolating them from any help, except by two-way radio.

One light after another blinked and faded to black. There would be no rescuing cavalry. "Tower clear," he said into a portable radio and stood up.

Tango two dug a number of small satchel charges out of his backpack and stuffed them into the pockets of his jacket. He gathered up his gear and moved toward the door. "C'mon, let's stay on schedule."

The intruders pulled the two-man crew to their feet and hustled them out. It was the last time they would see the observation tower. It might be the last time they saw anything if they didn't cooperate.

Where did they come from? John turned the possibilities over in his mind and nothing made any sense. The alarm panel had reported the perimeter and all gates to be secure. Still, they were here. *They tampered with the system.*

John followed Landon down the stairs and hoped he didn't trip. Descending the slippery metal stairs with his hands tied behind his back was tricky.

Intruder two stopped at each landing and duct-taped one of the packets to the steel supporting beams of the tower. They reached ground level five minutes later and walked a hundred yards or so further. John could see one of the SRT crews sitting on the ground next to their vehicle. They were handcuffed and one of them was bleeding profusely from a head wound.

A series of explosions breached the still night air. He could see the other SRT racing toward the perimeter fence. *Maybe they'll have better luck.* The sound of a diesel engine announced a civilian tractor trailer moving van that appeared as if out of nowhere.

"Move along, newbie," the first intruder commanded.

He mumbled a prayer under his breath, "Dear Lord, bless us in our hour of need..."

They certainly needed somebody to watch over them. He thought of his mom and dad in Story City, Iowa and prayed he would see them again. The intruder nudged him in the back with his rifle and John picked up the pace.

They were another hundred feet away from the tower when a quick series of explosions ripped through the night air and nearly knocked him down. The shrieking sound of twisting, tortured steel made him move even faster. He glanced back in time to see fiery puffs of smoke coming from steel supports. The tower began to collapse, like mud sliding down a wall.

He concentrated on staying on his feet as the ground shook even more violently. A cloud of dust enveloped them and made breathing difficult. He could smell the acrid stench of C-4. Numbness began to overtake him. *Can't believe it...the tower's gone...gone.*

His captor jammed the rifle into his back again and growled, "Move, before I shove this rifle up your ass!"

Airman First Class John Tomczak shivered and plodded on to an unknown destination with an indefinite future.

NEAR GUARD POST SEVEN

The searing pain in the back of Jake Thomas's head matched the intensity of the explosion from the RPG. His first attempt at raising his head brought a wave of nausea.

He lay back down, slowed his breathing and calmed himself. Years of martial arts training and conditioning served him well, and he was pleasantly surprised that everything seemed to work.

The shoulder roll out of the car and the explosion that followed left him relatively unscathed. "Thank you, Jesus," he said out loud.

He slowly rose to a crouch. The patrol car had flipped over him and slid into the drainage ditch on the other side of the road. It was upside down and roaring flames lit the immediate area.

Gotta find cover. He rolled into the ditch on the opposite side of the road as the fire reached the gas tank. The resulting fireball vented itself harmlessly into the night sky.

He waited a minute and raised his head above the level of the ditch to look in the direction of Guard Post 7. The wavering glow from the fire revealed a crouching figure about two hundred yards away moving slowly toward the burning patrol car. It was too big to be Joanna Davies.

Not the time to stand up and identify myself. There was no question this tango needed to be taken out. Jake belly-crawled to the end of the ditch closest to the attacker and huddled into a tight ball.

He keyed the mike clipped to his uniform shirt epaulet and whispered, "Base, Ops One, you copy?"

"Ops One, Base, wow, you're actually alive?"

"No, I'm faking it."

"Davies thought you were toast."

"Probably should be…Need to thank her. I'm mobile near Post Seven. It's wiped out…don't see her…"

The keying of another mike and the awed voice of Joanna Davies interrupted him, "Oh, man…Thought you bought it…"

"Sorry to disappoint you two, but I have a problem. A tango's moving toward me, over."

"Got one…Other's coming for you."

"Let's see if I can ruin his night. Send backup, just in case…Off while I take him out."

The conversation ended with a muted blast of static. He wished he had a pocket periscope from his response team kit. Unfortunately, it was in the trunk of the wrecked patrol car. He would have to depend on finely-tuned senses and training.

It wasn't long before the sound of crunching gravel reached him. The burning patrol car silhoutted him moving slowly, trying to be as stealthy as possible by walking on the gravel shoulder. It gave him away as an amateur, since the gravel announced his position and left him just a few feet from the ditch. *Come to Papa.*

He tucked his body against the end of the ditch and sensed the dark-suited figure moving past him far enough to get a glimpse. He was holding a short-barreled weapon and watching the fire across the road. *Probably figures nobody could have survived that.*

Jake slid quietly out of the ditch at a low crouch and approached from behind. He stopped just short of his adversary, set his left foot solidly, and used his right to deliver a powerful kick to the back of the intruder's left knee. It collapsed and sent him sprawling face first. He tried to catch his fall and the machine pistol skittered down the asphalt and out of reach.

He rolled over quicker than Jake expected and drew a commando knife from an ankle sheath. Jake pulled a collapsible baton from his belt and snapped it open. A quick blow to the right knee meant the other guy wouldn't stand without a cane for awhile. Another blow shattered the wrist that held the knife and it fell to the pavement with a clatter.

The tango threw both arms up and stuttered between pain-clenched teeth, "Ss…stop it, dd…dude! Ain't getting paid enough for this abuse."

The encounter took less than thirty seconds. Jake reached behind his back for a set of handcuffs from his belt and quickly secured the black suited figure. A quick search revealed another knife in an ankle pouch, two spare magazines and a can of pepper spray.

Only two mags? This guy either had another source of ammo or didn't expect to fight for very long. No wallet or identification, so it would be up to squadron investigators to find out who he was and who was paying him.

A quick flick of his wrist brought the radio back to life.

"Base, Ops One back in business…One tango cuffed…ready to stuff. What's the current sitrep, over?"

"Multiple instances of unauthorized entry…One guard post totally destroyed, along with your unit and two Peacekeepers. Alert Pad Control Tower's history. Fence breached in at least two places. Power down for most of the base. Half a dozen structure and grass fires and the Fire Department's working with low water pressure. Senior staff is set for an Emergency Disaster Response meeting at the command post in twenty-seven minutes."

Jake heard the crackle of another radio in the background as John continued with his report, "No identity on the tangos…They appear to be in control of the Alert Pad. Hang on a sec, Sarge…Getting a transmission over TAC2…I'll leave the mike open, over."

Haverhill picked up another mike. "Security Police Base…Why are you on Tac 2?"

Tactical Frequency Two was used mostly during exercises or an occasional stakeout.

An unfamiliar voice brought a steely chill with carefully spoken words, "Security Police Base and all others, be advised…The Alert Pad is now under control of the Black Diamond Front. No effort should be made to approach it. Our own security system is in place and will detect movement within fifty feet of the outer security fence.

"We have nine hostages and access to nuclear weapons. The Base Commander can hear our demands by telephone in the Base Command Post at 0730 hours. Black Diamond Front out."

36

The stillness was broken only by static hum from the radio and sirens in the distance.

Jake spoke first, "Black Diamond Front? Who are they?"

There was no reply, so he continued, "Base, send somebody out to pick up my prisoner ASAP. Davies and I'll stay on her post until you get replacements. Ops One, over."

"Affirmative, Ops One. Who was that, anyway? Sounds like some cheap action movie…"

"Affirmative, Base…Maintain radio discipline. Ops One standing by, over and out."

WINFIELD RESIDENCE
OFF-BASE IN RANCHO CORDOVA

Lieutenant Colonel Bart Winfield, Operations Officer for the 323rd Air Base Group Security Police Squadron spoke softly into the phone, "Thank you, Desk Sergeant."

Bart sat for a moment at the edge of the king size bed, one of a limited number of mattresses that did not leave his feet hanging over the edge. At a little over six feet-six, he towered over most people and challenged most furniture.

He ran his fingers through his thick brown hair and worked to shake the cobwebs from his mind. The call had interrupted an intense dream about a past mission in Europe when he was forced to engage in hand-to-hand combat with a knife-wielding assailant.

Bart had just twisted the knife from the bad guy's grip when the harsh ring of the phone tore him away from the dream.

"What in the name of God is going on over there?" He didn't realize he had said it out loud until Nora, his wife of twenty-three years, answered in a drowsy tone.

"Going on over where, honey?"

"Sorry, darlin'…Didn't mean to wake you. Need to get to the Command Post."

"Something wrong?" The question was rhetorical in nature, since a recall was initiated only when something critical had happened.

"Probably nothing more'n some drunk running through the Alert Pad fence again. Need to go sort things out."

"Not again…Hope it's nothing too bad," she mumbled. "Though, I know you can handle it…Call me when you know what's going on. I'll have breakfast waiting when you come back."

He leaned toward her and planted a kiss on her forehead. "Call you soon as I can."

She rolled over, pulled the covers over her head and mumbled, "Uh, huh…Love you."

"And I love you too, my little darlin'."

He pulled his uniform and boots from the closet as quietly as he could, closed the bedroom door behind him and moved softly down the carpeted stairs. The Desk Sergeant could not tell him everything, since the conversation was not on a secure line, so he stepped into the attached garage and retrieved the encrypted radio from his pickup truck.

"Security Police Base, this is Admin Two, come in please."

"Admin Two, Base, over."

"Sitrep?"

"Yes, sir. We have a full-fledged intrusion into the Alert Pad with multiple tangos who are well-armed and fighting SRTs."

"Copy that, Base, should be there in less than ten minutes."

"That's good, sir…All hell's breaking loose."

"Roger that…on my way." He finished pulling on his combat boots, reached over and pushed the button for the garage door opener. He was wide awake now and ready for whatever awaited him at the base. His next job was to make sure the entire squadron was ready…

***

CHAPTER 4

JASON'S HOME
OFF-BASE IN RANCHO CORDOVA, CA
SIX WEEKS BEFORE ALERT PAD ATTACK

"The working man ain't never supposed to be totally happy...least that's the way I see it." Rick Eichner puffed on a cigar and picked up the cards from the table. He raised one eyebrow as he glanced down at two queens, a three, and two fours.

He sorted them casually and looked around the table. It was a typical suburban Thursday night out with the boys bunch, including a plumber, an electrician, a bureaucrat and a retired military cop. Their baggage consisted of eight wives or ex-wives, five mortgages, two second mortgages, two cardiac episodes and enough extra weight hanging over three of their belts to make a small-sized sixth one of them.

Their idea of excitement was limited to the few times each summer when Judy Manlon, the divorcé who lived at the end of the cul-de-sac, sunbathed nude in her backyard.

The biggest neighborhood event in the past couple of years was when the TV show *California Cons* filmed the recreation of a car jacking at Sunrise Mall.

Dull? You bet your sweet ass they are.

He waited a few seconds, swiveled in the old gray office chair with the cracked Naugahyde upholstery and addressed the group again, "Think about it…You get just enough to feel more or less satisfied, right?…A lot less than what you'd like, but a little more than what you need to get by. So you don't ever get motivated to try something with real potential…Am I right?"

His fellow players shuffled their cards a few more times and glanced back and forth at each other. Finally, Bud Anderson took a deep, wheezing breath. "Think I know what you're trying to say," he mumbled as he sorted through his hand. "Take my job, for instance…"

"I wouldn't take your job for all the tea in China," observed Jack Hamilton, his closest friend. "You spend half your life crawling around in sewers, knee-deep in shitty water…Yeah, that's a dream job."

"Screw you," Bud shot back. "Somebody's gotta do it." The look of annoyance on his face was immediately replaced by one of self-satisfaction. "Besides, I put two kids through college with that crappy job."

Jack smiled at Bud's unintended pun. "Sure you did...But let's face it...Joe, Jr. only made it through 'cause he's the best tight end the state's ever seen."

"We can't all be geniuses, you know." Bud felt his face flushing and turned his attention back to Rick. "As I was saying, before I was so rudely interrupted...My job's typical. Been at the base eleven years and I'm the lousy third shift assistant supervisor. Nineteen more years of busting my hump and if I'm lucky, maybe I'll make WG-11 by the time I retire...In the meantime, guys like Bill Marston brown-nose their way up the ladder. Don't make no sense at all...But what am I gonna do, quit and throw it all away?"

"That's my point." Rick slapped two cards face down on the table. "You get enough to live, but never enough to do the things you really want to do."

"So what are you saying?" Jason Pressley asked. His slick gray hair shone under the imitation stained-glass Michelob beer sign that hung over the game table. Gray was his color, even at leisure. Tonight he wore a gray pullover sweater on top of gray slacks with light gray loafers. Most of the suits he wore to work in the Plans and Programs office on base were gray, as were most of his ties.

He continued, "Personally, I get a little tired of people who say you should go for more...If you've got a place to live, food on the table and you get laid now and then, how much more do you really need?"

"How about some dreams?" Rick replied, and sat back in his chair.

It was a moment before Bill Johnson shifted in his chair and spoke for the first time. "I think I hear what Rick's saying."

Bill had been sitting back observing, a trait learned in twenty-two years in the security police field, followed by four years as a Department of Defense civilian police officer. He usually thought of himself as nothing more than a glorified security guard, but it was better than working off base at two-thirds the pay.

Besides, the transition after retirement from the Air Force had been quick and easy. He took a few weeks off and showed back up in the gray uniform of the DOD police. No TDY trips to deal with and he was familiar with the surroundings. The work was easy and the pay was good. *Okay, maybe it is a cop-out.* He smiled at his own pun.

It kept his wife happy with the steady pay coming in and he would only have to do it for another eight or ten years—if he was lucky.

It was fairly painless, except for the occasional forced overtime during inspections or exercises and even that wasn't bad. Just more boring hours sitting in a plain-Jane patrol car. The vinyl upholstery was hot in the summer and cold in the winter, but the air-conditioning worked most of the time and the cars didn't smell like day-old puke, like most of the off-base cruisers.

The active duty guys knew he was only marking time until his next retirement. They more often than not thought of him as just another warm body to fill a seat—little more than a name on the roster to help fill out a shift and that was fine with him.

He turned his attention back to the smoky room where Rick had posed another question. "Haven't you ever wondered what it would be like if you didn't have to show up for work at all? You know, it didn't matter if you even got out of bed?"

"Sure, man," Jason snorted. "Who hasn't had that dream? But let's get real here....It's not part of the plan. In real life, you work your ass off for thirty or forty years and hope to break even by the time you retire, with maybe a little left over for later on. I mean, that's the way it's supposed to be, isn't it?

"Yes, but maybe it doesn't have to be that way for everybody," Rick replied. "There might be an easier way. Jason, let's use you as an example...What if you could walk into a casino with a hundred thousand bucks in your pocket and sit down at any blackjack table you wanted to...No more searching out the minimum tables. And what if you could bet as much as you wanted to?...Would that change your outlook on life?"

"Well, sure it would...Are you kidding? I could place bets in a logical pattern...You know, against the percentage the house has. That'd give me the advantage for a change. Could maybe even do a little card counting, if it was less than a three-deck shoe. Course, that's unheard of anymore...Even the loosest casinos have at least a three-deck shoe."

He sat back and started silently going through the possibilities, oblivious to the others around him.

Rick let him think for a few seconds, glanced around the table with a conspiratorial look and drew the others into a huddle. "Okay, let me ask you...what if you had help keeping track of the cards?"

"You mean cheating? If that's what you're saying, than you're crazier than I thought…We're talking about the mob! They don't take kindly to anybody screwing around with their business and they play for keeps. You could end up in the desert with scorpions crawling all over your dead face."

Rick sat back, took a long puff on the cigar and belched loudly. "Yeah, if you got caught."

"Oh, you'd get caught alright," Jason snapped back. "They'd have a thousand eyes on you the minute you started winning big. I mean really, they pay people to watch the people who look like cheaters…There's no way to beat their security, at least that I've ever heard of."

"True, if you went in by yourself," Rick conceded. "Being on your own would be a recipe for disaster. To get away with it, you'd have to be part of a well-organized team that was committed to the plan…You know, guys who'd back you up, no matter what. Besides, even if you did get caught, they'd still have to prove you were cheating."

"Well, I guess," Jason admitted.

"And you could spread the action around…Make it harder to pin you down. Plus, I have a source for some very specialized equipment nobody can trace…kind the CIA uses. It's sophisticated enough that you'd be gone before they even knew you were there."

"Whoa there, amigo," Bud interjected. "Let's slow this thing down a little. You've really thought this through, haven't you?"

Rick smiled and said nothing.

Bud sat up and looked Rick in the eye. "You're serious

about this, ain't you?" He let go a nervous little laugh and looked around the room.

Jack Hamilton jumped in, "Yeah, where'd all this talk about taking on the casinos come from all of a sudden? One minute we're playing cards and the next thing you know, you're acting like you wanna take on the casinos. You know you're talking about some major league bad boys, don't you? What did you do, go nuts all of a sudden, or something?"

Again, Rick smiled and said nothing.

They all started talking and the commotion made it hard to understand what was being said and by whom. It steadily increased in volume and intensity and words like crazy and stupid popped up more than once.

"Now wait just a minute, everybody!" Jason stood up. "Here you are getting all worked up and we're just daydreaming, right? I don't understand…where's the harm in that?"

He turned toward Rick as he was talking. "Look, Rick, don't get me wrong…I'm not saying I'm buying into all this craziness or anything…I mean, you got to admit, it is a little far out there. But still, being honest, I am a little bit intrigued. I mean, seriously, who hasn't thought at one time or another about ripping off the casinos? You see it all the time on TV and in the movies. I'm just wondering why you're bringing it up now?"

Rick shrugged. "Don't know…making small talk, I guess. It's not like I'm breaking the law, or anything, right? So, long story short…what's wrong with talking about it?"

"Nothing, I guess," Jason answered. "I've actually thought about doing something like it myself. I mean, come on now, who hasn't? Haven't you ever wondered what it'd be like to knock off an armored car? You know, just like in a movie. An organized team of guys swoop down with every second planned out in stopwatch precision…Black hoods over their faces and high-power weapons in their hands. It'd be a snap, unless, of course, one of the guards gets the drop on you…Then, things could go south in a hurry. Sure, I've thought about it…just never bothered talking about it 'til now."

He paused and looked around at the others who sat with mouths half-open, staring at him.

He smiled sheepishly. "Whoa, where'd that all come from, anyway? Guess I got a little carried away…"

The others laughed and it was easy to tell Jason was expressing thoughts they all had at one time or another.

Rick rubbed his hands together and stood. "I think it's time for another beer…Anybody?" Bud and Jack took him up on the offer. He stopped on his way to the small refrigerator behind the bar and turned back to the group.

"Look, guys, I'm not trying to start any arguments or anything…Just thought you might find my little plan interesting."

"Little plan…Wait, you've actually got a plan?" Jason spoke for the group.

"Matter of fact, I do…Even made a few notes. Anybody want to hear about it?"

The others nodded in agreement. Why not? It looked like the card playing was over for the night and none of them wanted to go home early. It might be fun to hear what Rick had to say.

They settled back, ready to listen…

BART WINFIELDS HOME
RANCHO CORDOVA, CA.

Nora made a vain attempt to return to the pleasant dream she had been enjoying before the phone jarred her awake. She left the pleasant tropical beach locale to have the brief conversation with Bart before he left and then rolled over. Unfortunately, the sparkling blue water was replaced with blood that was splattered on the street and walls in a back alley in London.

The effort to force the terrifying thoughts away failed and she kept returning to the last covert mission she and Bart had done for the White House.

In spite of Bart's assurances it would be the last time they ever subjected themselves to that level of danger, she knew the dark world of international espionage would somehow hunt them down and draw them back in.

Although there was no indication of involvement from their former enemies, her intuition told her that there was more to the attack on the base than local criminals seeking a quick score.

She sat up in bed, reached for the organizer she kept on the night stand and dialed a number for their old contact on the National Security Council. Half expecting to intrude into his sleep, she was only mildly surprised when the voice that answered was crisp and concise.

"Hello, Jules, it's Nora Winfield…hope I didn't wake you…"

"Hardly, Nora, I've been up for an hour reading intel briefs…How are you and how is that rapscallion you're married to?"

"Fine, thank you…although at the moment I'm not sure what's going on. There's been some kind of an incident…"

"Before you continue, remember this is not a secure line. Yes, I am aware of what is happening. Can you get to a secure line?"

"In less than an hour. Are the events connected to our former work?"

"Difficult to ascertain at this point, which is why we should talk on a secure line."

"I'll call you at this number as soon as I can."

She hung up the phone and tried to arrange her thoughts. Bart was one of the best intelligence assets she had ever worked with. So much so, that she felt comfortable in marrying him. He was a legend among international operatives and would keep her safe—no matter what happened.

Her job would be to gather information needed to analyze the threat and ascertain how it affected them. A quick shower and she would be on her way to the local office of the CIA. Fortunately, it was only a few minutes away. She headed for the bathroom.

JASON'S HOME
RANCHO CORDOVA, CA

"This is probably gonna sound a little weird, but yeah, I think

I'd kinda like to hear this so-called plan of yours," Bill said. "I mean, I may be a little crazy or bored, or maybe there's something in the water...But, hell yeah, I'd like to hear what you have to say...You know, just for the sake of it...How about you guys? Anybody else wanna hear what he's come up with?"

They nodded and shrugged and Jason said, "Okay, Rick, so why don't you go ahead and tell us about your little plan. Bill's right...Might be kind of interesting."

They took a break to go to the bathroom and refill their drinks.

When they came back, Rick sat down at the table and cleared his throat. "Let me just start by saying that if you wanted to get away with a whole lot of money from the Tahoe casinos, it really wouldn't be all that hard...for the right bunch of guys, that is...Let me explain how I'd do it with a little help from my friends and what's involved. Then, make up your own mind about whether or not it'd work."

The card playing was put on hold indefinitely and within a few minutes they were listening intently. Rick laid out a plan that grabbed their imagination and touched something deep within each of them.

"I gotta admit, you're right about a lotta stuff," Bud offered. "You hear guys talking about it now and then over a few beers and lets face it, nobody likes the casinos takin' their money. It's just that most guys don't have a clue what to do about it, and wouldn't know diddly-squat about how to pull it off, even if they did."

"We're not the only ones thinking about it either," Bill

added. "Look at all the movies out there about robbing casinos and banks. Casinos may be legal, but just barely. They're only there to take your money away from you and they do everything they can to keep the little guy down."

"You're right about that," Jason offered. "Odds are stacked against you the minute you walk in the door…Be nice to have a little edge for a change."

"Ain't that the truth," Bud commented. "I understand that they gotta win now and then to stay in business, but why do they have to take such a big cut?"

"Maybe that's why there are guys who do cheat a little… figuring the casinos take a whole lot more than they should."

"You bet they do…You gotta have a leg up on 'em just to keep their hands outta your pockets."

"Question is, how do you go about getting the edge over them? What do you think, Rick?"

"I think it can be done…All it takes is teamwork and a little gear."

"We got the team right here…Just needs a name."

"How 'bout Casino Cats?" Jason offered.

"Seriously? Sounds like a high school chess team."

"What's wrong with that?"

"Nothin'…'cept we're supposed to be tough."

"You got anything better?"

"I don't know for sure…But it's gotta be something that tells who we are."

"Hey wait, I know," Bill exclaimed. "How about the Thursday Night Mafia?"

"Well, we do meet every Thursday...And it's gotta be something strong..."

"Everybody else like it?"

Heads nodded and the name stuck. A pizza delivery kept them going until well after midnight as they kicked the plan around, modifying and discussing it as they went.

"It's kind of funny." Jack Hamilton scooped salsa out of a cereal bowl with a tortilla chip and addressed the group, "Never thought about doing something like this, but now that I have, it's kinda...Whadda they call it, liberating? Yeah, that's it...Really frees you up."

Bud paused from his attack on a bag of sour cream and onion potato chips. "You're so full of crap....Only thing that'd free you up'd be about a ton of laxative."

The group laughed and Jack stopped with a chip halfway to his mouth. "Screw you! Whadda you know, anyway? You're just another two-bit pipe wrench slinger." Salsa dribbled down his chin and he wiped it off with his sleeve.

"Hey, I charge a hell of a lot more'n two bits...Besides I was just messin' with you. Actually, I kinda know what you mean. I might've daydreamed about doing something like this after seeing something in a movie or on TV. But to actually go out and do it? Now, that's a whole different ball game."

Jason was sitting at the table with a plate of cold-cuts in one hand and a beer in the other. "You're right, Bud, it is a whole different thing and I'm not sure it's good. I mean, has anybody stopped to think about what will happen if we get caught? Anything could go wrong and if it does, we are in a world of hurt…Think about it, we could lose our security clearances and our jobs, to boot."

He grimaced as bile rose up in the back of his throat. "On top of that, we could be facing a lot of time behind bars…and we're not talking about one of those country club prisons, either. We could end up spending the rest of our lives doing hard time in the big house."

Bud stopped laughing and leaned forward. "So friggin' what? I don't know about the rest of yous, but I'm ready for some adventure. Besides, Pressley, I've had just about enough of your constant whining. Every step of the way you've come across like some weak-kneed punk and I'm fed up to here with it. Nobody's puttin' a gun to your head, so quit your bitchin' and make up your mind…You in, or out? I mean, that's what it comes down to, ain't it, paper-pusher?"

Jason started to stand, stopped, and sat back down with a sigh. "You're absolutely right. I'm in, no matter what…Just saying, what with the security and all, there's a chance we might get caught."

"Yeah, and you can step off a curb and get hit by a bus," Jack replied. "I'm with Bud…We can't do this thing halfway. We gotta commit one hundred percent or it'll go straight down the crapper. So shut up with any of this dumbass talk about getting caught, 'cause it ain't gonna happen."

He jabbed his forefinger in the air for emphasis. "Besides, with all the gear Rick's gonna get from his buddies, there ain't no way we're gonna get caught.

"Wait a minute…I thought this was just for fun. Sounds to

me like you actually want to go through with it," Jason replied.

"Sure, why not?"

"Jail, for one thing. Losing everything else, for another."

"Jail? Are you back to that? We'd be first time offenders and like Rick says, most they'd give us is easy time in some minimum security joint and then parole our asses back into the real world. Little slap on the wrist and we start all over...Course, we don't get caught and we're fixed for life!"

"You're missing my point, Jack. I'm not talking about the cops...I'm talking about the mob."

It was Rick's turn to join the conversation. "The mob? Are you serious? They got chased out of the casinos years ago with their tails tucked between their legs. Starting with the Kevauver Commission and down through the RICO Act, the Feds have had them on the run for years. They're afraid to so much as jaywalk within a hundred miles of a casino for fear they'll be thrown in jail for the rest of their natural born lives. I wouldn't give the mob a second thought. All we gotta worry about are the cameras and the pit guys."

Everyone nodded. "That's right," Jack said, "You been watching way too much TV."

Rick softened his tone. "Look, buddy, you're letting your doubts get the best of you. I'm telling you right here and now we're not gonna get caught. We've been through this a hundred times and it's foolproof. Besides, you can't back out on us now...We need you. You're the key player in this."

Jason stared at the beer bottle in front of him and picked at the label. *Been a long time since anybody said they need me.*

"Well, since you put it that way, yeah...guess I'm your man, and like you said, we can always back out if something doesn't look right."

"You got that right...One sideways glance from anybody in the casino, even the janitor, and we're long gone. All they'll have are bits and pieces of recordings and the hazy memories of a few bored dealers. We'll be gone so fast it'll make their heads spin. So, what do you say, you in or out?"

"Damn straight, I'm in! Like you said, it's just a case of the jitters. Although, you gotta admit, some of those guys look like they could be 'made men'..."

Jack let out an exasperated sigh. "There you go again with that TV talk...Made men! Gimme a friggin' break. They hire guys that look like that to scare the tourists. Most of 'em couldn't spell mob if you gave 'em a dictionary and underlined the word."

"All right, all right, I get the point. Like I said already, I'm in. I just wondered if anybody else had any doubts...How 'bout you, Bill? You haven't said much."

Bill's head popped up. "Hey, don't you girls drag me into your little spat. I was just lettin' you geniuses do all the talking...But yeah, you bet your sweet ass I'm in! I say go on...Roll the dice and hope they're good to us"

"I guess that about clinches it." Rick walked over to the couch and held out his hand, palm down. Bill put his hand on top of it, as did Bud and Jack.

Jason hesitated for a second, grinned and placed his hand on top of the others. "Like the Musketeers...all for one and one for all. Long as nobody gets hurt…I'm behind it."

"That's the plan, my man, that's the plan." Rick smiled back.

Their hands separated and he continued, "Okay, let's go through it one more time and if everybody thinks we're ready, we'll try it next weekend…assuming the gear comes in on time." *The stuff that's already in my garage.*

Rick watched as they filed out the door. His plan was advancing nicely. A few more training sessions and even stronger doses of drugs added to their drinks and he would have them right where he wanted them. *Life is good when you have a plan.*

***

CHAPTER 5

MAJESTIC CASINO AT LAKE TAHOE
STATELINE, NEVADA

Jason's hand touched the shiny brass door handle and he paused for a moment. The view through the tinted glass doors beckoned to him in a way he could never put into words. A shrink might be able to explain the steel grip casinos had on him, but it didn't matter. He never felt more alive or in charge than when he was inside waging the battle for what he thought of as his money.

His heart was pounding nearly out of his chest as he swung the door open and crossed the threshold. The jangling sounds and loud conversation engulfed him like an avalanche and swirled around him like a warm blanket on a cool night.

The smell of stale cigarette smoke and spilled drinks wafted through the doors. He half-expected the action to stop and hear the PA system announce his presence.

Instead, a half-drunk stumbling gambler with the dejected look of a loser bumped into Jason without apologizing and mumbled under his breath as he pushed past him.

A few more steps and he was in the middle of the call of coins clattering into the tin trays of slot machines. The chink a-chink sound quickened both his breathing and his pace.

He hurried past the rows of quarter machines with their whirling wheels and clinking cacophony of sounds and headed toward the open area in front of the card tables. The rich burgundy and gold carpet led him toward the blackjack tables like the landing lights on an airport runway.

This was where he belonged. This was where skill and timing outweighed the ability to merely pull down a handle or push a button. Leave the smalltime action to the salivating seniors and chattering conventioneers. This was where the real action and the biggest thrills were.

His hand went to the fake hearing aid in his right ear. He adjusted it and appeared to hum to himself. "Dum, de dum, dum, can you guys hear me?"

The reply was immediate. "Yes, we can hear you." The voice of Rick Eichner blasted into his ear.

He winced, reached up, and turned the volume down a little. The clarity and strength was unbelievable. Jason had no idea where Rick got the gear, but it was great.

The laptop computer in the van would calculate the odds and Rick would tell him which bets to place and when. All he needed to do was silently transmit the card information to them.

Tiny switches in the toes of his shoes let him tap out a code that nobody around him could hear. That, combined with the occasional voice cue as he talked to himself or the people around him, would give Rick the information needed to compute the bets.

They had already figured out which casinos used the largest shoes and avoided them. So far, the strategy had rewarded them.

A dark-suited man standing against the wall made eye contact with him and then looked away. The coiled wire of his ear piece screamed security, as did the bulge under his jacket. It served to remind Jason that even the sloppiest casino security people would begin to watch him closely as he started to win big.

He sat down at the first twenty-five-dollar minimum table he saw and started laying hundred-dollar chips down. Small bets at first, that were soon followed by larger and larger wagers. The pile of chips in front of him grew as his winnings increased.

A squat pit boss in an ill-fitting suit made a big deal of replacing the dealer after a dozen hands or so. The switch didn't slow his winning streak, so a floor supervisor consulted with the pit boss, after which the entire shoe was replaced. The supervisor closed the table a couple of hours later and the other players wandered off.

Jason sat and toyed with a stack of thousand dollar chips, separating them carefully from a larger pile of hundred dollar chips. He guessed that he had about sixteen thousand dollars in winnings and was contemplating his next move when a tall swarthy man in an expensive suit sat down on the stool next to him.

He offered his hand and an introduction, "Good evening, sir. I'm Nick Boretti, one of the managers here. I couldn't help but notice how well you play."

Cool...He's acting like I'm somebody. He smiled and shook hands. "Pleased to meet you...My name's Jason Pressley."

The group discussed whether or not he should use his real name and decided it was a necessary risk. There would be tax forms to fill out when he cashed in his chips and some form of valid identification would be required. It hadn't been a problem at the other casinos and he didn't see why it would be one here.

"I do have a nice little winning streak going...guess the cards are running in my favor. Anyway, what can I do for you?"

"Actually, I was hoping I could do something for you. After all, you're our guest and you seem to be much better than the average player. I'm sure you must be bored with the slow, limited action at these tables. A player of your caliber usually likes a bigger challenge than what the public casino offers. What would you say to a game with a higher level of action...Would you be interested?"

Keep your cool. "Would I?" Jason was trying hard not to appear too eager. "Let me think about that...Yes, it sounds like it might be fun. You are talking about the high-roller casino, aren't you?"

"Yes, although we call it the Preferred Players' Lounge."

He chuckled. "Oh, sure, of course. Yes, I'd like to give it a shot...that is, if I have enough to get into the game."

"Blackjack seems to be your favorite and the minimum bet is a thousand...Is that a problem?"

Jason had over thirty thousand dollars in his pocket from the last casino, but still pretended to do some quick calculations.

"No, not at all...I mean, what the hey, I already have enough of the house's money to stake me. So how and when do I get started?"

"Right now, if you're ready." Nick stood and motioned for him to follow.

Jason scooped up the pile of hundred dollar chips and stuffed them into his pockets as he followed Nick to an elevator that could only be operated with a key.

A short-skirted hostess opened the door for him and stepped inside as the door closed. She smiled after a perfunctory greeting and stared straight ahead. He softly hummed to an instrumental version of *I Shot the Sheriff* as the elevator rose skyward.

Eleven floors later they stepped out into a richly decorated lobby that led to a smaller casino lavishly furnished in a decor more likely to be found on the European Continent or Singapore. The elevator hostess provided a summary introduction to the amenities and stepped back into the elevator. She smiled at him as the doors closed and he couldn't tell if it was friendly or smug. Dozens of gamblers rode with her each week and most left on the losing side. No matter...he had his buddies watching his back. What could go wrong?

There were no annoying clanging bells from one-arm

bandits in this refuge for the rich. The only discordant sounds came from a prize-wheel in the corner. A bored-looking man of Middle Eastern origin was laying ten-thousand-dollar chips down in piles and watching the wheel take one clacking turn after another.

Jason felt like he had come home to a place he had never before been allowed to enter. The casino hostess led him to a glass-partitioned corner of the room where she held a set of double doors open for him to enter. The three tables inside were mostly empty and requests to hit me or stay were muffled by the plush carpet and heavy drapes over the windows.

Their plan called for him to gain access to the high-roller's casino, but now that he had, a knot of tension settled into his stomach like day-old chili.

This was the big time and the scrutiny would be ten times more intense than ten floors below. He knew he had been watched in one way or another from the moment he sat down and even more closely when he started winning.

His play had indeed drawn the attention of security people firmly ensconced in a windowless control center in the middle of the building. Nick Boretti walked into the secure room and called for a summary of Jason's activity.

"I'll tell you what, Boss, this guy's slick," reported Stan, one of the technical specialists. "We recorded every hand he's played with both overhead and close-up cameras and then went over them a frame at a time…Looked for any way at all he might be recording the action. Close-ups of the fabric in the sleeve of his jacket don't show any divisions that can be used like an abacus. Hasn't touched any pockets, either, so it don't look like he's using a hidden calculator."

"What about accomplices?"

"Now that's where we maybe got him," answered Brian, another technical specialist. "I called a buddy of mine over at the Gold Mine, Nat Lucchese. He's bringing over a frequency scanner to check for stray signals."

"Why?…And what's this frequency scanner thing?"

"He seems to mumble to himself a lot and that hearing aid he's wearing could be a two-way radio. Frequency scanners check for signals they give off and track them."

"Okay, so why don't we got one of those things?"

"Not sure, Boss…They're kinda pricey and besides, I think they're sorta restricted."

"Restricted?"

"You know, as in classified…I think you gotta be government or law enforcement to get one."

"But you're telling me the Gold Mine's got one?"

"Well, I, umm…not exactly sure how they got their hands on it."

"Find out and get me one…I don't care what they cost. If bozos like this are gonna come in here using the latest gear, then we gotta have a way to spot it…right?"

"Yes, sir, Mister Boretti, I'll get right on it…"

"After we nail this guy…By the way, hire this buddy away from the Gold Mine."

"Don't know if we can…He's a made man."

"How? I know all the made men in this town…I ain't never heard of him…So where'd he come from?"

"Not sure…I think he works for Mister Lemonica."

"No problem…I'll give him a call. Now, back to the business at hand. Odds are in our favor…"

"You mean because we're watching him like we are?" A new technician asked the simple question.

"What? Oh, I forgot, you're still wet behind the ears…No, because the house's only got a three per cent advantage over any player…"

"Three per cent…that's all?"

"Quit interrupting me and I'll tell you. Blackjack's the best odds for any player which is why we watch it real close…Slightest bit of cheating tips it in their favor."

"Makes sense…So I see why we're so careful…That's a good thing…"

"Glad you like our methods," Boretti answered sarcastically. "Now, like I said, shut up and listen. This guy's playing real good…not getting too far out there and placing bets at just the right time…He'd be okay even if he wasn't cheating."

"This is gonna sound dumb, but how do we know he's cheating?" Stan asked.

"Gut feeling, mostly…Like all the way down to my toes. If he was to win a few games and score big, we could overlook it. But he waltzes in here and all of a sudden he's up forty big ones in just the first hour. He's up almost two hundred large after a couple more hours…Something fishy's going on…I'd bet my last dollar on it."

"So what you're sayin' is experience and instinct make all the difference when it comes to spotting these guys?"

"Now you're catching on, kid...You might just make it here, after all."

Jason wiped the sweat off his forehead with a cocktail napkin and glanced at his chips. *Two hundred and fifty grand, plus three hundred in the van...Not bad for three days work.*

The voice in his left ear was showing the strain. "Think we pushed it 'bout as far as we should. Let's cash out and blow this pop stand." Rick's voice was no longer casual.

Jason used the toes in his left shoe to tap out their code for "NO." At the same time, he used the big toe on his right foot to tap out their prearranged code indicating the dealer had dealt himself the seven of spades and the jack of hearts.

A sudden burst of static in the earpiece was loud enough the people around him must have heard. It was replaced by dead air and Jason's hands stopped halfway to the twenty thousand in chips the dealer was pushing toward him.

He started to reach again and found his arm restrained by the strongest grip he had ever felt.

A glance to his left revealed a black man in his mid-twenties wearing a bulging dark blue business suit. He had a coiled wire running from an earpiece to a shirt pocket.

Jason peered to his right to find the player next to him had been shouldered aside by another dark-suited figure.

"This table is closed," the black security man said in a calm voice.

T.C. Miller

The other players shrugged their shoulders, scooped up their chips and wandered off. The two security men began hustling him toward the elevator. Four floors later they shoved him toward a door marked Authorized Personnel Only.

"You'll want to come quietly," the first one said in the same calm voice. "We have questions and don't want to damage you any more than necessary."

Jason almost lost control of his bladder. *Gotta let the others know.* "I don't know why you want me to go in that white double door...What'd I do?"

"Don't bother trying to warn your buddies. We know they're in a gray van outside. They'll be joining us in a few minutes."

He entered a code into a keypad, pushed the door open and motioned for Jason to enter.

Thirty steps later they passed through another door that required a key card and retina scan and entered the internal security area of the casino.

The hum of computer fans and the ozone smell of electronics at work greeted them. Five operators sat at banks of video monitors and used joysticks to direct cameras to zoom in on the action in the casino.

Dozens of hidden directional microphones directed hundreds of voices into the headsets they wore. They monitored the action continuously and their eyes were glued to a dozen screens in front of them.

He saw a frozen picture of himself on one of the screens and his confidence slipped a little more.

The operator glanced up and smirked with obvious delight

66

at Jason's predicament. He twisted his head and watched as Jason was led down a hallway toward another set of double doors.

The security men rudely shoved him into what looked like an industrial break room. Bright fluorescent lights overhead cast a harsh glare off two bare six-foot banquet tables. A cheap Formica counter held a worn-out microwave oven and an ancient coffee maker that was crusted with spilled coffee.

Cupboards above and below concealed their contents behind fingerprint smudges and a broken handle. The smell of stale coffee and trash cans that needed to be emptied hung in the air.

It was not the kind of ambiance the public areas of the casino displayed.

The rest of Jason's crew sat grouped around the far end of the tables in plastic chairs like you find in tired old Laundromats. They had their hands secured behind them with plastic zip lock cable ties that cut off circulation. Their faces showed a mixture of fear and defiance and squares of silver duck tape covered their mouths. The right side of Jack's face was red and already showing signs of bruising.

Nick Boretti glanced up at Jason from his seat at the head of the table. The silky smooth tone in his voice was gone as he pointed toward a chair and gestured toward Jason. "Have a seat, scumbag, we got some questions."

"So what? You've got no right to…"

Stars filled his vision as a flash of white-hot pain exploded all around him. He lurched forward from the blow to the back of his head and folded onto the table. The smell of the mildewed rag that had been used to wipe the table off sometime in the past filled his nostrils. A hand grabbed the back of his neck, pulled him upright and slammed him into a chair.

"Sit your ass down and listen," his escort commanded. "You're in a shit load of trouble."

"That's right, Mister Pressley," said a middle-aged man who had been observing from the back of the room.

His charcoal gray suit was custom-made, with a white dress shirt and dark gray tie with silver specks. A neatly folded matching handkerchief peeked out of the breast pocket of the jacket. Silver cufflinks secured the shirt sleeves that shot out of the jacket sleeves at a fashionable length. Italian loafers were polished to a high sheen and his smooth dark hair had streaks of silver that nicely matched his clothing.

"Oh yes, we know who you are, where you live and where you work…so don't bother trying any tricks. In fact, we know more than you know about each other…So don't waste my time trying to hide anything. I'm Mister Lemonica, Director of Security for casinos here and in Las Vegas, and don't bother asking around. For all intents and purposes, me and my associates don't exist in those jobs…at least not as far as the Gaming Commission is concerned.

"We been watching you since you started winning at the Grand Dame. Nobody escapes our attention, especially mooks who suddenly win big. We get paid a lot of money to settle things like this without ever getting the cops involved…understand?"

The group looked at each other and nodded.

"I gotta admit it did take a while to figure out how you were pulling it off...Course, what you don't know is we got the latest in monitoring gear. That stuff you're using is old news according to my guy...at least three or four years old. He picked up your radio signals earlier this evening at the Stardust and we tailed you...Figured you'd end up here or at the Brentwood...You know, looking for the low-count shoes."

A chilling smile faded almost as fast as it appeared. "Sure enough, you didn't disappoint us and here we are."

He pointed to each of them in turn. "Now, I don't know which one of you is the leader and, quite frankly, I don't give a damn. It's up to your little group to figure out exactly how to get our money back to us. All I have to do is figure out how painful today is gonna turn out to be for you."

He said it as a matter of fact and Jason came close to losing control over his bladder again.

Lemonica went on, "For instance, let me introduce you to Toby, one of my best wet-work guys...Found him a coupla years ago working for a loan shark in Trenton...specializes in breaking body parts, so they heal slow and don't ever work quite right again. And Craig over there knows the nervous system better than most third-year medical students...He's what you'd call a pro in the dark side of pain management. Most guys pass out in seconds from the pain and shock."

Jason started to stand. "You greasy sack...."

His words were cut off by Toby dropping him back to his chair with a precision blow to his collarbone. Pain shot all the way down to his toes, back up to his head and settled in his stomach. His testicles tightened like they were in a vise and his stomach did a dozen flip-flops in a matter of seconds. He felt like he needed to vomit and suck in his breath at the same time.

"Mind your manners, punk...Unless you want a lot bigger dose of their skills," Lemonica commanded. "Didn't I tell you they were good? And for your information, I'm not trying to scare you. Oh no, we're way past that. I don't have time to play games with yous...so, I'm gonna lay this out in terms you can understand. You owe us the three large that you already got away with and, as you can imagine...we want it back. My guys searched the van and came up with squat and that's a real problem. Wherever you stashed it, we want it!" His face turned beet red in a flash and he slammed his fist on the table.

Jason looked around at the rest of the crew. "How would I know? I was in the casino!"

Toby shuffled toward him.

"No, wait!" he yelled. "I'm not trying to be a smart-ass. The three hundred thousand was in the van when I came into the casino."

He swept the table with his eyes. "Ask them where it is."

The duck tape over their mouths muffled his teammates' excited responses.

Lemonica leaned forward with his hands curled into fists and rested white knuckles on the table. He gave the impression of a silver-back gorilla preparing to charge. "I told you I don't got time for this and I'm through arguing with you...So get this straight...I don't care where or how you come up with the dough, so long as you do...Understand what I'm saying?"

They nodded in unison and he continued, "Now, I know you got houses, vehicles and retirement accounts and you can borrow from your families and friends. Push comes to shove, that's the only reason your bodies ain't rotting away in the desert as coyote hors d'oeurves."

Jason slumped back in his chair as their predicament sank in. *Gotta stall for time.* "Look, I'm sure we can get the money…In fact, I know we can," he was almost shouting.

The others were nodding in agreement and screaming strained approval through the duck tape.

Only Rick sat with no expression, seemingly ignoring the panic around him. He looked as if he was an observer who wanted this scene to finish so he could get on with the next phase—whatever that might be.

Lemonica straightened up and slowly replied, "I gotta tell you, you're putting me on the spot here…ten years ago you woulda been dead by now. In fact, my bosses would probably like it better if I just had my men kill you and got it over with. But, there is the matter of the missing money and we are a business. You can come up with it if you make as much effort as you did at trying to cheat us.

"So listen up, and listen good. First of all, I'm tired of this whole mess already, so don't even think about screwing with me or I'll do what the bosses want…But first, let's talk about how much time it's gonna take for you to cough up the bucks."

"Well, that depends…I mean, I don't know for sure," Jason stammered, "We'll have to find buyers for our houses and I'm sure it'll take a while to get loans against our retirement funds.

It could take a few weeks, even a few months…It's not like we can snap our fingers and make it happen. What I'm saying is, I don't know how fast…"

"I do know!" Lemonica yelled at the top of his lungs as his fist slammed down on the table again. "I'm gonna make this perfectly clear…You got thirty days to come up with every penny you owe us or your body parts'll start showing up all over northern California…Got it?"

The group nodded in unison.

He straightened his tie and adjusted his suit jacket. "Like I said before, we know where you live and where you work…And that goes for your families, too. You run and I guarantee you…we'll find your sorry asses. Contact any cops, even the local dogcatcher and we'll know about it and you'll regret it for the rest of your unnaturally short lives…Is that clear?"

"Crystal," Jason mumbled. "We're not stupid enough to double-cross the mob."

"Oh, yeah? Seems to me like you already done that…so come up with that money damn quick or you're history…In the meantime, you probably need a reminder of what happens if you don't."

He nodded toward Toby, who walked to the other end of the table and grabbed Bud Anderson by the arm.

Bud's eyes went wide. He shook his head from side to side and began shouting something through the duck tape as he jumped up and down in the chair as far as the restraints would allow.

Toby took a heavy rock hammer out of his suit coat pocket

and brought it down squarely on Bud's forearm.

The muffled snap of bone breaking was almost drowned out by the stifled cries from the group. Another strike and the arm was broken four inches away. A third blow wasn't necessary. Bud passed out and slumped over.

Lemonica nodded and Toby stepped back.

"You got one month from today...not one minute more...Or broken bones will be the least of your worries."

He opened the door at the end of the room and led Nick Boretti through it.

The two security guys cut the cable ties binding them and one waved smelling salts under Bud's nose to bring him back to consciousness.

Bill wrapped some of the duct tape around Bud's arm to hold it steady. They could properly dress it later.

The group hastily tore the duck tape from their mouths and began talking at once while interrupting each other.

Jason held up his hands to get their attention. "Guys, I think we're in a shit load of trouble."

The others rolled their eyes and returned to exchanging comments in high-pitched voices that conveyed panic and fear. Again, Rick was unusually calm and quiet.

Jason started to move toward him and stopped. *Maybe he's in shock.* There would be time for questions later. All he wanted now was to get out of the casino and face the fact their lives would never be the same.

CONSORTIUM MAIN OFFICE
CENTRAL EUROPE

"I do not like to bother you during your afternoon file review, Commissioner, but I have had an inquiry from one of our clients in Las Vegas."

"This is something you cannot dispense with?"

"Only because of the amount, sir, and because they wish to file a claim against another of our clients."

"What is the amount and who is the other client?"

"The claim is for three hundred thousand US dollars. The other client is Rick Eichner."

The Commissioner touched a gold-plated cigar lighter to the end of a Cohiba and puffed until it glowed persimmon red. He leaned back in the chair and blew a fanciful smoke ring toward the ceiling, quickly following up with a more forceful ring that passed through the first.

"What are the particulars?"

"It would appear Eichner is pursuing the operation of which we previously spoke and, while in the process, he and his team defrauded the client's casino."

"Is the casino owner connected to the American Mafia?"

"Yes, sir."

"And their accounts are in good standing?"

"Yes, sir, as usual. They have approximately three and a half billion dollars in our care."

"How much does that yield in interest?"

The aide did a quick calculation in his head.

"Approximately seven hundred sixty thousand dollars per day."

"Pay the claim for five hundred thousand, with the condition they do not pursue the matter any further. I do not want Eichner's operation compromised."

"Should I inform Mister Eichner?"

"Not immediately…You may eventually tell him we are providing protection and there will be repayment at a later date. If he asks for details, tell him we have been fair with him, as we are with all our clients. Tell him to ask the client who runs the smuggling ring in California if we have not been more than generous with him."

"Very good, sir. I will see to it immediately."

"Also, make notes in Mister Eichner's file indicating my approval of the transaction. Five hundred thousand is a trifling sum compared to what his operation may yield, but none the less, it is still a debt."

"Yes, Commissioner. Thank you for your direction."

"Not at all, Conrad…I am pleased you brought the matter to my attention. Now, if you will close the door behind you, I wish to continue with my work."

"Indeed, sir." The heavy wooden door closed with little effort and a double electric lock secured it.

***

CHAPTER 6

JASON'S GAME ROOM

Bet they haven't gotten eight hours sleep between them. Rick looked at the subdued and sullen group. *And they look defeated...How gullible these Americans are.* Living among them for twenty years had given him a keen insight into their psychology, including the need to gamble to relieve boredom.

Gambling brought the group together in the beginning and helped him identify their individual talents. He pushed out anybody who didn't possess a skill he needed to fulfill his plan until he had distilled the group down to the essence he required.

It was easy to steer conversation over endless card games to the subjects he desired. Their complaints of job dissatisfaction revealed secrets about the Air Force base and its operations that allowed him to perfect his plan. The scopolamine he added to their drinks made them even more pliable. Its nickname was the "Zombie Drug", and it made people more susceptible to suggestions.

The game room, as Jason referred to it, was an ordinary two and a half car garage that had been partially converted to recreational use. A Budweiser sign buzzed and flickered occasionally on an unfinished wall.

A pool table with cigarette burns and scratch marks on the rails and a green frayed felt table took up much of the space and served a variety of purposes. At the moment, three empty Domino's boxes were spread open on it. Scraps of cheese pizza crust were discarded in one and dried pieces of pepperoni stuck to the bottom of another.

Jason sat on the edge of the table, picking at chunks of oily pepperoni. Bud, Jack, and Bill sat side-by-side on the couch sipping beers and munching cold day old pizza.

Rick took a slug of beer. "All right, guys, I think we need to admit that we're well beyond the old rock and a hard place thing…"

"No shit, Sherlock," Jason broke in. "Thanks to you, we're in it up to our asses! And before we go on, I still want to know what happened to the three hundred grand that was in the van?"

"What the…Why the hell you asking me? The goons who searched the van probably took it…I remember one of them taking a gym bag over to a car when they pulled us out of the van. Besides, if you were so worried about it, why didn't you bring it up with Lemonica? Or in the van on the way back from the lake. Why wait 'til now, hotshot?'"

Jason licked his lips and stammered, "Well, I wasn't exactly sure what was going on…I thought maybe you guys hid it…Or that Lemonica might be playing us…I mean, we're talking about a lot of money and I didn't know…"

Rick spat out, "You didn't know if you could trust us, is that it?"

"No, not exactly…We're under a lot of stress and like I said, I thought maybe you hid it," Jason sputtered and tripped over the words.

He looked at the others for support, but no one came to his defense. His voice rose in pitch and volume, "Look, I don't know who to trust anymore! All I know is we're screwed…No two ways about it."

"So you start blaming your friends?" Rick calmly replied as he stood up and just as quickly sat back down. "Tell you what…Let's both take a step back here, okay? Pissing all over each other's shoes will only give us wet feet…and blaming each other won't clean up this mess. We need to think things out, right?" He looked around the room for approval.

The others slowly nodded. "We need to figure out how to come up with the money or the mob'll make an example out of us. I know you told Lemonica about borrowing against our houses, but they're already mortgaged to the hilt. We couldn't sell them, even if we wanted to…In fact, I imagine foreclosure notices will be hitting our mailboxes any day now."

"So, what you're saying is if the mob doesn't get us, the bankers will?"

"I'm not worried about the bankers…They don't bust heads or cut people's throats. All they do is take back their collateral…No, we're in way deeper than that. In fact, let's start by going over where we stand, point by point."

He raised one finger. "First, we tried to cheat not one, but three casinos out of half a million bucks and got caught…Which means three groups of bad guys are gunning for us."

Another finger went up. "Before that, we borrowed thousands of dollars from friends and relatives on top of the second mortgages. No way we're ever gonna be able to pay them back in a hundred years."

A third finger went up. "And last, we maxd out our credit cards…We can't even afford the minimum monthly payments. So, the way I see it, our resources have pretty much dried up, right?"

Rick paused long enough to make eye contact with each member of the group and continued before they could interrupt, "We also used up all of our cash, figuring we'd make a killing. We don't even have the money to run, even if we could get away. We're all tapped out and short about, oh, two hundred and ninety five thousand, I'd guess. Unless one of you has a fairy godmother, we're dead men…Pure and simple."

Jason shot to his feet. "That's exactly what I said, remember? If this thing goes south, we're all screwed…Didn't I say that?"

His look of satisfaction brought no comfort to the others.

"That's right, champ," Jack spoke up. "You get the 'I Told You So!' award of the month. We'd have a T-shirt made up that says that…but we're too broke. Now sit your ass down and let Rick go on."

Rick lowered his voice, "All right then, I'll ask the question again…Am I right?"

Rick was right. The logic of his argument sank in and buried them like an avalanche.

Jason jumped to his feet again and jabbed a finger at Rick. "And you got us into this mess with your bullshit talk of dreams and riches! So, Mister Bigshot Idea man, how are you going to get us out?" He started to move toward Rick, who stood his ground. "Plus, I'm still not sure it was the mob who took the three hundred grand!"

Rick took a quick step forward and shoved hard on both of Jason's shoulders, causing him fall back on the couch. "Okay, that's it…I've had it right up to here with you getting in my face. I'm in the same boat as everybody else…No, I don't have an answer for you and probably never will! But it's time for you to quit your bitching and move on…This blame game won't put bucks on the table. Bad mouth me all you want, but we need to come up with some kind of plan. The clock is ticking and the noose is getting tighter as we speak."

Jason started to rise from the couch again until Bill stepped in front of him and blocked his way.

Jason puffed up his chest and yelled at Rick, "It's just a little too damned easy for you to explain the money away, just like that!" He snapped his fingers for emphasis.

Bill continued to block Jason's way. "All right, you two, settle down. I'm serious…put a cork in it! Rick's right…Gettin' all pissed at each other ain't gonna get us out of this hole. And tryin' to beat the shit outta him won't do no good neither."

"No," Jason shot back. "...but I'd feel better."

"Oh yeah?...Bring it on, chump."

Jason saw he had no support and sat down after a few moments. "Okay, okay, maybe you're right...Time's running out and we're no better off than we were yesterday."

"True," Jack added in a conciliatory way. "And we're supposed to be partners in this, so we gotta work together like Rick says...Otherwise, we all go down the shitter together."

They nodded their heads in agreement. Desperation hung thicker in the air than a Tulé fog in the Sacramento Valley. They stared at each other with a sullenness born from fear and the scopolamine drug.

Bud stuck his finger as far down in the cast as he could trying to scratch his arm. Pale faces and dull eyes displayed the resigned shock that settled in after their release from the back room of the casino and was still evident.

Bill attempted to restart the conversation. "Man, those casino owners sure were eager to let us go...Guess they figure we can't come up with the money if we're tied up with arrests and court appearances and such."

"What it comes right down to is they don't want any official record of us...You know, in case we should have an unfortunate accident or something," Bud noted sarcastically.

"Plus, you gotta figure it won't take long for other casinos to find out we cheated them," Bill replied. "We could end up facing guys who use baseball bats instead of croupier sticks."

"They gotta give us more time…I mean, it's not like they're dumb." Bud offered. "They gotta know it's gonna take more than a month to come up with that kind of money."

"Push comes to shove, I don't think they give a damn about our money problems," Bill shot back. He wrung his hands and looked around. "How could I let you guys talk me into this, anyway?"

He slumped back on the couch as he posed the question. "My Mary's gonna go ballistic…I mean, she'll dump my ass in a New York minute. She warned me not to throw money away on gambling, but did I listen? Nooo! Went right ahead and did it anyway…Should never have listened to you guys…"

"Now, wait just a freakin' minute there, amigo," Bud yelled. "Nobody put a stinkin' gun to your head. You was in this right from the beginning and went along with it just fine…Truth is, we all let greed get the best of us and now it's time to pay the piper."

Jason joined back in, "Look, I'm as brave as the next man, but those casino guys scare the hell out of me. No way we can put anything over on them…So we need another way out of this mess and the way I see it, this is Rick's fault. Yeah, you, chump…You need to come up with a big chunk of the money on your own. Sell some of your construction equipment or get a loan…Do something, anything to help get us out of this mess."

Rick started to move toward Jason but stopped in midstride. "Okay, maybe I should've come clean right from the start…So let me tell you where I stand. First of all, the equipment is all leased…I don't own it. My office is rented and

I'm three months past due. And I owe the government half a million bucks in back taxs…I couldn't get a loan to buy lunch if I was eating by myself.

"Sure, I have account payments coming in, but the guys at the bank are getting what the IRS doesn't. That's why I was so eager to try this…Figured it'd be cash nobody could trace. So, as Bill put it, push comes to shove, I'm in this as deep as anybody, maybe deeper. Nothing I can do about it, so let's drop the subject and remember why we're here."

"Yeah, because time's ticking away and none of us have the slightest idea how to get out of this mess."

"That's just it!" Bill clenched his teeth and slammed his fist down on the arm of the couch. "There ain't no damned way outta this bind we're in…Unless we start robbing banks or something."

"Actually, that might not be a bad idea," Rick said it so calmly it caused the others to stop in mid-sentence and turn toward him.

He went on, "Although, robbing banks is for losers… Prisons are filled with guys who tried. They usually end up with a few thousand bucks and an exploding dye pack for their efforts. Putting the casino thing aside, we're not that dumb, are we?"

His comment was met with a couple of rude looks and they all began to talk at once.

Rick waved both hands to get their attention. "Look, guys, I think I may have an answer to our problems…I really do. If you'll just give me a few minutes, I can lay it all out for you."

Frustrated, they fell silent and waited.

"I'm not saying that what's happening is the way it should be...I'm just telling it the way it is. Our day-to-day lives are a thing of the past...long gone and deader than road kill. I've wracked my brain day and night, like I know you all have and can't come up with an easy solution. But that doesn't mean we're all doomed.

"And by the way, you're right, yelling at each other won't do any good at all...And it's sure not gonna get the mob off our backs. I imagine you've already figured out they'll need to set an example to show they won't be cheated. My guess is they'll take every penny we come up with and kill one or all of us in slow and painful ways."

The idea had already occurred to each of them and it showed in their faces.

Gotcha. "Let's face it, if you'll pardon the bad pun, we took a gamble and lost. Our options aren't just limited...They flat out don't exist. On the bright side, though, this whole thing did prove we can work together as a team, didn't it?"

They nodded.

"Well, in that case, I may know a way out of this mess. It might not be my first choice, but it may be the only one we have left."

Heads came up slowly at the encouraging note in his voice.

"I admit the plan I'm about to lay out for you is so far out there it sounds like some kind of Hollywood movie script...But, if it works, it could solve all our problems in one fell swoop.

"What I'm proposing is that we go in for one gigantic

score…And not just what we need for now. I'm talking about something that is so big it'll set us up for the rest of our lives. I mean, if we're gonna be dead men anyway, what do we have to lose, right?"

The others moved to the edge of their seats and looked to Rick for their salvation.

***

CHAPTER 7

SECURITY POLICE COMMAND POST
MATHER AIR FORCE BASE, CA
ONE HOUR AFTER ATTACK

"All right, people, let's settle down so we can get this meeting going. Where's Lieutenant Baxter?" Bart posed the question to the five section chiefs and two guests seated around one end of the conference table."

"Still on his honeymoon at Lake Tahoe," Chief Master Sergeant Tony Russo, Operations NCOIC stated. "Not supposed to be back 'til tomorrow."

"I thought it was today…Okay, whatever…let's move on. I want to thank Captain Clark from Intel for joining us, as well as Captain Brown from Bomb Wing security.

"Nobody likes being thrown out of bed by a recall, including me…Especially when it's the real thing. I've been studying the initial reports, so I'll start with a recap…Feel free to jump in if you have anything to add…You get a radio call, step away from the table to answer it, understood?"

Heads nodded and he continued, "Boss has a Command Post meeting at 0730, so we need to get all our ducks in a row…Don't want him blind-sided. What I get from the reports is that a small band of tangos did what everybody figured was nearly impossible…The wrong people are now in control of thermonuclear weapons and have hostages to boot…Which puts not just us, but the whole Sacramento area squarely behind the eight-ball.

"They used a multipronged, well-planned maneuver that isolated key parts of the base while creating maximum confusion. Diversionary actions at the O Club and base housing sent backup units clear across base while we were investigating and clearing a traffic accident at the front gate…That one appears to be a drunk driver and may or may not have been their doing…Only time'll tell.

"We do know they started fires at two power transformer stations and two switching substations…Fire Chief tells me there was clear evidence of arson. Base power grid got knocked off-line, so no pumps meant a lack of water in the hydrant system and made fighting fires a real bear…"

"Don't mean to interrupt, sir…" Captain Clark broke in. But what about backup generators?"

"Looks like they knew exactly how to cripple those, too.

They're working now, but not quite at full-capacity. Hospital and Command Posts are back online, as well as the Comm Center. Fire Department pumped water from golf course ponds to put out the fires and CE is doing their best to get everything working again.

"Whoever did this seems to know exactly what they're doing and the timing of everything is way too precise to be coincidental...Which, to my way of thinking, suggests an inside job. It's the kind of event they cover in Air War College to test senior base leadership...Only this time it's far too real...By the way, before I forget to mention it, all records of this event are classified...So, make sure you secure your notes.

They nodded.

"Now, to continue...The Broken Arrow notification went out as a Flash message...First one I've seen since Nam...Should tell everybody how serious this is...Something that we here at the local level already know.

"They woke up POTUS and key members of Congress. They'll be briefed by the National Security Advisor after we know what the tangos want. It just so happened the SAC Commander was taking his turn in Looking Glass, so they didn't have to wake him up. He's still circling on an EC-135 that's been refueled on the fly...They'll extend the pattern 'til we know what's goin' on."

"They say how he reacted? Captain Brown asked.

"No, but can't imagine he's happy about it...Nobody likes something like this happenin' on their watch, including me. Besides, he's probably tap-dancin' on roller skates on an ice rink trying to run down the EAB checklists...It's got forty-two action items on it. Speaking of action items, DOE called a SAFEHAVEN and pulled all its couriers in..."

This time it was Lieutenant McMahon interrupting, "I know this is gonna sound kinda dumb, sir, and I've heard the word before, but what exactly is a SAFEHAVEN?...And what couriers are you talking about? Like UPS or FEDEX?"

Bart suppressed a smile. "No, not exactly...Department of Energy is responsible for securely transporting nuclear material around the country. They use disguised semis that are guarded by agents in nondescript vans. When there's a problem like this, they order them to report to the nearest secure facility, usually a military base...So, it's called a SAFEHAVEN."

"Makes sense."

"Sense is the only thing that works when you're dealin' with nukes. Anyway, thirty-eight of them were on the road yesterday and now they're all behind secure fences and locked gates that are double-guarded.

"Thank you, sir. I'm still getting used to security jargon."

"No problem...Always a good idea to ask if you don't know something...Now, let's see, where are those other items," he mumbled as he shuffled through his notes. "There it is...NSA's sending two people over from their San Francisco office to help. Apparently there's a piece of their comm equipment on board the bomber....Should be here within the hour."

Lieutenant McMahon interrupted again, "Excuse me, sir. Why would the NSA have equipment on an Air Force plane...Just curious."

"And you know the old cliche about what curiosity did to the cat, right? Whatever it is, it's classified way above our level. Short answer is, I have no idea and it was never mentioned here, got it?"

"My lips are sealed, sir."

"Good...A secure comm unit from Tinker left Oklahoma about ten minutes ago. They'll pick up some Intel experts on the way and be here in about five hours. FBI's sending an Anti-Terrorist team from Quantico, along with the Pentagon security team that designed most of the Alert Pad alarm systems.

"It'll take about six hours for all of them to arrive, but I want to stress something...They're only coming to advise us. Technically, our base commander and staff'll still be in charge. Although, most of us know that outside agencies tend to want to stick their noses in wherever and whenever they can and that's where I see a potential problem.

"Chain of command tends to get a lot longer in situations like this. Too many of them runing around looking for something to justify their existence and next thing you know, they'll be forming committees to decide what brand of coffee to serve in the Command Post."

First Lieutenant Jim Branson, an Individual Mobilization Augmentee Reservist spoke up for the first time, "Speaking of extra help, sir...I'm only here for my one day a month Inactive Duty Training...Think you might need me longer than today?"

"Good question, Lieutenant...Quick answer is we have no idea how long this might go on...But it sure would be nice to have your expertise…And I know I can trust you…You could help run things here while we're in the field. Can you be here longer or will your full-time job call you back?"

"I'm a Sacramento police officer…And they have to let me be here if you need me…It's Federal law. I can either do a few more IDT's or request man-days."

"Sounds good either way. Let me know if there's anything I need to sign.

"Yes, sir. I'll contact Senior Master Sergeant Miller, the Base IMA Administrator…He'll take care of it, no matter what."

"Great, now let's go over a few security concerns…I've been trying to put myself in the tango's shoes to figure out what their next move might be because, quite frankly, something just doesn't add up here. Take a look at their security layout and you'll see what I mean."

Bart pointed to the diagrams he'd drawn of the Alert Pad and the terrorists' present position. "They haven't even tried to include tankers in their perimeter, which seems a mite strange. Besides taking over the entire Alert Pad with their alarm sensors, all they really did was lock down one BUFF."

"You think they're planning to escape in it?" Captain Clark asked.

"Don't hardly think so. If they know our procedures as well as they seem to, they'd have to know we'd never let that plane take off. Too much chance they'd head for San Francisco, or LA."

"And yet, like you said, they seem to be concentrating

mostly on that one bomber for some reason…" Clark noted.

"Now you see what I'm trying to say. They could've taken over the entire perimeter…Controlled three B-52s and three KC-135 tankers…Wouldn't be that hard to do. They'd have a double whammy…Bunch of nuclear weapons and enough jet fuel to light up half of Sacramento.

"Instead, they concentrated on that one bomber…Like it's special or something. Of course, it could also mean they're a lot smaller force than we think…Or they're not planning on staying that long."

"Not being in security, I'm not quite sure I understand, sir," a puzzled Captain Clark interrupted again.

"Well, it's like this…They can't be on guard twenty-four hours a day without having enough men to split into shifts. And a small force is easier to control and more nimble…It could somehow escape right out from under our noses.

"Notice how they chose the bomber closest to the fence? Base perimeter road's on the other side…Few hundred yards beyond that it's scrub land and river…Kind of a stretch, but all they'd need is a diversion of some kind and they'd be gone faster'n a scalded hound."

The captain nodded. "But they'd have to be fools to try that…Everything's sewn up tight…I mean, a flea couldn't get out of there."

"That's how it looks on the surface…But I see some real problems here. We're responding as fast as we can, but it may not be fast enough. Attackers got the jump on us, no doubt about that.

"Only mistake they made was thinking Post 7 would be easy to take out. Lost two of their people, thanks to one tough security policewoman and a skilled shift supervisor…And that might have put a crimp in their plans…'though I'm not even sure about that. They either had the flexibility to shrink the area they captured or they never intended to take more than one plane.

Bart leaned far back in his chair and stretched his lanky frame. "No, if I had to guess, I'd say this is gonna be a hit and run raid…They'll get what they came for and be gone faster'n ice cream at a church social. It's a gut feeling, but my gut's right more often than not…Thoughts?"

Captain Morgan raised one finger. "Hard to argue with that, sir…So how do you want to handle it?"

"Not my call, Captain…All we do is offer suggestions to Colonel Hadler…He'll pass them on during the Base Staff Meeting and the Base Commander makes the final decision.

"For now, let's review our setup to make sure we're ready to go, whatever he decides. We've already gone to THREATCON Charlie, since an attack has occurred and we're keeping the reason classified…Don't want wild rumors flying all over the place. Tell off-base people, especially the press, that we're in exercise mode until further notice."

Master Sergeant Bill Dobson spoke up, "Problem with that, sir, is we didn't announce it…Press releases are usually put out way in advance of any exercise."

"Good point. Maybe a press release announcing a surprise inspection might help keep things calmer."

"I'll put something together that Colonel Hadler can take to the staff meeting," Hobson answered. "Something needs to happen, since civilians are sure to notice long lines forming at the gates."

"Another good point, and you're right…Press release might help stall questions…On the other hand, it won't be long before the media picks up on all the activity. Get another release ready saying we suffered a power problem that resulted in some small fires."

"Base Public Affairs is supposed to do that, sir."

"Civilians know our job's making sure the base is secure and we want them to feel that way…Which means they don't need to know about this event. What they do want to hear is the world's not gonna blow up in their face. Any hint there's a problem and all hell'll break lose. Besides, protesters gathering at the front gate would draw manpower away from other ops. We need to get control of the Alert Pad back. That'll solve just about everything."

***

CHAPTER 8

JASON'S GAME ROOM
THREE WEEKS BEFORE THE ATTACK

"Let me ask you all a simple question…What has this country done for you?" The group looked back and forth at each other, not sure where Rick was headed with the query.

"You've all given a big piece of yourself to public service and what have you gotten in return? Gratitude? Hell no! Respect?…Not a chance. When it comes right down to it, you don't owe anybody a damn thing and that includes your families. You got wives who ask for way too much far too often. Your teenagers laugh at you behind your back…Sometimes right to your face. So tell me, why should you bust your butts for them?…I say let's go for one big score and disappear forever."

"Uh, we tried that, remember?" Jason answered. "Look where it got us."

"That's the way it looks on the surface, but if you step back and look at the big picture, there's a deeper story. We had the right idea and found out we make a pretty damn good team...Problem is we didn't shoot high enough. A few hundred grand?...That's chump change compared to what I'm talking about...I say we go for hundreds of millions, instead."

Bud groaned and let out an exasperated sigh. "Yeah, right, Champ...I'm sure the casinos'll see the error of their ways in busting us. In fact, I bet they'll feel so bad they'll get in line to hand over millions to us...Probably put us up in high-roller suites while they get it together and offer us a private jet to fly away in!" He paused long enough for an exasperated sigh, "What the hell's the matter with you, anyway?...You gone crazy or something? Must have if you're talking about robbing the casinos again."

"Not casinos," Rick said emphatically. "Or banks, for that matter. They're small change compared to the nine hundred pound gorilla on the block...the federal government."

Jason spoke for them, "Okay, I'm thinking Bud must be right...Did you flip out or something?"

"No, in fact, I'm saner than I've ever been...and now that I have your undivided attention, let me finish without interruption. There's a pretty good chance you'll like what I have to say...especially if you keep an open mind, okay?"

Nobody responded, so Rick repeated it, "Okay?"

They slowly nodded.

"Now, how could we go about getting the government's attention so they'd give up hundreds of millions.?

Again, he paused for effect. "When nuclear weapons are involved...That's when." He grinned.

He went on before they could voice the shock that was showing on their faces. "First off, does everybody agree to keep whatever is discussed in this room totally secret?"

Their expressions showed they were trying to absorb his words. "No, I mean it. Raise your right hand and swear on your mama's grave you'll never reveal anything that's said here...Ever."

"I don't know..." Bill mumbled.

"I'm not saying you have to commit to it just by being here...But take the time to listen to my plan and decide if you want to join in."

"Well, I am kinda curious...Guess there's no harm in just listening..."

"Exactly."

Hands slowly went up.

"Look, I don't want to beat around the bush, so I'm just gonna come right out and say it...I think we should hijack a B-52 on the Alert Pad at Mather and threaten to blow up all the nukes on board unless they pay us an amount with about eight zeros behind it."

They started to interrupt, so he hurried on. "I know it sounds crazy...But I've thoroughly researched it and have a plan in which nobody gets hurt and we get away scot-free...Just hear me out and if you don't like it, that's fine…You can back out at any time. But I don't think you'll want to…once you hear what I have to say.

"Our choices have been whittled down to doing something drastic or dying…And I don't know about you, but I'm not quite ready to bite the big one…So, do you want to hear the details?"

"Hold on now, wait just a frickin' minute." Bill started to get off the couch and realized he had a plate of pizza on his lap. He settled back with a thud and his face turned crimson. "I spent a big chunk of my life protecting those weapons and now you're asking me to help steal them?"

"No," Rick's reply was calm and firm. "That'd be really stupid, now wouldn't it?…They'd hunt us down to the ends of the earth to get them back. What I'm suggesting is we threaten to blow them up or steal them…That alone will get them to pay.

"Besides, what would we do with them if we stole them… sell them at a local flea market?…I don't think so. All we have to do is show them we're capable of getting away with them or setting one off and if there's the slightest chance we might actually do it, they'll pay."

He slowly looked at each man in the room. "Oh, yes, my friends, they'll pay big time!

"Furthermore, I have a surprise in my plan that let's us get away nice and clean, right out from under their noses. I have friends who'll help us disappear to a country with no extradition treaty. Next thing you know, we're sitting on white sand in the tropics, taking drinks from pretty little topless waitresses."

"Sure," this time it was Jason who spoke. "And what about

all those armed guards? You think they're going to let us waltz right in and take them?…Gee, maybe they'll help us load 'em up…Duh! You know they are paid to keep people like us away from those bombs, don't you?"

This time Jack jumped in, "So what? We got the mob after us and you're worried about a bunch of snot-nosed rent-a-cops? Ever look at 'em close?…Nothing more than a bunch of pimply-faced kids…They run around pretending they know what they're doing 'cause they give 'em weapons. So what?… Push comes to shove, they'll wet their pants and go running home to their mamas first time somebody points a gun at them."

"Are you serious, man?" asked Jason. "I mean, they do get paid to guard those planes, don't they?…And they do know how to use those guns, right?"

Rick sighed. "Look, guys, I never said it'd be a piece of cake…If it was, other people would've done it…But I've thought it out and think I've covered everything that might happen…For instance, part of the plan is to sneak drugs into their food, so they're not thinking clear. I got a contact in food service that'll make it happen. Then we swoop down and take over before they figure out what hit them…We have all the know-how we need sitting right in this room and can hire other help as needed."

He could see by their confused looks the scopolamine was working. "It'll take planning and perfect timing…as well as some preparation on our part. But keep in mind, I have my contacts. It'll also take a certain amount of luck…But, if anybody can do it, the guys sitting in this room can."

T.C. Miller

"So, tell me again why we should do this?" Bill asked. "You know, so everybody's clear on it."

"You mean other than avoiding a second go 'round with Toby and his hammer?" Rick answered.

They all winced at the mention of Toby.

For the next hour they listened to the outline of his plan.

"This might actually work," Jason finally admitted. "It is kind of weird though, how our little group that somehow came together has all the know-how we need to pull it off..."

"See, what'd I tell you?" Rick replied. "Fate's on our side... I'm telling you, we're gonna come through this in great shape."

The old cuckoo clock above the bar wearily signaled midnight as Jason yawned and stretched. "Look, I hate to break up this little party, but I've got to get some sleep. They catch me snoring at my desk again and I'll be in deep doo-doo."

Bud gave him a caustic look. "Deep doo-doo? Man, you're weird..."

"Some of us are just a little more sophisticated than others, that's all...We don't feel the need to use vulgar language."

"Yeah, you and old ladies...But whatever...You're right, it's probably way past time to hit the rack."

"And put your plates and empties in the garbage can before you go," Jason added. "I shouldn't have to clean up after everybody."

That brought a few rude looks, but they stood and, for the most part, complied.

Rick offered a parting statement, "Okay, guys, sleep on it and we'll meet back here tomorrow night at seven to start working out the details."

Bill and Bud walked out to their trucks together. They weren't free yet, but there was at least a tiny ray of hope. A dog on the next block over was barking for some reason only it knew and the full moon shone off windows of the houses across the street.

"Smell that night air," Bill commented.

"Hope it's not the last free air we breathe, buddy…So, what do you think of Rick's plan?"

"Not sure what to think at this point…He's right, though, our old lives are pretty much over…dead and gone. No matter what happens now, I'd say it's time to move on to something else."

"Even if it means giving everything up?"

"I already cashed in everything worth selling…so yeah."

"Not the money part…I'm talkin' about family and friends."

"Let's face it, they won't understand what we did, since we don't understand it ourselves."

"So what do we do now?"

"You're asking me for advice? I'm one of the biggest dummies in this mess…I shoulda known better. But, do I stop?… Noooo! I jump right in with both feet and go along with it….Why, you got some other way outta this?"

"Nope. That's just it."

Bill paused and cleared his throat. "I've never told anybody this before, but since you're my friend, I think you'll understand…When Rick starts talking about his plan, I think, wait, he's asking me to betray my country"

He looked up at the stars in exasperation. "I oughta jump up, grab him by the throat and punch his lights out…I mean, given my job, I should be madder'n hell…But the thing is, I'm not.

"First of all, I ain't got the energy…Life's taken all the fight outta me and most days I feel like I been beat down like a stray dog. Just countin' the days 'til they put me in a cheap suit and plant me in the ground…Know what I'm sayin'?"

"Been there, too…Like we got some kinda mid-life crisis… ain't that what they call it?" Bud offered.

"Guess so…Can't think of what else it might be…It's not like we're on drugs or somethin'. And to be honest, this ain't the first time I thought about doin' something like Rick's talkin' about."

"For real?"

"For real…You can't be a cop for more'n a few months before you start thinkin' about grabbin' your own little piece of the pie. You stand by while a currency shipment is being loaded or walk through a warehouse full of expensive stuff and think about how easy it'd be to grab some for yourself…Boy, do you think about it!"

"Never thought about that," Bud mumbled. "Just figured cops were all upstanding citizens and everything."

"Most of the time…But sometimes you daydream and, if you're smart, that's all you do. Guess I stepped over the line this time and what's done is done…Time to clean up the mess."

"I hear what you're sayin'," Bud answered. "Anyway, see you tomorrow night."

The headlights on a car parked down the block came on, the

engine started and it moved toward them.

"Wonder who that is?" Bud asked nonchalantly.

"Shift worker, maybe," Bill replied.

The car screeched to a halt just before it got to them and the driver and passenger doors flew open. Two figures sprang from their seats and rushed toward them.

"Oh, shit, it's them!" Bill mumbled.

"Them who?"

"Toby and Craig…"

"What'll we do?"

Bill pulled on Bud's arm to get him going. "Run back in the house."

Toby and Craig caught up to them halfway across the yard and gang-tackled them with ease. Bud felt like he had been hit by the NFL's biggest defensive lineman. He landed with such force it knocked the wind out of him.

Craig hissed in his ear, "What you running from, Fatman…you don't wanna talk, or something?" Bud could barely breathe.

Bill lay on his back, looking up at Toby towering over him. The moon was low enough on the horizon that the front yard was in shadow. The goon didn't see him reach into a pouch on his belt and pull out a stun gun.

"So, you twos, our bosses want we should pick up whatever money you got," Toby said. "Sort of a down payment on what you owe."

"And what if we don't have any?" Bill hoped Bud could come around enough to at least run to the house and alert the others while he stalled. A steadily increasing whine from the device he held next to him reached a peak and changed to a long beep.

"What's that?" Toby asked in a voice that was more inquisitive than fearful.

"Something for you, asshole." Bill sat up and jammed the Taser into Toby's inner thigh as he pressed the trigger. Nine and a half million volts of raw energy coursed through the hapless mobster's body. He vibrated in a St. Vitus dance for a few seconds, fell to the ground and shook all over as he curled into a fetal position.

Craig had his back turned away while he tried to fasten Bud's hands behind him with zip ties. He didn't see what was happening and only knew there was something wrong when he heard a loud thud as Toby's twitching body toppled to the ground.

Bud had recovered enough to take advantage of the distraction. He sat up, and as Craig turned back toward him, delivered a swift punch to the kneeling thug's Adam's apple. Craig's hands instinctively went to his throat and he dropped the plastic cable ties. Bud scooped them up and moved toward Toby to subdue him.

At the same time, Bill heard the long tone again and applied the prongs of the weapon to Craig's neck. A quick push of the button took him out of action. Bill reached behind his back and removed a set of handcuffs from another pouch. A minute later the restrained Craig lay on the ground, still twitching from the after effects.

Bill heard the door of the house close behind him and motioned for Rick and Jack to hurry over. "We need to get these two into the game room before somebody sees us.

Bill and Rick helped Toby and Craig to their feet and led them toward the house. "Bud and I'll take their car over to the commuter parking lot on Highway 50," Jack said. "Come on, Bud...follow me in your truck."

Two minutes later the street returned to its usual quiet state.

"Okay, now what are we supposed to do?" Jason posed the question as he stood in the game room, hands on his hips. The query was rhetorical in nature, but seemed to be directed at Rick, since he had become the de facto leader.

"I don't know...This wasn't part of the plan," Rick said to nobody in particular. He seemed to be thinking out loud and nobody commented. "Give me a minute to clear my head."

Bill was the first to come up with a plan. "I can get some leg chains from work...We can hold them here until we put our plan into action."

Toby had been sitting on the couch with a sullen look on his face since recovering from the shock. "What plan?"

"None of your business, asshole," Bill answered. "Sit still and keep your mouth shut, or we'll have to gag you."

"Might be a good idea, anyway," Rick offered.

The action of gagging the two men seemed to break the group from its lethargy. One after another, they offered suggestions.

"Okay," Rick said as he motioned for silence. "Here's the

105

way I see it. These two are under control for the time being, but their buddies up at the lake are bound to come looking for them sooner, not later. We just need to move up the time schedule a little...like a week or two."

"I don't know." Jason looked at the two mobsters. "Do you really think we're ready?"

"Doesn't matter...This changes everything. We'll have to adapt, that's all."

"Yeah, but..."

"No buts about it," Rick broke in. "Is all the equipment in place at the base?"

The group nodded.

"You all know your roles, so I just need to make sure the temporary help I hired is available. I say we go for it Wednesday."

"That's just two days from now!" Jason noted.

"Plenty of time."

"I wasn't ready for it so soon."

"Then you need to man up and wrap your head around it, you hear?...Forty-eight hours from now we go for it...Agreed?"

Nobody could come up with an alternative, so they simply bobbed their heads.

"All right, then," Rick summarized. "Bill, I guess you'll have to go to work tomorrow to get the chains...Everybody else, call in sick or take leave tomorrow. In the meantime, we'll take turns guarding these two."

Bill started to leave, but turned back to Rick. "So, what are we going to do with them two days from now?" His words hung heavily in the air and both goons turned toward Rick.

"Only thing I can think of, is we'll call their bosses on Wednesday and tell them where to find them," Rick answered. "Sound fair?"

"Yeah, sure…they can stand another day of watching TV, I guess."

"Good, now go home…Get some sleep and meet back here tomorrow at noon."

They filed out as Rick used a plastic clothesline to bind the captives legs together.

CONSORTIUM MAIN OFFICE
CENTRAL EUROPE

"Sorry to bother you, sir, but you asked for an update on the Eichner operation."

"Yes, yes, Conrad, come in and take a seat."

"Thank you, sir. I have confirmed the transfer of the five hundred thousand US dollars to our Mafia clients in Las Vegas as you ordered."

"Good, I trust they were satisfied?

"Not entirely. They expressed the opinion they should be allowed to send a message to other gamblers they will not tolerate being cheated. In other words, they want to make an example of at least one of the members of Eichner's group."

"Hmm, this is somewhat troubling. While I understand their position, they do not have an overview of what Eichner is doing. We have a very strong interest in his success, although that is unknown to these gangster persons. I suppose Eichner might be willing to sacrifice one of his operatives…once the operation has concluded. I will speak with him about the matter."

"Very well, sir. Do you require anything else of me?"

"One other item…Have you assembled the dossiers on the replacement for the deceased head of the Consortiums' North American Headquarters, Smithfield?"

"Work is progressing nicely on them…I am waiting for recommendations from Division Chiefs, as well as background investigations of the potential candidates. One has already disqualified himself due to womanizing."

"Perhaps I should intervene in the matter to encourage the Division Chiefs to expedite their replies."

"If you wish, sir. I think they are reluctant to make hasty comments that might be misconstrued…After all, it is one of our largest income streams."

"That is true, although I find it curious that such a bastion of freedom produces corporations that are so quick to deal in covert operations to achieve their business goals. Conversely, I suppose we should be grateful for the funds they provide to us…It has proven to be quite lucrative."

"Indeed, sir…I'll redouble efforts to gather the information you require."

"Good. The absence of a permanent replacement seems to have slowed progress on completion of the consolidated headquarters in Colorado."

"Regrettably, sir. It appears the Acting Director may be somewhat overwhelmed by the task, if you do not mind me saying so."

"No, I believe that is an accurate assessment, although I trust that, as usual, you will not offer that opinion to anyone else."

"Of course not, sir. I do my utmost to assure discretion."

"It is one of the reasons we reward you so well and so often."

"For which I am grateful. Will there be anything else?"

"Not at this time…You may return to your work."

***

CHAPTER 9

WINFIELD RESIDENCE
RANCHO CORDOVA, CALIFORNIA

"Bart, is that you, honey?" She had only been back from the local CIA office for a few minutes. The visit there had told her little, other than there was a working incident at the base involving intruders and nuclear weapons. She knew as much as the people in DC.

"Sure is, baby…Back for a five-minute shower, then on to the Command Post. Coffee sure smells good."

She came into the foyer wiping her hands on a towel. "I'll get you a cup…So, what did it turn out to be?"

"Unknown subjects took over the Alert Pad."

"Took it over? You mean controlling the gates, right? They

don't have the planes, do they?"

"'fraid so…A BUFF with nukes on board, to be exact…Supposed to tell Johnson their demands at 0730." He started undressing as he was talking to her, dropping his clothes on the floor.

"That's easy to believe…You've been warning them forever that Alert Pad security needed to be beefed up."

"Kind of a moot point, now."

"Maybe they'll listen to you now, even though it's like closing the barn door after the horse is out. So what can I do to help?"

"Nothin' at the moment…'less you wanna make me a fried egg sandwich to go."

"You betcha, big guy…Then I need to make a few calls…"

BASE COMMANDER'S OFFICE
MATHER AFB
0530 HOURS, PRESENT DAY

Colonel Jim Jackson, or J.J. as he was known to his friends, usually thought of his position as Base Commander as little more than a stepping stone to his first star. Years spent at assignments all over the world allowed him to shoulder increasing responsibility with ease.

He spoke softly into the phone to his wife, "No, baby, I can't tell you why I was called in…Just do as I say. Grab your go-bag and head for Lake Tahoe. Call it a quick getaway vacation…You know, a surprise."

"You can't tell me why? At least tell me when you'll be there."

"That's just it, I don't know…day or two, at the most."

"So what am I supposed to do in the meantime?"

"I don't know…Gamble?"

"You know I don't like gambling…"

"Then see some shows or go shopping…think of something."

"I don't know, my book club meeting is tonight…I think I'll wait until you go."

"I'm only going to say this once, so listen up. I want you on your way to the lake in less than thirty minutes…No ifs, ands or buts…"

"And just who do you think you're talking to, mister, one of your Air Force flunkies?"

"No, Sugar, I, uh, didn't mean it quite that way…Take my word for it, though, it's the most important thing I've ever asked you to do…"

"Besides marrying you?"

"Believe it or not, it's a very close second…Look, we're getting ready to start an emergency meeting…"

"What kind of emergency?"

"You know I can't say, but please do as I've told you and leave now."

"Okay, now you're scaring me…Does this have anything to do with those nukes? I told you I don't like being assigned to a base that has them…"

He cupped his hand over the phone. "A little privacy, please...We'll start the meeting in two minutes."

The first people into the room turned around and motioned for those following them to back out. A young lieutenant was the last one through the door and closed it behind him.

WINFIELD RESIDENCE

Bart stopped on the stairs and turned back toward Nora. "Look, I know you know how to be careful...But everything about this is real hush-hush...'though, I guess you'd know that better'n anybody."

"It's one advantage of having worked in OSI...I know how to talk-around something like this. Besides, a few of my girlfriends and I developed our own emergency-action codes to use over the telephone to let each other know when there's a problem."

"Any way of lettin' them know to leave town, without comin' right out and sayin' it?"

"Of course...All I have to do is tell them we're having a girl's night out in the Bay area to celebrate Mary's Birthday...Means they should take cover away from here."

"Who's Mary?

"No idea...We made the name up to use in the code."

"Hot damn, I love being married to a super-smart woman. Okay, give them the code phrase, but no more'n that, okay?"

"Roger that, my darling husband." She put her arms around him, laid her head on his warm chest and breathed in his scent.

"Please be careful."

"You know I will. Otherwise, I have to answer to my lovin' wife and you know what a bear she can be."

"I mean it...I thought we put all this behind us when we quit doing covert missions..."

"We did and I have...Especially for other agencies. I'm just a run-of-the-mill cop now."

"You're not a run-of-the-mill anything, sweetheart. I wonder how people in your squadron would feel if they knew they worked with the legendary Tupelo?"

"Oh, I'm sure they'd want my autograph at the very least. Men would envy me...Women'd wanna have my baby."

"Fat chance as long as I'm around...You're one hundred per cent mine... Seriously, though, what about exposure? I thought you were going to keep a low-profile."

"I'll do my best to stay out of the limelight...Let others do the photo ops."

"Hope so, especially after London..."

LONDON, ENGLAND
SIX YEARS BEFORE

Bart, or Tupelo as he was known in the shadowy world of spies, had set up the meeting with a double-agent named Martin who insisted that it be in a secluded locale to reduce the chances of being followed. It was not an unusual request, so Bart agreed, fully aware of the possibility of a double-cross.

He arranged for the only two agents available at the time to post themselves at a hidden spot at each end of the deserted street. The warehouses and offices that lined it provided ample opportunity for both hunted and prey.

Bart and Nora turned the corner from a side street and the smell of rotting garbage and wet cobblestones assaulted their senses. They had not started the two-block walk to the center of the district when their earpieces crackled with a message from one of the hidden agents.

"Hey, Boss...Adams. Think I see something in one of the second story windows...possible sniper."

"Has he spotted you?"

"No, I'm on top of the building above you looking down at him. He's focused on the center of the street...Hasn't looked back up my way."

"Sure he's an enemy op?"

"Don't know why he'd be holding a rifle with a scope?"

"You have a suppressor on your weapon?"

"Don't leave home without it."

"Can you take him out without a commotion?"

"Easy shot...But won't Martin be looking for him?"

"Don't think so...He'll be afraid to give him away by looking up...Anybody else in the room?"

"Can't tell...too dark."

"Not a good idea to leave him...Take him out."

They heard a muffled pop from above and the tinkling sound of glass falling on the sidewalk ahead of them. They paused to wait for a reaction—but there was none.

Nora looked up at Bart. "What now? Do we go on, knowing

it's a trap?"

"Could be, but also could be Martin put that guy up there in case we were settin' a trap. Everybody in this business looks over their shoulders...including us. We'll have to continue so we can draw him out. One way or another, we need to know where he's coming from...friend or foe."

"Might not be a friend after we killed one of his men..."

"One of the risks in this business...Told him to come alone...He chose to put the man up there...it's on his head. One of the risks we all take."

"I know...just hope we don't plan on doing this forever... don't think I could take the tension."

"Like I said, it's our last mission."

"Unless something more important comes up."

"Not likely...I'm ready to settle down and live a normal life..."

Bart was interrupted by a car turning onto the far end of the street. It stopped after a few yards and the headlights blinked twice. Nora raised the flashlight she was carrying and blinked back twice. The headlights went out and the driver's door opened. It was impossible to make out the facial features of the driver as he stepped out and walked around the door, but he appeared to be the same height and build as Martin. The streetlight behind him shadowed his face and made any attempt to see inside the car futile.

A heavy fog had begun moving into the street—which was not surprising, since the river was only a few blocks away. It brought with it the primordial smell of the river. *Wonder if*

Martin thought about fog moving in when he set the time? Nora nearly stopped in mid-stride before abruptly continuing.

"Everything okay, Baby?"

"Don't know…strange feeling just hit me. Call it a premonition, but I feel like there's something wrong with the whole setup."

"I don't much like it either, but we're here and we need to let it play out. It's never easy working with double-agents."

"Who did you say Martin works for?"

"AVH–Hungarian Intelligence Service."

"And we're supposed to trust him?"

"Like I said, a double-agent. Those Soviet encryption codes could prove priceless…"

They had moved close enough to the shadowy figure for his face to come into view. Bart suddenly shoved Nora away from him and she sprinted across the street. He yelled loudly enough for their backup agents to hear, "It's not Martin!"

The figure in front of them drew a pistol from his pocket and aimed it at Nora. At the same time, Bart pulled his 1911 from a shoulder rig and fired. The .45 round caught him in the chest and knocked him back, causing his shot to race harmlessly skyward.

Nora drew a Walther PPK from her purse and fired another round into the spy. He collapsed to the pavement like a wet newspaper.

A noise behind them caused them to whirl around as an old Mercedes sedan turned from the side street and steered in their direction. Its headlights blinded them and they moved into doorways across the street from each other. Nora made note of the rear windows rolling down and fired three consecutive rounds into the back.

The driver's head exploded from the well-placed shot rendered by Adams from his perch above the street. The out-of-control vehicle moved past before crashing into a store front.

Bart and Nora approached the sedan from both sides with pistols at the ready. It was unnecessary, both rear seat occupants had taken rounds from her weapon.

"Nice shootin' pardner!" Bart said.

"Thanks, Honey."

They turned their attention to the vehicle at the other end of the street. Another spy climbed into the driver's seat and started the car. He put it in gear and turned to look out the back window when a .45 caliber round caught him just above the ear and removed the top of his head with a spray of blood and brain matter. Nora looked over at Bart, who had assumed a two-footed, square shooter's stance. His pistol had a trace of smoke coming out of the barrel and the smell of cordite hung in the air.

"I can't believe you made that shot!" she whispered. "Has to be thirty yards or more."

"Luck," he replied. "And maybe a little help from above."

"Whatever it was, looks like nobody got away," she observed. "So what just happened?"

She asked the question as they moved cautiously down the street toward the stalled car. Again, they approached the vehicle from opposite sides, working as a team.

"Don't know for sure, but it's obvious they aren't friends." Bart walked to the back of the car and opened the trunk with his weapon drawn. The precaution wasn't necessary. The dead man's hands and feet were bound and there was a single shot to the temple.

"Looks like they figured Martin out and killed him after getting the information about this meeting. Hell, for all we know, they could've been holding a gun to his head while I talked to him on the phone."

"So where does it leave us?"

"End of the line for this investigation and my cover is blown…Time to return to my day job.'

"Can't say I'm sorry about that." She sighed. "I'm ready for a little peace and quiet."

"Me too, Baby…me too."

The silent figure stayed in the shadows of the second floor room. His associate lay twitching and bleeding on the floor, beyond any medical help. The quick gun battle had unfolded in the street below, yet he felt no urge to join in. Years of intelligence work for the Soviets taught him that it was better to let brash young operatives expose themselves to danger and dying and let more cautious agents live to continue their work.

He removed his comrade's identification folder and placed it in the pocket of his raincoat. *Let MI-6 earn their pay.* He was fairly certain the tall figure worked for British Foreign Intelligence—not that it mattered. He had gotten only a glimpse of his face, but he would remember it. Martin had not revealed the agent's identity, even while being forced to endure an extremely painful interrogation. The only clue he gave was a whispered name as he passed out from the pain. "Tupelo…"

BASE COMMANDER'S OFFICE
MATHER AFB

"Yes, Margie, you should be scared out of your wits….Does that tell you enough?" Colonel Jim Jackson spoke firmly into the phone.

"Yes," she replied in a trembling voice. "I'll leave right now.

"Leave a message with my office when you get to Tahoe and I'll call you back."

"I'll be waiting for you."

"Be there soon as I can." He listened to the static on the phone for a while and finally hung up.

"Come on in," he said in a loud voice. The door opened and they filed in, taking their usual places around the conference table.

"Everybody here?"

"Nobody from Food Services," Lieutenant Colonel Schmidt replied.

"We'll start without them…Fill 'em in later."

"Yes, sir."

J.J. cleared his throat to bring the room to silence. "Most of us have lived near nukes long enough to fear them…and getting them back may be the most important thing we do in our entire careers. So let's buckle down and start running the checklists."

He turned the page on the EAB red binder and looked at Item 1. "All right, let's see here...In case you haven't done it already, we're on twenty-four hour manning as of this moment. Start with twelve hour shifts and see how it goes. Fifteen minute recall status and I don't mean just essential personnel...I want everybody available. We don't anticipate this lasting long, but I want us at full manning while it does."

The Director of Civilian Personnel motioned to him. "What about civilians? You're talking a lot of overtime."

"We can leave them on their usual shifts for now. Any section that feels they need extra civilian bodies should coordinate it through you to my office.

"Item 2...I'm placing my executive officer in charge of the rest of the base while I act as the on-scene commander. Lieutenant Colonel Schmidt will take over until further notice. If you need anything from me, run it through the XO.

"Public Affairs should get a press release out that says we're conducting a base-wide exercise and going to DEFCON Three as part of it.

"Before we go on, and this is critical...Go back to your people and tell them I want a solid lock on rumors. I'll personally crucify anybody who talks out of turn. Their careers and maybe even their freedom will go down the toilet...and I'll be the one pulling the chain. Any questions?"

They sat quietly.

"This situation's like most exercises, although I have to admit it sure raises the pucker factor when it's the real thing...

Now, if you'll excuse me, I need to get to the Mobile Command Post. "

He grabbed his BDU camouflage hat from the table, tucked his organizer under his arm and stood as they snapped to attention. They sat down as soon as the door closed and started mumbling to each other in hushed tones.

323rd ABG MOBILE COMMAND POST OVERLOOKING THE ALERT PAD

Colonel Jackson cleared the last step as the occupants sprang to attention. "At ease," he said automatically and they resumed their duties.

The custom command and control center was built on a commercial bus chassis and resembled the massive recreational vehicles that cruised the local freeways—at least on the outside.

The inside had little in common with its vacation counterparts. A bank of television screens that occupied six feet of one wall was used to monitor local and network newscasts, or to review video recordings.

A satellite dish on the roof supported remote communications capabilities, including secure teleconferencing. The distinct smell of stale air conditioning mixed with the aroma of half-burnt coffee. The constant hum of electronics equipment produced a blanket of white noise as a backdrop to hushed conversations.

Half of the interior walls contained consoles for communications technicians and supplies were stocked in

122

overhead bays.

He walked over to the most important item, a thirty-eight cup coffee maker, grabbed his white mug with the embossed colonel's eagle from a wall-mounted rack and filled it. Four sugars later, he took his first sip. *Better than my wife's.*

A small conference table occupied the rear of the command post. Half-filled coffee cups and pads of paper with scribbled notes and doodles lay strewn about. Members of the Emergency Response Team from Disaster Preparedness wandered in and out with reports.

J.J. plopped down in the chair at the head of the table and opened his ever-present organizer. He pulled a silver pen with an engraved eagle out of his shirt pocket and drew a line on a yellow legal pad two inches from the left margin from top to bottom, labeling the smaller side TIME, and the larger side ACTIONS. After noting the time of the attack, he drew a line under both entries from the left margin to the right margin and moved down one line.

His command staff entered and sat around the table. "We'll get started in a minute. First, though I'd like all nonessential personnel to wait outside. Stay close in case you're needed."

A half-dozen mumbling people filed out the two doors, one at the front and one in the middle of the unit. Another six sat shoulder-to-shoulder in folding chairs at the opposite end of the command post. They would be called upon to address the group.

"All right, Chief Worth, let's get started."

Chief Master Sergeant Bill Worth, the Senior Enlisted Advisor, was also his key assistant and aide.

"Yes, sir," came the crisp reply. "This briefing is classified Top Secret and all personnel present have been confirmed to be authorized."

A Staff Sergeant administrative assistant took notes on a hardened computer that was designed to contain classified material. It could have been any corporate meeting, except for the camouflage BDUs and the guard outside with an automatic weapon.

Chief Worth locked the front door, walked to the middle door and checked the lock. "Ready, sir."

MATHER AIR FORCE BASE
BASE COMMANDER'S STAFF MEETING

Lieutenant Colonel Schmidt spoke in a determined voice, "All right, everybody, Let's start by going over every check list that's available. Call your people together when you get back to your sections and brief them on the situation, especially the need for utter secrecy.

"I know they'll want to tell their families what's going on, but tell them to keep it close and personal. We don't want to start a panic with our dependents.

"Some will want to send their families out of state…That's understandable, but tell them to do it discreetly. Also, quietly call your essential personnel in from leave or any other authorized absences."

The Director of Personnel raised one finger.

"Yes, Colonel Scott."

"What about personnel who are TDY or away at tech schools?…You want them recalled?"

"This should be over by the end of the day…tomorrow at the latest…Now that I think about it, it might send the wrong message if we start yanking our people back for something we haven't admitted exists."

"I agree, Bill…But it's part of the checklist." Scott pointed to the red binder in front of him.

Schmidt glanced down at the notes he had been taking. He had led numerous staff meetings as vice commander of the base when Colonel Jackson was unavailable. *Chance to grab a little command time.*

"Of course…Good call, Jim. Run through your section checklists to make sure we're at a hundred per cent and our sixes are covered. Meet back here in one hour for a base-wide status report…Keep your radios close and stay alert."

He stood to signal the end of the meeting. Readiness of base resources would be confirmed and no matter what happened out at the Alert Pad—they'd be ready. This could be the most critical day of their Air Force career—nobody wanted to come up short in any way.

WINFIELD RESIDENCE

Bart took note of her concerned look and walked back down the stairs. He held her face in his big hands and looked her in the eye. "I'm not tryin' to make light of the situation…You know as well as I do there's always a little danger in this job. What I'm trying to tell you is I'm not going to rush headlong into it. I'll stand back and let the younger guys take the risks…They heal faster. Besides, I didn't put getting shot on my to-do-list for today, okay?"

"I was just thinking back to London. If you hadn't taken out that Soviet agent…"

"But I did…And he's the only one who's ever seen my face…Everyone else's looking for a ghost."

"Long as you don't become a real one."

"Do my best to avoid the bad guys."

"Keep that streak going…Now go take a shower. I'll get your sandwich ready."

He gave her a kiss on the forehead, stroked her hair and headed upstairs.

The warm water ran down his shoulders and back and provided some relief from the tension.

He pulled a big fluffy sky-blue towel off the rack and began drying his face. The clean fresh scent of the fabric softener was also relaxing. *Sure would feel great to take a nice long nap…*

323rd ABG MOBILE COMMAND POST

"Thanks, Chief," said Colonel Jackson. "First, I need to introduce two visitors." He pointed to two civilians in dark suits at the other end of the rig and they stood. "Agents Mary Benson and Jay Johansen are with the NSA…They're here to assist in the investigation.

He turned his attention back to the group. "I want a brief

report on what's happened so far...then we'll discuss options."

A quick glance at his aviator's chronograph gave him the time accurate to within .01 seconds. "We have less than fifteen minutes before they..." He pointed out the window to the Alert Pad, "...contact us. Please, be brief...Colonel Hadler, you have the floor."

"Excuse me!" Colonel Eric Bateman, Commander of the 320th Bombardment Wing interrupted. "The Alert Pad is SAC...I should be directing this operation."

"Now hold on there a minute, Colonel," J.J. responded.

Johansen leaned over to Mary Benson and whispered, "What's going on?"

"Territorial dispute...Mather's an Air Training Command base that conducts navigator and bombardier training. Has a full-bird running it...Also has the 320th as a tenant...a SAC unit with a Colonel in charge...They bicker over base priorities. That's why there's a Base Commander...also a colonel. He runs the base facilities, sort of like a landlord."

"What keeps them from fighting?"

"Protocol, mostly, but they also know the Brigadier General Selection Board will review their performance during a crisis like this...Figure out whether they deserve their first star."

J.J. continued, "I think I know where you're going with this, but it's nothing more than apprehending criminals who have broken into the Alert Pad...has little to do with your mission."

"What the...how can you say that? Those planes and cargo

are my responsibility…Those intruders are in my Alert Pad." Colonel Bateman's face turned redder by the moment.

Colonel Jackson held up his hand like a traffic cop. "Point well taken and, notwithstanding the failure of your security to prevent the intrusion, those planes and cargo will be turned back over to your control as soon as possible."

He paused for a moment and went on in a conciliatory tone, "Actually, I just talked with the SAC Commander. He suggested I secure the Alert Pad and wait for the advisory teams to arrive, since we're in the early stages of this incident. Depending on how it plays out, we'll turn the recovery phase over to them."

"Unless it falls apart in the meantime," Colonel Bateman snapped back. *Gotta get to a secure line…talk to SAC/CC.*

"Well, then, I guess we need to make sure it doesn't." He pushed on before Bates could come up with a retort. "Let's move on…Security, I'd appreciate it if you'd get things going."

Colonel Jim Hadler, Commander of the Security Police Squadron sat at Colonel Jackson's right hand. He swiveled his chair toward the rest of the table and began in a calm, low-pitched voice, "It appears this was an extremely well-planned attack, executed with impeccable precision and timing…The intruders are either trained mercenaries or ex-government operatives…"

"Excuse me," J.J. interjected. "Let's stick to what we can confirm to avoid speculation."

"Not speculation…We have a positive ID on the attacker our young airman killed…Fingerprints popped up on NCIC… Hired thug with a twenty-year rap sheet of robbery and assaults."

"You think this is a botched robbery?"

"Didn't say that. If you want me to speculate, my guess is he's a local thug hired to help gain access....May not have anything to do with the core group...Had no provisions or equipment for an extended stay and only four mags on him...Probably would have left as soon as the Alert Pad was taken.

"Again, I'm not sure we should be labeling them...But I do see your point about the hired gun...What else do you have?"

"No contact beyond the one message. No visuals, so no ID. Our sensors are picking up activity, but we have no idea what's going on in or around the plane. That's why I've asked Lieutenant Colonel Winfield, my Ops Chief, to brief you. Colonel..."

Bart stood up and walked the length of the conference room in long strides. His six- six frame barely fit under the ceiling and he lowered his head to gain a little space. His distinct southern drawl evoked memories of Elvis Presley in its resonance.

"I've put together a timeline of the attack to gain a perspective on what we're facing. The entire sequence, from initial contact through complete control of the Alert Pad, took just over twenty-two minutes...including destroying two power transformers and disabling alarm system relay boxes to slow response time...They also laid tripod-mounted sensors...It's all but impossible to get close.

"There's a moving van parked next to the plane and a commercial generator for power. They also put up a plywood barricade under the B-52."

"Why?"

"So they can move around undetected...Or they may be getting ready to move nukes to the semi."

Everyone sat up straighter and Bateman slammed his hand down on the table. "We need to rush the damned plane before they get away!" Loud murmurs of agreement showed many were in favor of the idea.

"Hold on there," Jackson. commanded. "This isn't the time for a knee-jerk, cavalry-charge reaction..."

Colonel Bateman started to pursue his point, but was interrupted by Captain Clark, a young intelligence officer who waved his hand to get the base commander's attention. "Sir, could I make a point?"

"What is it?" J.J. motioned for silence.

"I agree with you that rushing the plane's probably a bad idea."

"Glad you're with me on that," he replied with a condescending smile "Tell us what you have."

"We've been analyzing raw data from communications traffic and electronic sensors...We think there's a pretty good chance they got one of the nukes out of the plane."

"So? We expected that...But they don't have the activation codes..."

"No, but they may be able to override them. I mean, up until a few years ago there was no way...But now, with new desktop computers and off- the-shelf software, it's more than possible. A third year computer student with store-bought gear could crack those codes."

"You think there's major flaw in security we're totally unprotected against…Is that what you're saying?"

"Unfortunately, yes, sir. The working group I'm part of, tried to get the Justice Department to put a lid on public access to the software…Turned us down…Said it would put too many constraints on commercial use…Civilian access to this type of encryption breaking-program is a fairly recent development. It's been argued against in just about every symposium I've attended…A real hot-potato issue."

"May turn out to be the hot-potato issue of the century," Jackson noted. "Nothing we can do about it at this point, but we'll include it in our report…let's move on."

He nodded to Bart. "So what are my options for retaking the Alert Pad?"

"We've come up with a couple of assault plans. I know you said you only wanted to secure the Alert Pad, but with the possibility of those people being able to detonate one of the weapons, seems like it's more crucial than ever to retake the plane. And as fast as the intruders appear to be working, we should probably move ASAP."

A telephone on the console at J.J.'s side began a distinct beeping sound. He glanced at the technician at one of the wall consoles who took off his headset and half-turned in his seat.

"Excuse me, Colonel Jackson…It's the intruders for you."

***

CHAPTER 10

UNDERNEATH THE B-52
INSIDE THE ALERT PAD

Jason gathered Bill and Bud under one end of the plane and spoke in a hushed voice that betrayed his anxiety, "Where's Jack?"

"With Rick," Bill replied. "Rigging the bombs with something…"

"Rigging the bombs! Why, in God's name, are they messing with them?" Jason demanded.

"How the hell should I know? I ain't their boss," was Bill's annoyed response.

Bud broke in, "I heard Rick tell Jack it was so nobody could accidentally set one off…"

"Oh, come on…Sounds a little fishy to me," Bill interjected.

"I'm with you on that, but what was I supposed to do, get into it with Rick?" Bud asked.

Jason jumped back in, "That's what I wanted to talk about…I'm starting to worry about Rick…"

"Starting to?" Bill commented. "I been worried since we took over this plane…He's wound tighter than a two-dollar watch and getting jacked up more every minute."

"But why? Everything's going just the way we planned…"

"Which makes me wonder what's really going on…Like maybe he has some hidden agenda or something."

"Look, fellas, I'm no genius," Bud said, "but most anybody can tell there's more to this than what meets the eye…Maybe he's planning on cutting us out of the ransom…You know, use us to finish things and then leave us high and dry…Whadda ya think?"

Bill answered, "It's possible…Especially since the ransom is going to be transferred to an account only he knows about."

"So, what are we going to do about it?" Jason asked. "Get in his face now, or wait until the ransom's been transferred?"

"Be a little late then, don't you think?" Bill seemed to be thinking out loud. "He could tell us all to go to hell…Then what could we do, threaten to kill him?…Either way, we don't get the money."

Jason's voice went up a notch, "Thing is, he's acting like we're his paid flunkies…or worse yet, his slaves. Barking orders and yelling at us…like he's gone over the edge or doesn't care what we think anymore."

"Still, it ain't no good," Bill said. "Problem is, we're kinda stuck...We gotta see it through...After all, he's made the arrangements to get us out of the country and he's the one with the contacts...Which means they probably won't give us the time of day, even if we knew who they are...Especially without no money to back it up."

"It all comes back to the money, doesn't it?" Jason observed. "I say we talk to Rick right now and get some answers...You know, like the number of the bank account and where it's located. What about you two?"

Bill sighed. "Can't argue with you on that point. We need to know where it's going...If nothing else, in case something happens to Rick."

"Hadn't thought about that," Bud said. "But you're right...Ol' Rick gets hurt or has a heart attack...We're up the creek."

"And from the way he's acting, he might just drop dead from the pressure," Jason added. "I think it's time we had a little heart-to-heart talk with him."

"Heart-to-heart? Man, you're weird," Bill commented as they climbed up into the plane to look for Rick.

Jack had told them Rick went to the other end of the plane and they found him peeking around the plywood barricade at the rest of the Alert Pad.

"What do you want?" he demanded. "I'm kinda busy right now...getting ready to go back into the plane and give them my demands."

They had decided Jason would be their spokesman. "That's one of the things we want to talk about…Like just now…you said 'my demands' instead of our demands. We need to know stuff like where the money's going, in case something happens to you. You know, you get sick or have a heart attack, or something…"

Rick interrupted, "So, you want the most crucial information in case I keel over? Is that what you're saying?…'Cause if it is, I say bullshit! How do I know you're not hoping to steal the money and split it four ways instead of five?"

"We'd never do that, man…What kind of guys do you think we are?"

"Don't know…thought you were my friends. Now, I'm not so sure…What, or who, brought this all up?"

"You've been acting a little strange."

"Look, this isn't a cozy little card game in your garage anymore. This is the big time and one wrong move could send us to prison…or worse yet, to an early grave…."

"Well, I…um, hear you, but what we're saying is there's no reason why we all shouldn't have the account information."

Bill stepped in closer to Rick and towered over him. "Yeah, what's the big deal, anyway? Seems to me there ain't no harm in everybody sharing everything we know."

Rick started to spit out a retort, paused and rubbed the back of his neck. "Hold on just a minute here…let me think. Guess I see your point and you're probably right. I'm so used to running construction crews where I have to think of every little thing that I forgot about you being partners. It's usually just me running the show."

"See?" Bill turned to the other two. "I told you it was something simple."

Bud and Jason nodded, but didn't seem entirely convinced.

Rick pulled a notebook out of his shirt pocket and began to write. He tore out a page a minute later and handed it to Bill. "Why don't you copy that for everybody else?"

"Sure, no problem. Let's see here…Grand National Bank… Cayman Islands…these are the account numbers?"

"That's right. The six-digit PIN code is required for any withdrawals, so don't lose it…Just having the account number won't do any good."

He set up the automatic transfers when he opened the account. It was information that his so-called partners in crime didn't need to know. They would be left with a PIN code that was useless without funds. Not that it mattered—they would never get a chance to use it anyway.

"Now, if you'll excuse me, I need to make a call."

323 ABG MOBILE COMMAND POST ALERT PAD

J.J. looked at his watch. "Looks like they're a bit early, Owens…Put 'em on the speaker." The connection was made, "Colonel Jackson here."

The voice had a flat tone that was chilling and devoid of accent or emotion. "First of all, Colonel, tell your teams to pull back at least 100 yards or I will incinerate one of the tankers on the Alert Pad…I'm counting now, nine...."

"Wait, hold on a minute, what happened to ten?"

"Eight, seven…"

"Dammit, stop counting, whoever you are, so I can give the order… They'll withdraw as soon as I do."

"Good…I'm glad to see you know how to pay attention. It'll make our relationship so much easier."

"I don't want a relationship…I want my Alert Pad back and I mean now!…And who are you, anyway?" his voice had gone up in volume and pitch.

Captain Clark tapped him on the shoulder and whispered, "Don't anger him…need to keep the dialogue open."

The annoyed look he got caused Clark to sit back in his chair. *Last advice from me.*

Jackson muttered, "Just a minute." He hit the mute button on the console and turned to Colonel Hadler. "Jim, pull your teams back a hundred yards."

"That's not a..."

He was interrupted with a raised hand and a curt look. "Make it happen."

"Yes, sir." The security police commander turned to the communications technician to issue the order.

J.J. returned to the terrorists. "Okay, they're moving back…Now, can we continue?"

"Certainly, Colonel," the intruder replied. "…and for the sake of future communication, why don't you call me Number One…Will that suit you?"

"Sounds like a Bruce Willis movie, but sure, Number One it is…And while we're at it, how should we refer to your location?"

"To add a little color, why don't we call it the Blackjack Bomber?" Rick suggested.

"You mean like the Russian bomber?"

"Yes, like the Russian bomber…sort of an inside joke. A little humor can make difficult situations so much easier."

"Whatever…Blackjack Bomber is fine…Now tell me, what do we need to do to end this situation? I want it over with as soon as possible."

"Let me assure you, Colonel, I want it over even sooner…and to help make that a reality for both of us, I've prepared a motivational device…I'm sure you must have timers in your command post that display elapsed time, as well as a countdown clock…Am I correct?"

"Of course we have them."

"Good. On my mark, please start the countdown clock at twenty-four hours…I'll wait while your people prepare."

"Twenty-four hours it is…Ready whenever you are…"

"In three…two…and mark!"

Six-inch high red numbers above the center console came to life and displayed a digital countdown in hundredths of a second from twenty-four hours, zero minutes and seconds. A beep over the speakers indicated a timer had been started in the bomber.

J.J. leaned over the microphone. "Okay, Number One, what's the timer all about? We're going to try to meet your demands as fast as we can, clock or no clock."

"I thought you might like a little incentive…I am the only person who can stop the countdown and I will, if all of my demands are met by tomorrow at this time."

"Well, like I said, we'll do our best…"

"Let's hope that is adequate," Rick replied. "Although, it won't matter if you don't. You see, I've rigged a detonator to two of the nuclear weapons in the bomb bay. They will not only produce a spectacular explosion, but will also destroy all other devices on the aircraft. The added nuclear debris will make the biggest dirty bomb the world has ever seen…Hundreds of square miles of northern California will be unusable for centuries…Millions of people will die immediately. Those who don't will wish they had…rather than suffer the effects of radiation poisoning."

"You can't be serious…"

"Oh, but I'm deadly serious…Meet my demands, or face the worst catastrophic disaster your country has ever seen."

"Has it occurred to you that you'll die, too?"

"So what?…I'll be serving my cause."

"What cause would that be?"

"Doesn't matter…I'll fax the demands as soon as we finish this conversation and you might want to get to work on them immediately…My demands are few and are not negotiable. You have twenty-four hours and either I will be gone or a good-sized chunk of northern California will glow for a very long time. This is Number One from the Blackjack Bomber, out."

The intruder's voice was replaced with the gentle hum of a dead line.

139

Colonel Jackson's reply froze on his lips. "The son of a bitch hung up on me...can you believe that?" he said to nobody in particular. "Although, I guess that went about as well as could be expected. Anybody think of something else that needed to be covered?"

Nobody answered the rhetorical question. They waited for the fax machine to spit out the demands and a few minutes later one of them began gently whirring. Chief Worth grabbed the single sheet as it finished printing and gingerly carried it to the head of the conference table as if it were contaminated. J.J. looked up,

"Thank you, Chief." J.J. took the paper from his hands, pulled a set of bifocals out of his shirt pocket and placed them on his nose. The rest of the room remained silent, with only the soft hum of the air-conditioners to break the tension.

"Let me start by saying none of what was said on that call leaves this room, understood? I'm not going to bore you with the details of this message...Most of their demands are need-to-know, anyway. They're asking for pretty much what we expected...whole boatload of money deposited in an overseas account with more delivered to the Alert Pad and, of course, transportation...including passenger vans and helicopters. Don't know where they think they can go without being followed, but they do seem to have a well-thought-out plan.

"Let's see...They want a manifesto released to the public...not uncommon for terrorists. Also want a list of high-profile prisoners released and brought here...and a fortune in uncut diamonds delivered in very specific satchels. Food and water for them and the hostages…the usual stuff. I'll send the demands we can't handle locally up the chain.

"Let's get back to our sections now and work those Red Book actions. Twenty-four hours is not a lot of time…we need to get cracking. This meeting is adjourned. Colonel Hadler, would you and your team stay behind?"

He stood and the rest of the room followed suit. They began filing out with determined looks on their faces and notebooks in hand.

UNDERNEATH THE BLACKJACK BOMBER

"Well, I guess that settles that!" Jason had a smile of satisfaction from ear to ear.

"Does it?" Bill challenged.

Jason's smile faded and was replaced with a perplexed look. "We stood up to him, didn't we?…Forced him to give us the account numbers…"

"And how do we know they're real? Could be any string of numbers…Besides, that bank might not even exist. How do you feel about all this, Bud?"

"Hard to say…I mean, he seemed sincere…"

"But do you think he was telling the truth?"

"Couldn't tell one way or another."

"Exactly, and we got no way to verify nothing."

"So what do we do now, just give up?" Jason asked.

Bill smiled. "Actually, that's one possible scenario…Throw up our hands and walk out to the gate…Let them take us in.

'Course, that leaves us back where we were…Facing jail time and still being chased by the mob."

"Doesn't have any more appeal than it did when we broke in here," Jason noted.

"Yeah," Bud chimed in. "I was kinda hoping this would work out."

"It still might," Bill offered. "Won't know for sure until this is all over…will we?"

"How in the world did we get ourselves in this mess?" Bud asked.

"Been through that too many times already," Bill answered. One thing I have noticed, though, is how fuzzy my thinking's been the last couple of months…Like I was on drugs, or something…any of you guys feel that way?"

Jason stood silent, but Bud spoke up, "Yeah, now that you mention it, I have felt a little spacey…Which don't make no sense, 'cause I don't even take the stuff the doc gives me…makes me feel like a zombie."

Bill turned toward Jason. "How about you, Champ? Ever feel like somebody's slipping you a mickey?"

"Sort of, I guess…"

"Huh?"

"I used to see a doctor for anger management…My temper's got me into a little trouble now and then and I had a fight with Bill Smythe at work…They made me go or else they'd take me before the Disciplinary Board…Anyway, I went for a couple of months and the doctor gave me a prescription to calm my nerves. It worked…but I remember now that it made me feel like I was isolated from the whole world, so I quit taking it."

"How long ago was that?" Bill asked.

"Six months or so…although, I've sort of felt some of the same feelings come back a little the past couple of months… been way too calm."

"That's what I thought," Bill replied. "I know this is gonna sound kinda far out there, but I think Rick's been slipping something to us."

"Oh, come on, man," Jason exclaimed. "You turning paranoid on us?…Gonna join the local conspiracy theorists group?"

"No…In fact, I'm thinking clearer now than ever before and there's a reason. I quit eating or drinking what the rest of you have…Been drinking the food and water they bring to us through the fence…And the thing is, I'm noticing a big difference already."

"Glad to hear that…But why do you think it's Rick?"

"He seems to like hovering over our food and drinks, that's why. It's not like he helps fix it, so I asked myself why he'd do that and the answer came to me in a flash…could be he's putting something in it…"

Bud broke in, "I never said nothing before, but I came out of the john at Jason's place one night and Rick had a pill bottle in his hand near the pizza. He looked real surprised and then covered it up by saying it was some stuff his doctor gives him. I didn't think no more about it…but he coulda been putting something in the food."

Bill put a hand on their shoulders. "I don't wanna get carried away with this, but I think we should talk to Jack and all of us need to keep our eyes open…Maybe he has, maybe he hasn't. Who knows? But there's another reason…He's the only one who don't work at the base. He's not one of us."

323RD SPS BRIEFING ROOM

"Sergeant Thomas, would you join us to say how you'd handle this? We're racing the clock."

Lieutenant Colonel Winfield had hurried back to the security police squadron building from the meeting in the mobile command post and gathered together the team that would lead the response.

The area where guard mount was usually held was set up like a classroom, with rows of student desks and a chalkboard in back of him. He leaned his tall frame on the lectern while the team copied information from the board behind him.

Items were grouped under headings that broke the facts down into logical sections: Subjects, Weapons, Transportation, Physical Characteristics and Personality. Side notes added information about a particular item and footnotes directed certain security police elements to take charge of individual tasks.

The smell of stale coffee and body odor permeated the room. Most of them had hurried in without going through their usual morning routines—there'd be time for personal hygiene later.

"Sorry, sir…" Jake Thomas stopped tapping a camouflage

pen against the side of his hand and directed his attention to the front of the room.

"I want to hear how the NCOIC of Special Ops Response Team A would go about retaking the Alert Pad...But first, let me make a few comments.

"I received some information during the Base Commander's phone call with the intruders that can't be discussed...But I can tell you that we need to find a solution to this problem fast. We know this squadron can take whatever's thrown at us...The key now is to do it with speed and precision. Our fate, and that of the entire area, is on our shoulders like never before. That's nothing new...We face the inherent dangers of this job every day...Maybe not like this, or we'd all quit."

The comment brought a few smiles and he returned them.

"Intruders seem to know our procedures better'n we do...Been a step ahead of us the whole time. That ends today when we put our heads together and come up with a solution.

"And don't be afraid to step outside the lines. We need to listen to every idea...no matter how far out there it is. With that in mind, what do you have for us, Sergeant Thomas?"

Jake stood up. "Well, sir, this isn't much different than scenarios we've run a hundred times during training. We simply need to analyze the setup and apply the right fix, with maybe a few twists thrown in. For instance..."

He held up one finger. "First, we gain access to the plane through the auxiliary power unit hatch in the tail."

He held up a second finger. "Two, we coordinate killing the ground power at the same time we feed CS gas throughout the plane using the external air-conditioning cart…"

Bart interrupted, "Don't you figure they'll have gas masks?"

"Be shocked if they didn't, sir…They're obviously pros. I'm sure they expect us to begin any attack with gas, which is why we'll stop it as soon as it gets going. They'll also expect us to charge the plane…and that's why we won't."

"Now wait just a daggone minute…You're telling us all the things we're supposed to do, but not gonna do?…So, what should we do?"

"We need to throw them off balance a little to gain the upper hand. By testing them, we may discover a crack in their armor. At the very least…might find out who we're up against. At the moment, we don't know anything about them."

"I agree, we don't have enough intel…What else?"

"They've had two local radio stations playing full-blast inside the plane so we can't filter out the masking noise. We need somebody inside to feed us info…The fake assault is our cover. I'll access the aircraft through the APU hatch and crawl along the old tail gunner walkway to the forward crew area. There's an avionics bay where I can get close to them…Won't be able to talk, but I can text in what I see."

"Don't you think they'll react full-force to an attack?"

"Absolutely, sir…So we'll need to back off as soon as we get started…Keep from totally spooking them. We could turn off the security lights on the ramp to start the attack and turn them back on…Make them think we aborted the attack because of a mix-up. Or do a fake transmission over Tac 2….You know they'll be monitoring it."

Bart rubbed his chin. "Commander may not buy into a plan that makes the subjects that edgy…Still, we should be willing to take a risk. These individuals aren't hampered by any set way of doing things…We shouldn't be either…"

An administrative assistant knocked and entered the room to hand him a note. The background hum of conversation rose in volume as the security policemen compared notes.

He read it and raised his hand to get their attention. "Quiet down, please…I have an unfortunate announcement to make."

Conversation subsided immediately. "Just got word that Colonel Hadler has been taken to the base hospital with a medical problem. I know your thoughts and prayers are with him, so I feel like a moment of silence is in order."

He paused and continued a minute later, "Y'all are the best unit I've ever had the honor to work with. I know we'll take these thugs down and get the Alert Pad back in short order…right?"

Fists were thrown in the air. "Hoo, rah!"

A senior airman yelled, "Let's go kick some terrorist butt!"

"Sounds good to me, but first, let's brainstorm this a little more…Come up with the strongest possible plan I can present to Colonel Jackson, since I'm now the Acting Squadron Commander."

"Best work we've done in a long time," Bart proclaimed thirty minutes later. "Lieutenant Johnson and Sergeant Thomas, grab your hats…let's go brief Colonel Johnson."

"Think he'll like what we've come up with, sir?" Jake posed

the question.

"Gotta like it...Uses caution and patience while acting expeditiously...Best way to keep a situation under control. This is no time for cowboyin'. We got a lot of people counting on us...even if they don't have the slightest idea what's going on. It's our job to regain control of the Alert Pad and the nukes in the planes before the world blows up in our faces...and theirs."

He looked at his watch...*Twenty-two hours and forty-two minutes.*

***

CHAPTER 11

HEADQUARTERS BUILDING
323 AIR BASE GROUP

Agent Mary Benson retrieved an ebony-colored aluminum case from the jet-black Suburban with the darkly-tinted windows and followed Colonel Jackson into the base headquarters building. The secure conference room was in the basement down a long hallway. Fluorescent lights overhead cast a greenish glow on the highly polished tile floor and their footsteps echoed off concrete walls. An armed security policeman stood outside the door to the conference room and came to attention as they approached.

J.J. tapped a code into the crypto-lock and beckoned them into the room. He pressed a privacy button to prevent anyone from entering. The musty smell of a room that was seldom used hung in the air. He walked to the head of the table and opened a concealed drawer to reveal a security control panel.

"I need to sweep the room," he explained to the two agents.

A press of a button on the console brought a small computer screen to life. He chose the option for a full debugging and waited patiently as the computer checked for phone taps, eavesdropping devices and concealed microphones. A beep indicated the sweep was finished.

"All clear. Good, I don't like surprises…Which is why this incident grates on me so much."

"Nobody's blaming you, sir…Could've happened anywhere and at any time."

"Yes, but it happened on my base…so I want everything done by the book. My people can handle these criminals…Although, it does have a certain surreal quality that's hard to shake."

"Not just for you, sir," Mary Benson noted. "We're all new to this type of overt attack. We deal constantly with minor threats and intel gathering. Something this massive in scale shocks your whole system."

"Indeed it does." He pushed a button on the side of his chronograph to display elapsed time. It matched the timer in the Command Post and had just counted past twenty-two hours and thirty-four minutes. "I'm sure you didn't ask to see me privately to offer sympathy. What do you have? Something good, I hope…I need a little positive news."

"Unfortunately," she replied in a businesslike tone, "it probably doesn't come under the heading of good news and may relate to what's happening on your Alert Pad."

She placed the briefcase on the mirror-like finish of the conference table and inserted an odd-looking key that was shaped like a double M into a lock on the case. Johansen did the same with another key that was shaped like a double V.

A small door opened to expose a digital keypad and the two agents took turns punching in half of a twelve-digit security code. At the same time, they held their thumbs over small smoked glass windows on top of the briefcase. There was a gentle whirring sound and the case popped open.

WINSTEAD RESIDENCE

"Hello," Nora said firmly into the phone.

"It's me, Darlin'…On my way to meet with J.J.…only have a minute. Thinking maybe you should go to Mary's birthday party after all. Where'd you say it was…Tahoe?"

She was taken aback and it took her a moment to respond. "I…uh, yes, that's right. Will you be able to come?"

"Not sure at this point…He glanced at his watch. "I'll know by 1640 tomorrow, one way or 'nother."

"Let me think…Sure, I'll call the South Shore Lodge and see if they have a cabin available. I imagine you'd like the idea of a few days with no phone to deal with." *And the security of a CIA safe house.* "I like the idea of spending time with my big, handsome husband."

"Let me know when you arrive at the lodge."

"Will do, big guy…See you as soon as you can get there. I

love you, my darling."

"And I love you more than you'll ever know…Later."

Nora sat still after the call ended and tried to sort out the hidden implications of the call. It sounded like he knew there might be a major disaster in the near future. She entered the numbers by rote.

HEADQUARTERS BUILDING
SECURE CONFERENCE ROOM

After removing a folder marked Classified, Level Seven-Alpha, Eyes Only, Benson noted the date and time on a tracking sheet. She returned Colonel Jackson's military ID card after recording the serial number.

"We've confirmed this room is secure, so we can begin the briefing."

"Go right ahead."

"This is a classified briefing intended for your information only. The contents are not to be divulged under any circumstance, unless specifically authorized by POTUS under written executive order.

"Disclosing information can result in prosecution under Title 10, Section 978 of the U.S. Code and result in penalties of not less than a ten thousand dollar fine and not less than six months in prison, and penalties can be administered without trial. Do you understand, sir?"

"Yes, of course," J.J. said, "I've been in hundreds of classified briefings." He paused for a moment. "Although, I don't believe I've ever heard of an automatic conviction without trial."

"Then you understand the importance of absolute secrecy?"

He nodded and she continued, "More than four decades ago, the NSC approved the implementation of a program to prevent the unauthorized acquisition of nuclear material by entities hostile to the United States which might occur from the downing or accidental landing of an aircraft, or the illegal transfer of nuclear devices by a misguided or mentally deranged crew member."

Jackson interrupted, "Misguided or mentally deranged crew?"

"They were concerned that a crew might defect for political or financial gain..."

"But, that's what the Personnel Reliability Program is all about. Crew members undergo constant physical and mental testing...There's no way it should happen. Of course, the part about mechanical trouble is always possible."

"You're mostly correct...PRP has worked well, with only minor deviations."

"Minor deviations?"

"Sorry, you're not cleared for that."

"I see."

Mary went on, "Plans were formulated to insure that irretrievable devices would not be available to hostile forces. There might be a need to terminate the event with extreme prejudice."

"English, please?"

"Certainly...Small-yield nuclear devices code-named BlackStar are installed on all aircraft that carry nuclear weapons under the guise of being a piece of ultra-secret communications equipment and can be remotely detonated."

"What!" J.J. came half out of his chair. "Are you saying we'd blow up our own plane with a crew on board?"

"Yes, Colonel...The possibility of the crew being in the aircraft is unfortunate...The bigger issue, of course would be the consequences of nuclear devices falling into the wrong hands..."

Jackson interrupted her, "This sounds like something right out of Hollywood...Don't see how it hasn't leaked..."

"Not a hint. Think how catastrophic it would be if some ragtag terrorist group or rogue country got control of some of our nukes...They could reverse engineer them or use them against us. The BlackStar Investigative Section was created to insure that will never happen...I'm proud to be part of the program."

"I can see that. But tell me, is there one of these devices on the Blackjack Bomber..."

CONSORTIUM HEADQUARTERS
CENTRAL EUROPE

"Commissioner, Rick Eichman is calling via encrypted satellite phone and demands to speak with you directly."

"Really? I understand he is a new client, but does he not comprehend our organizational protocol? He should contact his regional director first."

"Yes, sir, I told him that, but he insists upon talking with you, saying it is a matter with many zeros behind it."

"Thank you, Conrad. I will take his call this time."

The Commissioner would usually refuse, but he was intrigued by the cryptic nature of the message. He pressed a button. "Mister Eichner, yours is an unusual request to which I would not normally respond...You have thirty seconds."

"How about in five words, Commissioner?...Hundreds of millions of dollars."

"I suppose I can overlook the breach in protocol...At least long enough to hear a proposal. Please continue."

Rick laughed and switched to Russian. "Interesting isn't it?...How large sums of money transcend just about any impediment to conversation. I have only recently made use of your services, but am pleased with your agency's response to my requests. Certain operations to which I am connected require access to even more sensitive data, however."

"You speak White Russian as though you were a native."

"I am sure you are undoubtedly aware of my provenance. Therefore, you must know that I can be taken seriously. However, in order to expedite our business relationship, I will ask a direct question...What amount of money do you require as a retainer for access to some of the most sensitive information about the American intelligence community?"

"When you say American intelligence community, to what specific area are you referring?"

"Deep-cover clandestine agents."

"That is, most assuredly, a sensitive area. We usually require a retainer of ten million dollars a year and billing by the hour for research of that sort...It can often run into many additional millions. How long will you need our assistance?"

"There is no set period...I prefer to think of it as an ongoing arrangement."

"That gives me a better idea of how much time you may demand from my staff," the Commissioner noted, "Is there an immediate desire for research?"

"Yes. I will give your assistant a list of names of United States Air Force personnel for which I need background material."

"How many names and how far back?"

"From university forward should suffice for now and there are five names on the list."

"Such a search will entail many hours and, therefore, be very expensive. How soon will you need the information?"

"Minutes would be better than hours," Rick replied. "I am in the middle of an operation."

"I am aware of that...Instantaneous service requires a two-hundred per cent premium and a deposit equal to a one year retainer."

"I see no problem, and will get the appropriate banking information from your assistant to transfer the money immediately."

"Are there, perhaps, other services we can offer?"

"Not presently. I will, at some point, require clandestine transportation and papers for me and approximately two thousand pounds of cargo to an overseas destination."

"I do not foresee any difficulty. Simply give Conrad possible destinations and he will research the matter. Will your present team accompany you?"

"That is undetermined at this time."

"Very well, I will transfer you back to Conrad. Thank you for your business."

The Commissioner smiled as he ended the call.

HEADQUARTERS BUILDING
SECURE CONFERENCE ROOM

"A BlackStar device is aboard all aircraft and vessels that carry nuclear weapons," Mary Benson stated.

Colonel Jackson brushed his gray-tinged hair back and exhaled slowly. "Really?...Still, if this is a highly classified program I would think the terrorists don't even know it exists."

"Actually, there may be a problem on that point."

She withdrew a personnel folder from the briefcase, opened it and took out a picture. "Look familiar?"

Jackson studied the picture. "Maybe...can't say for sure. I've got over 2300 military, 2700 civilians and who knows how many contractors on base at any given time...Can't be expected to know all of them."

"Of course not. John Paul Hamilton...goes by Jack. WG-11 electrician in Civil Engineering...Worked there for eleven years. Before that, he was a classified weapons technician in Project BlackStar."

"You're kidding!"

"I seldom kid, sir...especially when it comes to BlackStar. As soon as we heard of a possible Broken Arrow we did a search of our database. Three former employees popped up within a two hundred-mile radius and we've interviewed two of them. Hamilton is the only one we haven't found."

"Think he's one of them?"

"Distinct possibility. Wife says she doesn't know where he is...Been calling friends and relatives trying to locate him. Given his background and heavy gambling debts, we can assume he's involved.

"On the positive side, he had limited access to the devices and compartmentalized knowledge of the overall program. His primary task was to insure electrical systems on aircraft were adequate to handle the increased load. After all, the BUFF was designed during World War II and has been upgraded piecemeal since.

"Furthermore, his work was closely monitored and recorded...Still, there's always a possibility that casual conversation with other maintenance personnel may have disclosed more information than necessary. Hamilton is competent enough to deduce BlackStar's intended purpose. He's also competent enough to figure out how to remove the device. Which means Johansen and I need to gain access to the aircraft as soon as it's secured to see if the unit is intact."

"By all means," J.J. replied. "Hard to believe that a foreign terrorist group found Hamilton and got him to cooperate. Although, if he has heavy gambling debts, who knows?...So what do I tell my people to explain your participation?"

"Tell them nothing about BlackStar. The constraints of SALT II make it more important than ever for the U.S. to have an ace in the hole."

"It violates the treaty?"

"Not in the technical sense...It existed prior to SALT and is not a weapon, per se. Tell your people the President asked the NSA to oversee the incident and report directly to him...that we're comm experts here to secure classified encrypted equipment. They should understand they don't have a need-to-know."

"I can do that." Colonel Jackson was already considering the possibilities. *What a leg-up for the BG Selection Board.*

"By the way, how big is this BlackStar device?"

"About the size of a small office photocopier, although somewhat flatter than cube shape...Good comparison would be an oversized piece of luggage. Dark gray in color...with locking pins that keep it secured to the aircraft."

"That should give my security people an idea of what to look for...Anything else I should know?"

Johansen broke in, "Two things...You have a Technical Sergeant Jake Thomas assigned to your security police squadron..."

"Matter of fact, I do." J.J. smiled. "Second best softball player on his squadron team...tags more than his share of runners."

"That's nice...but we're more interested in his job skills. He's been extremely valuable to our agency on more than one occasion. We're not planning to use him in this event unless absolutely necessary, but wanted to make you aware of his history with us."

Benson added, "Same goes for a Lieutenant Colonel Bart Winfield."

"Best softball player on their team. I wasn't aware…"

"And you still aren't…understood? A remarkable asset. but, there's no need to mix his background in with this event, at least not at this point."

"In light of what you just told me, should I call them in for a private chat?"

"No…Our superiors feel it would be better to let things unfold naturally. We'll let you know if it becomes necessary to use them. In the meantime, though, you might insure they are involved in face-to-face contact with the intruders whenever possible….could prove valuable."

"Certainly, I'll make sure they're front and center." He consulted his chronograph again. Twenty-two hours and four minutes. "Look, I hate to cut this short, but I need to get back to work as On-Scene-Commander. As they say, the clock is ticking…So, unless you have something else…"

"No, that's all for now." Johansen glanced down at his watch. "Written executive orders detailing what we've told you should have been transmitted to your comm center by now."

They stood and began gathering their materials.

"Good," J.J. replied. "Comm Center's right here in the basement…We can stop by on the way out."

He waited while the agents secured the briefing material and led them from the room. *Could be the biggest career boost I've ever had.*

He locked the door and pointed them down the hall in the opposite direction from which they had come. *Looking better every minute.* He couldn't help but smile.

MOBILE COMMAND POST
NEAR THE ALERT PAD

J.J. stood at the wide back window of the mobile command post with feet spread apart and hands clasped behind his back. He chewed on the stub of a cigar and stared into the darkening evening.

"Be nice to light that up, wouldn't it?" Colonel Bill Howard, the Flying Training Wing Commander stepped up beside him.

"Sure as hell would," he answered. "This politically correct crap's gone too far when I can't even light up in my own Command Post. Supposed to set a good example…What a crock!"

"I hear that.…Least we can hope it'll be gone next election."

"Don't know about that…This no smoking thing may be here to stay. Anyway, what's going on?"

"Training's mostly shut down, since we can't use the runways…Thanks to whoever they are." He nodded toward the Alert Pad. "Thought I'd stop by and lend some moral support. Sorry I couldn't make your staff meeting this morning…Been busy all day trying to sort things out for the current class of nav students. This'll put them behind on their training schedule, which means adjusting all of their follow-on report dates."

"Wish it could be avoided...Too chancy to let anything take off right now."

"I know...You holding up okay?"

"As well as can be expected with this hot potato thrown at me. Wish we were both back on Okinawa flying routine patrols...Thousand times more fun than this and we could have a beer or two at the O Club when we got back."

"Yeah, I miss those days...Young and dumb and hardly a care. Nice rig you got here...New?"

"Sure is...first op I've used it on."

"Good way to break it in...Well, guess I'll head on home...Been one long day."

"And gonna be an even longer night."

"Expect so...See you later and good luck...Be praying for you."

"Thanks...Pray for all of us...and watch your six."

"Roger that...Back atcha."

He wanted to tell Bill about the timer but, even though he knew the secret would be safe with him, decided not to. He might be tempted to send his family away and that could start a mini-evacuation. *Fire up the old rumor-mill a bit too much.*

J.J. turned back to the window in time to see part of SORT Team A cut a hole in the fence and roll custom made dirt bikes into the Alert Pad. The sun had set an hour before and the moonless night left any area outside the security lights in total darkness.

Speakers crackled behind him as the rest of the team moved into place. The secure frequency was scrambled and gave their voices an alien quality that could not disguise the tension they felt. This was not an exercise.

He moved from side-to-side to loosen his back and wished he could go for a workout, or maybe even play a little basketball. The quest for physical fitness that started before high school took him to the base gym three or four days a week to play some hoops with men and women half his age.

He not only kept up with them, but usually left them bent over and gasping for breath while he sailed down the court. He longed to be there now with sweat pouring out of his body while they practiced the mild version of trash talk they used.

An administrative specialist handed him a message. "Sir, do you have any idea how long this will last? My boys go to a civilian childcare facility in Rancho Cordova…"

"Nobody knows how long. I hope it's over today or tomorrow, but it's not up to me…Only the people who've taken over the Alert Pad know for sure and they're not talking."

"My mom lives in the Bay area…I can probably get her to come over to watch them."

"What about your husband?"

"A cop…In fact, he's on the team getting ready to go into the Alert Pad."

"Talk to your bosses…See if they can put you on opposite shifts. Have them call me if need be."

"Yes, sir."

The event affected most base personnel, as they held their breath and hoped they could soon drop back from rotating twelve-hour shifts. The cover story spoke of a SAC exercise and warned them against discussing the events with anybody, especially the media. They knew this was no exercise.

Closure of the road that passed by the Alert Pad meant a longer drive around the base to get home, but produced only a few minor grumbles. Base housing residents understood the need for occasional inconveniences.

His reverie was interrupted by the Chief of Services, Major John Miller, who was coordinating the delivery of food and water to the Black Jack Bomber.

"Sorry to bother you, sir, but Number Two is at it again…Dictating new terms every fifteen minutes and generally being a pain. It was a lot easier dealing with his boss."

"I know, but they're in charge…at least for the moment. What's he doing now?"

"Same thing he's been doing all day…Asks for items and makes our people go through a song-and-dance routine to deliver them…Says it's part of their security measures. Personally, I think he's just gone power mad."

"Not surprising, but how?"

"Rejected the first delivery…Made the airmen strip to their underwear and carry the supplies by hand from the fence to the concrete just short of the bomber. Insisted they open and randomly taste the food and water. Ordered it to be removed and replaced. Repeated that twice more before he allowed two of the hostages to carry the food into the trailer."

"Okay, now give me some good news."

"I negotiated the release of two members who were injured while resisting the attack…one with a possible concussion from a rifle butt to the back of the head and the other gut-shot. Both had to be carried out by two volunteers who also had to strip to their underwear."

"They okay?"

"Pretty much, other than cuts on the bottom of their feet…"

J.J. smiled. "No, I meant the injured SRT members."

"Oh, right,…Being treated at the Base Hospital. One with the concussion came to…Should be able to question him in an hour or two. May be a day or more on the other, but he should be okay."

"Good…Anything else?"

"No, sir, just wanted to fill you in."

"Good job, John…Carry on."

He thought again about stepping outside the door and lighting the cigar, until a comm tech motioned to get his attention.

"Pentagon for you, sir."

***

CHAPTER 12

UNDER THE BLACKJACK BOMBER

"What do you mean, you can't tell us what Rick has you doing to the bombs?" Jason posed the question to Jack as Bud and Bill looked on.

Rick was up in the bomber talking to the base commander. They had coaxed Jack out of the bomb bay a few minutes before.

"You heard me," Jack answered. "Rick says it's for everyone's good."

"Whose side are you on, anyway?…Ours or his."

"How about mine?" Jack replied. "Gotta look out for my own interests, don't I?"

"So he's offering you a special deal, that it?" Jason's face had reddened and his jaw had a firm set to it.

"Didn't say that…But he pointed out a few things…"

"Like what?"

"Like the fact you're a little hotheaded, for a start…and that we need to stall them or we won't have enough time to get away. Says he threw a couple of red herrings at them in the demands…Wants to upset their balance. He's also worried they might screw things up when they try to take back the Alert Pad and accidentally set one of the nukes off. So he's had me wiring a couple of the bombs so they can be destroyed by remote."

"And who has the remote?"

"Rick…Says he'll only use it if things get out of hand."

"And you believe that?

"Why wouldn't I? He's got a pretty good head on his shoulders…Been one step ahead of the whole base…"

"And that includes us." Jason pointed out. "Which leaves everybody one step behind him…That doesn't worry you?"

"Well, maybe a little…"

Rick walked toward them with a purposeful stride and the conversation ended.

"Come on," he ordered. "We need to finish getting the nukes out of here."

"Only two left," Bill replied. "I don't see why you're so worried about something happening to the nukes…And tell me again why we need to move them to the truck?"

"Because I don't want to be responsible for half a million people being vaporized, that's why!" Rick answered. "Besides, we don't have time to argue about it…we're almost done."

"Something just don't seem right, that's all."

""Yeah," Jason added. "This wasn't part of the original plan…"

"Plans change when the situation changes," Rick noted. "Have to stay flexible…Now, we can stand here and argue, or we can get the job done and get outta here…What's it gonna be?"

"We're not trying to make a federal case out of it…Just want to know what's going on."

"Like I said, let's do it before they bust down the gates and crawl all over us and I'll explain what I'm doing later…That good enough for you?"

"Whatever."

MOBILE COMMAND POST

"Pentagon?…They say who it is?"

"In no uncertain terms, and I quote, this is Major General Greg McIlvoy…get Colonel Jackson now, unquote."

"Thanks…Put it on my console phone. Colonel Jackson here…Who's this?"

"J.J., Greg McIlvoy."

"General…been a long time."

"Sure has…Air War College Seminar on strategic planning…three or four years ago, I believe."

"Good memory…What can I do for you, sir?"

"Other way around…somebody higher up decided they wanted a two-star overseeing the negotiations and I guess the bullseye's on me."

"When will you be flying in?"

"Won't be…They want me to do it by phone…"

"In case this all blows up?"

"God, no…unless you meant that figuratively…They thought it might draw too much media attention if I suddenly show up. This damn Internet thing's given them way too much access to information…They'd figure out who I was in a New York minute."

Nothing like an inflated ego. "True. So, do we have some answers for the terrorists?"

"I do, but let's not call them terrorists until we know what their motives are."

"They call themselves the Black Diamond Front…They're threatening to set off a nuke in…" He glanced up at the event timer. "…twenty-hours and forty-eight minutes, but whatever you say, General."

"Right…Boy, they sure threw a hot potato at us with these demands."

"Seven-hundred million dollars does seem like pie-in-the sky."

"Oh, that was no problem…Got it out of our black budget and transferred it to their offshore account. NSA will try to track it although, for all intents and purposes, it's probably gone for good. Second one was easy, too…Twelve unmarked civilian helicopters of the same make, model and color. Took us a little under four hours to locate them…On the way to you in four C5As…They'll unload at Travis and hop over."

T.C. Miller

"I'm still puzzled by that one, sir. They've got limited cargo capacity and only about a four-hundred mile range."

"Who knows?...They asked for it...they'll get it. You round up the vans?"

"Yes, Greg...I mean General...Six identical passenger vans from a local truck dealer."

"Great. Their next demand took a little tap-dancing, but we got it done...Ten million dollars in uncut diamonds from a San Francisco diamond exchange...Subjects were nice enough to tell us which stores carry the leather satchels they demanded. Twenty-two hundred bucks apiece...They've got good taste. All of that should be to you by midnight."

"And the prisoner release?"

"That's where it gets a little sticky. DOJ's been sending requests for the twelve guys all over the country with mixed results. Seems one of the inmates was killed in a prison yard stabbing and another's in the infirmary with viral pneumonia...Can't be moved. They'll have to give us two other names.

"What's strange is we checked their records and can't find any obvious connection between Eichner and them, or each other, for that matter. Most were convicted of crimes that don't appear to have anything to do with politics. Counterfeiting, bank fraud and bank robberies, mostly. One was convicted of weapons violations...armorer for a biker gang. Makes no sense. Have they said what the connections are?"

"Not a clue, sir...Will you be able to get them all released?"

"Looks like a qualified maybe, at this point in time. Problem is a bunch are facing warrants in other jurisdictions, so stops were put on their release. Had to do a little arm-twisting and promise a few favors to some prosecutors. Been hard, since we can't tell them why we want them…Old national security thing only goes so far nowadays…May have to get the White House involved."

"Speaking of…What about the printing of the classified ads?"

"Really had to go to the mat on that one. DOJ thinks they might contain coded messages and the NSA is sure there's some kind of hidden code…Just haven't found the right encryption key. White House says they'll allow them to be posted, but don't want their fingerprints on it.

"The ads will be printed tomorrow in the fifty-four cities specified. We put all federal agents in those locales on high alert. Gets complicated, though, when we can't tell them what to look for…only something suspicious…Pretty wide net to cast. We'll go back and take a look at those locations when it's over…see if anything ties in."

"Sounds like the pieces are falling into place."

"Damn well better…Got a lot of man-hours in on this one. Now it's up to you to make sure they don't get away."

"I'll do my best, sir. Now, if you'll excuse me, I have an intel-gathering op underway."

"No problem…I have a meeting with the big guy himself, Chief of Staff, in twenty-minutes. Good talking to you."

Jackson turned back to the command post staff. "All right, people, let's start recording. I want the topside camera zoomed in on the windows of the plane. Analyze every videotape, audio tape, and radio tape nine ways to Sunday…Need to get this right from the get-go."

A comm tech signaled him. "Sir, Team A is in place and ready to proceed."

"Tell them it's a go…Let's say a prayer for Team A."

J.J. reached for his coffee mug, rubbed his stomach and put it back down—stomach acid was boiling up in his throat. He picked two antacid tablets from the roll he kept in his pocket and popped them into his mouth. His command post staff was busy concentrating on various tasks.

Nobody wanted to screw up the most important mission they would face in their entire career. They wanted the Alert Pad back under military control ASAP.

MOBILE COMMAND POST

"A Team Leader, this is Alpha One, proceed with plan…Deadly force is authorized…repeat…deadly force is authorized."

The command was given over an encrypted frequency and transmitted to Jake Thomas's headset. He used a series of hand signals to provide directions to the other five members of the team.

All hell broke loose with his final gesture. The lights that had been illuminating every square inch of the plane faded slowly from brilliant white through orange and finally to black. Their dying glow threw only the slightest shadows. The intruders had apparently turned off the generator that powered the temporary lights they had rigged.

The other five team members were mounted on three dirt bikes. Jake sat down behind one of them and held on. They buzzed past the tripod-mounted sensors and stopped under the fuselage of the bomber long enough to knock down the plywood barrier that had been erected by the terrorists.

One team member found shelter behind an aircraft power unit, while another climbed up into the wheel-well of the giant bomber. The remaining three crouched behind the bikes and waited for any attempt to repel the team.

"SRT-2 to SRT-Leader, something's wrong…Why no fire from the bad guys?"

"No idea…Eyes on bogeys, anyone?"

"Negative."

"No tango in sight."

"Same here."

"Now what?"

"Team Leader to Team A, proceed as planned."

Jake crept toward the back of the huge bomber. *Glad I practiced covert entries on this bad boy bunches of times.* Its flat gray paint reflected none of the faint ambient light and the plane was more a presence than an object.

He reached the auxiliary power unit hatch and took a power screwdriver out of a belt pouch. It was similar to one you might purchase at a local hardware store, Tech Services had modified it for stealth operation. Black electrical tape was wound over a coating of non-reflective plastic to silence all but a faint whir when it was running. Para cord attached to the back prevented it from hitting the ground if dropped. The screwdriver bit matched the size and star shape of the APU hatch screws and was soldered in so it could not be lost.

It took less than a minute to loosen the locking handle cover, and swing the hatch inward. He reached overhand for a grip bar and swung swiftly and silently up into the plane.

Jake keyed his mike three times to let the other team members know he was inside and could almost hear them running for their dirt bikes. The security lights would be turned back on any second.

His night goggles adjusted instantly and he quickly surveyed the APU compartment. It was empty and the generator was silent. *Something's wrong.* Jake scanned the six-foot wide by eight-foot long compartment and noticed an open security panel. Lettering on the outside indicated it contained classified communications equipment and was to be opened only by authorized personnel. *Too late.*

He carefully eased the door aside and let the beam of his flashlight probe the interior. Electrical cables dangled uselessly from the top and rear of the yard-square space. Some looked like they supplied electricity to whatever had been there, while others appeared to be antenna leads.

A metal tag riveted to the door noted the missing equipment was to be serviced only by authorized personnel of the National Security Agency. He took a moment to copy a list of telephone numbers to contact in case there was a problem onto his notepad and closed the door. There would be time later to figure out how the piece of secure comm gear fit into the other pieces of the puzzle. Right now, he needed to continue surveying the rest of the aircraft.

He moved across the compartment with slow, carefully executed steps and looked through the saucer-sized window of the interior access door. Slightly hazy with age, it still allowed him to see the length of the bomb bay. A flip of a switch changed the goggles to infrared and showed no body heat in the plane. He opened the access door very slowly to avoid creaking hinges announcing his presence and eased out onto a narrow walkway. To the credit of maintenance, the door opened smoothly with no noise.

Soft rubber-soled boots muted the sound of his steps as he patiently made his way toward the front of the plane. Countless martial arts classes had taught him the subtle nuances of stealth. Raising his foot nearly knee high and placing it down toe first before settling into place, he moved soundlessly down the metal catwalk with hips and shoulders squared toward the front of the plane. His left hand was positioned at chest height in front of him to clear the way. His right hand rested lightly on the sling that supported the machine pistol hanging against his right hip.

A double beep in his earpiece told him phase two of the operation had begun. Although he couldn't see out of the aircraft from his vantage point, the ambient light increased as the sodium vapor ramp lights blasted back to life with a yellow orange intensity.

All other members of the SORT except Senior Airman Juan Flores, had already retreated and were almost back out of the Alert Pad. Flores was secreted away in the wheel-well of the bomber to provide cover in case Jake had to beat a hasty retreat from the plane.

He was midway over the bomb bay and decided to point his flashlight downward. What he saw caused him to freeze.

INSIDE THE MOBILE COMMAND POST

Bart Winfield had joined Colonel Jackson at his request and stood listening to the hum of activity as the mission got underway. He would much rather be outside with his men, but J.J. wanted him beside him to offer advice.

The red letters of the countdown timer displayed the time left as nineteen hours, thirteen minutes and twelve seconds. Not enough to move at the cautious pace he would prefer, but he had never been on a mission that let him move at anything but a hell-bent-for-leather, breakneck pace.

A flat-screen monitor in the center of the rig displayed time-elapsed in green numbers and the status of mission personnel in orange. Messages that Jake or Juan typed into their keyboard would appear in red.

SORT A had retreated from the Alert Pad, leaving Juan Flores and Jake Thomas to finish the recon. They would rush back in to support them if it hit the fan. Bart could see them through the windshield milling around near the hole in the fence.

J.J. tugged on Bart's sleeve and pointed to the message screen. Red letters started to appear as Jake provided an update. The words sent a chill through Bart as he read, T's wired two n devices together.

"Why would they do that?" J.J asked.

"Couple of reasons…neither of 'em good. Might could be a trap to slow us down, or a way to detonate two at the same time. Either way, it messes things up nine ways to Sunday."

CATWALK ABOVE THE BOMB BAY

The inside of the bomb bay smelled of hydraulic fluid and metal and looked like the inside of a factory with numerous racks and devices of different shapes and sizes mounted on the walls. Nothing seemed to have changed.

A scraping sound near the front of the plane jolted Jake back to reality and served as a call to action. Primal instincts screamed at him to rush forward and meet the unknown danger with a furious charge. Training and discipline held him back as he waited patiently to hear if there was a follow-up sound to indicate anyone moving in his direction.

He continued his studied advance and discovered the disturbance was caused by a cable strung from the cockpit toward the back of the plane for about fifteen feet. It ended near a crew hatch in the floor and was connected to some electronic gear. It rubbed against the side of the aircraft as it swung back and forth in a slight breeze from the crew hatch.

Moving closer, Jake focused first on a control panel on the box and then to the open hatch. He could see the tarmac below and the edge of what appeared to be a manhole cover that led to a storm drainage tunnel. A framework of heavy metal beams was mounted over the manhole and seemed very much out of place. The stillness both inside the plane and the limited view of the outside indicated the intruders had abandoned the aircraft. Still, protocol dictated clearing the rest of the area.

A search of the inside of the plane revealed he was the only occupant. He returned to the hatch area and examined the electronic gear, which was similar to setups he had seen in hostage-terrorist negotiation training sessions at the FBI training center in Quantico, Virginia. It was a relay system that allowed signals to be rebroadcast from another location.

A digital recording and replay system and a laptop computer were also attached to it. Bright red letters displayed a countdown timer that matched its counterpart in the Command Post. Similar systems were usually designed to allow remote operation of communications, as well as the control of lights and other devices. He shined his flashlight around the back of the unit and saw cables snaking toward the front and rear.

It was time to break radio-silence and let others know what was happening. He switched to the encrypted frequency. "Control, this is A-Team Leader, come in."

"Roger, A-Team Leader, Control, over."

"Be advised…Subjects appear to have vacated this location. As indicated earlier, two devices have been wired together…And there's some comm gear up here that also seems to be wired into the two devices, over."

There was a pause and a strong voice filled Jake's earpiece, "A Team Leader, this is Colonel Jackson, are you sure they're gone, over?"

"Affirmative, sir…I'm alone. Can't see much outside from here, but the outside area also seems to be negative on activity. There's an open manhole under the aircraft with some kind of steel frame and winch system built over it…Doesn't look like it's supposed to be there. Can't see far enough into the manhole to determine status…You want me to search it?"

"Negative. We'll have a team with a camera do that…Never know what might be waiting."

"Yes, sir.…Haven't touched the comm gear…May be booby-trapped. But, appears to be a relay and remote control unit, over."

"For the nukes?"

"Could be…Also looks like it's meant to put on a show for us…Connected to lights and speakers in the aircraft…Has a couple of antennas coming out of it. Only thing active at the moment is the countdown timer, over."

"Copy that, Sergeant…Stay put for now. A sensor search under the plane is negative except for you and Flores. I'll send in an EOD team to survey the devices and a security team to assist you in gathering evidence and securing the site."

"Yes, sir." Jake smiled for the first time in a long time. "Be nice to have company…I'll put the coffee on."

He sat back on his heels and pulled out a package of M&Ms from a pouch on his belt. The ritual of tearing a corner off the package and letting those sweet little ovals drop into his mouth helped him to relax and focus. It was his personal reward for a job done well.

The first few had just slipped across his teeth when a low

rumble filled the inside of the plane and dust and smoke roared up through the hatch. A section of the deck about five-feet from him bulged and Jake was knocked over. He ended up sprawled on his back—dazed and a little deaf. M&Ms were scattered across his chest. Thankfully, the frame of the venerable old aircraft had protected him from most of the blast.

He raised up on one elbow and was about to stand when Colonel Jackson's voice filled his earpiece. "What the hell's going on in there, son?"

Jake shook his head and coughed to get rid of what felt like a dump-truck full of dust. It was hard to breathe and he considered donning the gas mask on the back of his belt.

He dropped the bag of candy and pressed the mike button on the side of his neck. "No…idea…what's going on…sir," and he coughed again. "Don't think…it was a booby trap…Shaken up…still in one piece…just sitting here…Came from underneath the plane. Flores okay?"

"A little dazed, but yes…Says the main landing gear shielded him from most of the blast. No fire around the BUFF…Maintain current position…Recovery team's almost there…They're marking evidence and checking for unexploded ordinance as they go, out."

Jake shook his head to clear of the effects of the blast and did a series of breathing exercises. *Not everyday somebody tries to blow me up.*

He grew tired of sitting after a few minutes and knew it would take the bomb squad a while to clear the rest of the area under the aircraft and get to him. He crept to the edge of the warped hatch and cautiously peered down at the gaping hole where the manhole had been. Dust and smoke blocked most of the view, but it looked like twisted metal and broken concrete were all that remained of the drainage tunnel entrance and the lifting apparatus.

Buildup of gas, maybe?

The briefings A-Team received before the assault indicated two concrete-lined drainage tunnels ran to a creek about two hundred yards away. They were six feet in diameter, with a six-inch deep channel in the bottom. Electrified Titanium bars with 440 volts of flesh-frying power blocked access at the creek end of the tunnel.

Security teams had been stationed at those exit points since the initial attack and reported no disturbances in the metal grates that covered the titanium bars. The only thing manmade they found within twenty feet of the openings were some crushed beer cans and an old plastic bait bucket. They were blocked from any further search of the tunnels because the grates could only be opened from the inside.

Jake switched over to the operational frequency and listened to reports flowing in from other units.

"Ops, this is Tac Unit 3...Completed search of Alert Pad... No sign of subjects, over."

"Roger that, TU-3. Report to Lieutenant Colonel Winfield for further assignment. TU-2, say status, over."

"Control, TU-2 at the moving van clearing weapons and ammo left behind by unknowns. Four hostages unaccounted for...thirteen are secure, with only minor injuries, over."

"Hold them in place...Paramedics will be there shortly. They have anything to say?"

"Negative...Most are angry at having been overpowered. Seem to think their meals were drugged and weapons jammed during the attack, over."

"Investigators are on the way to debrief them. Have passenger buses arrived, over?"

"Affirmative, Control...Hostages are sitting inside them."

"Good, TU-2, you're clear for the moment. TU-1, anything from the moving van driver?"

"TU-1...Driver says he was hijacked from a truck stop on I-80 by masked men. Shaken up and unable to provide ID on any of the perps...Kept him blindfolded and tied up in the cab, over."

"Copy that, TU-1."

"Control, TU-2, over."

"TU-2, whatcha got?"

"One hostage is a vegetarian and brings his own lunch...Appears to be the only SRT member who wasn't drugged...Reports strange behavior from other members. Says they were lethargic and seemed confused, over."

"Control to TU-1, copy that?"

"Affirmative, Control, we'll talk to him first...Rolling up on their twenty as we speak, over."

"TU-2, Control...Have the vegetarian at the front of the line."

"Roger that, Control is on it."

***

CHAPTER 13

MOBILE COMMAND POST-ALERT PAD

"Damn, Bart…news keeps getting worse," J.J. spoke softly into the radio. He had asked for hourly updates on the situation in the Alert Pad—although he wasn't sure he wanted to hear one now. "Four SRT members dead?…Did I hear that right?"

"'Fraid so…According to Chief Fritz." Chief Master Sergeant Bill Fritz was First Sergeant of the Bomb Wing. "Didn't respond to a roll call and they found their bodies under the moving van covered with a tarp."

"I'll call Colonel Bates when we're done and offer my condolences. Is Mortuary Services on site?"

"Not now…picked up the bodies and they'll will notify the families…We're coordinating everything through the Bomb

Wing office."

"Good. John Miller, new Chief of Food Services, stopped by...Says they searched for trash from the mid-break meal to have it tested and came up empty. Intruders burned most of it... although they left a couple of fifty-five gallon drums behind the moving van filled with ashes. CSU is sending them in for analysis...Won't have results for a while."

"Certainly lends support to the drugged food theory," Bart noted. "Couldn't find the truck that was used to deliver the meals...or, for that matter, the driver. Asked Rancho Cordova P.D. to check his home...Found the government truck parked in his driveway. Driver and his wife seem to be in the wind...They put an APB out on them and their POV. "

"Guess that's about all that can be done at this point," Jackson let his breath out with a whoosh. "Man, this has been one hell of a day."

"I'm just glad we can shut off that dadgum timer...I was startin' to see red numbers whenever I closed my eyes."

J.J. chuckled. "I hear you...Raises the pucker factor when you're staring at something like that. You get a handle on how these people managed to pop up in the middle of my Alert Pad?"

"Sergeant Thomas and I have a theory."

"Thought you might...Let's hear it."

"We studied maps and geological features of this area and found there was a placer mining operation here a hundred years ago...."

Colonel Jackson interrupted, "Placer mining?"

"Old method not used anymore. They pumped water under extremely high pressure through what looked like huge fire hose nozzles...Washed away trees, rocks and everything else from hills to expose the gold ore underneath. Most of the dirt washed down the river, leaving the two and three-story high piles of rocks..."

"What do piles of rock have to do with my Alert Pad?"

"They're all around it."

"So?"

"Placer mining missed a lot of gold and didn't touch what was deep underground. Experienced deep-rock miners were brought in to dig mine shafts under the area. We think the subjects used one of those abandoned shafts to dig up into the Alert Pad drainage system."

"Seems a little far-fetched...How would they tie all that together? They'd have to have somebody familiar with the area and the know-how to bypass the intrusion alarms in the tunnel...Plus a construction background."

"Our thoughts too," Bart replied.

"Maybe they did pull off some kind of Houdini act, but you have to admit...seems a little far out there."

"Might be a stretch, but don't see how else they could've popped up in the middle of the pad and then disappeared without a trace. Sensors picked up squat the whole time...On the other hand, we didn't use ground penetrating radar...No reason to suspect they'd come from below ground. It all sounds like some kind of Hollywood film plot."

"Does, doesn't it? J.J. replied. "Good work."

185

"Well, as my mama used to say, 'Even a blind sow finds an acorn now and then.'"

"Except you seem to do it more often than not."

"Thanks, J.J....'ppreciate the compliment."

"Don't let it go to your head....Although, from working with you, I know it won't. Keep it up and the 0-6 Board will give you wings and you'll be gone somewhere to take over a squadron."

"Stranger things have happened...Except, truth be told, I don't want to leave Mather."

"Really? Figured a hard-charger like you couldn't wait to make full-bird."

"Didn't think I'd ever like settling in one place, but the quiet life sorta grows on you."

"Right...Then all of this comes along...Shakes you up a little."

"Speaking of that, I'd better get back to searching for evidence."

"Guess I'll make that call to Bates...then join you at the Alert Pad."

CONSORTIUM HEADQUARTERS
CENTRAL EUROPE

The conference room could have been in the corporate headquarters of any Fortune 500 company. Dark paneling lined the walls and a crystal chandelier hung over a thirty-foot ebony-wood table lined with high-backed upholstered arm chairs. The smell of lemon-scented furniture oil competed with freshly-cut exotic flowers to lend an air of quiet tranquility.

A dozen senior managers in custom-tailored suits offered their attention to one of five partners of the international intelligence organization. He and his four associates were usually referred to as the Commission and directed the affairs of the larger group.

Bernard Bergstrom, Acting Director of North American operations finished a lengthy report of progress since assuming his current position and sat down.

The Commissioner took a leisurely drink from a crystal goblet. "The establishment of the consolidated headquarters in an abandoned underground ICBM site near Deer Trail, Colorado is proceeding slower than the original schedule dictated....Why is this so?"

Bergstrom wiped his sweating brow with a handkerchief monogrammed with a double B as his heart pounded. "We had considerable difficulty adapting the underground silo for the communications antennas..."

"That was my idea and quite clever...if I do say so myself."

"Yes, being able to retract them when not in use will certainly help to keep a lower profile," Bergstrom noted. "On the other hand, it has demanded much time and money."

"I can see where it might, since the silo is over forty years old. The initial budget was one hundred fifty million for the entire project. Will you require more?"

"Probably not...If more time is allowed in the schedule."

"That is not possible...Events will soon transpire that

require us to be able to rapidly respond to client requests. Consolidation is the key to greatly enhanced capabilities for us. Are there other reasons for the delay?"

"Yes...concerns about getting adequate power into the facility."

"Will it prevent us from proceeding in a timely manner?"

"Possibly...I am hopeful this body will be able to provide guidance."

One of the managers raised a finger. "Is there only one person obstructing us and, if so, could they be eliminated?"

"No, Mister Ehrlinger, the major impediment relates to the amount of electrical power...They are afraid it will put undue strain on their distribution system and they might not be able to recover the cost of creating new infrastructure...It is a small electrical cooperative."

"What is the cost?"

"Three million dollars."

The Commissioner interrupted, "A pittance...give it to them."

"It is not the sum, sir, but the source...Under their bylaws, any expenditure over one million dollars requires approval by their membership...Which could take a year or more. The only exception is national security."

"Therein lies the answer...I will arrange to have the money transferred to their accounts for a secret government project. Tell the local officials funds will be routed through a shell corporation and will be classified...Their constituents will never know the source and the administrators will be protected from scrutiny.

"Let me further clarify something for you, Bernard…It is imperative that we finish this facility in a timely manner…If you are not capable of managing the project, may I expect your resignation?"

The acting director was now sweating profusely. "I hope that will not be necessary. Elimination of the problems we've discussed should put the project back on the original schedule, with the exception of design changes…"

The Commissioner startled the group by slapping the project file on the table. "Most of the changes were my idea and are quite innovative! However, I can see how they might cause some delay. Have you calculated the cost of overtime to compensate for the additional work?"

"Approximately seven million dollars."

He commissioner cleared his throat. "Unless one of you objects, I am going to approve ten million dollars to put this project back on track…Is that acceptable?

Heads nodded in agreement and the Commissioner smiled. The Consortium could quickly and efficiently accomplish tasks that neither government nor traditional business would be able to undertake.

ALERT PAD-UNDER THE WING OF THE BLACK JACK BOMBER

"I want what I'm about to tell you to stay close and tight, understood?" Colonel Jackson commanded. "Wing personnel

T.C. Miller

say five nuclear devices are missing from the plane, as well as a highly-classified piece of communications equipment...The worst has happened.

"I just got off the phone with the Pentagon...The mission to return all devices will remain at our level...at least for now. We'll continue to man the command post twenty-four seven on twelve-hour shifts. Off-duty personnel will maintain fifteen minute recall status. Check into billeting if you live beyond that...Now, how we can wrap this up?"

The group froze like an ice sculpture. Nobody wanted to become a lightning rod. Colonel Jackson waited a few moments and when nothing was offered, took a more strident tone. "Come on, people...I want some ideas."

The Chief of Public Affairs spoke, "I...think we're all still trying to absorb, uh...what happened, sir. So much doesn't seem to make any sense."

"Sense or no sense, we need a resolution," Jackson replied tersely. "I'm getting a lot of flak and you know what flows downhill."

They followed the chain of command, which meant they reported directly or indirectly to the base commander.

J.J. continued, "Every agency with an interest in national security will be down on us in a matter of hours...We need to make sure our ducks are in a row. Careers are on the line here and failure is not an option."

There would be consequences for mistakes. Airman Performance Reports would contain statements like...after careful consideration, Sergeant so-and-so is able to formulate a

190

measured response to a given situation...meant the person was slow to respond to anything other than normal events and tended to freeze in an emergency.

Officer Performance Reports would be more subtle. Puffed up statements would be replaced with career-killing statements like...does an adequate job managing resources."

It meant the same thing in the end, slow or no promotion for enlisted and early retirement or dismissal for officers.

Jackson cleared his throat. "Colonel Winfield, how do we find them?"

"That's the hard part, sir...'til we ID them, we don't have a clue...and most of our crime scene's under tons of rock and dirt."

"All right, then...Keep going through the Alert Pad and start a search up and downriver...They may have escaped by boat, since it flows into the Delta and on out to the ocean. They could meet up with a ship and go anywhere...We need to move fast."

"Yes, sir." Bart put his hand on Jake's shoulder and leaned in. "Good job on the research, son...Now, get yourself over to the base hospital and let them check you out. That was a pretty good-sized blast you took."

"If you don't mind, sir, think I'll wait 'til later...Like to check out a few things first."

"Whatever." Bart turned to the Operations Lieutenant. "Establish a search grid and let's get the ball rolling."

"On it, sir!"

They started to leave, when all the radios squawked at once. The voice of an excited young airman relayed the electrifying news, "All command post staff on this frequency, please report to the Alert Pad...We found one of them alive!"

HIGHWAY 50
EAST OF PLACERVILLE

The Class C motor home was a full-sized passenger van in front with an RV body attached behind the front seats. This allowed the driver or passenger to stand up and walk into the rear living area.

Rick Eichner sat in the driver's seat wearing a baseball cap that read, Retired: No Job, No Clock, No Worry. He took it from the owners before locking them in the tiny bathroom in the middle of the vehicle.

The unlit stub of a cigar he was chewing seemed to act as a gyroscope, helping to steer the wallowing vehicle around curves that were tight enough to slow most drivers down to thirty or forty miles per hour. Instead, he ignored the numerous yellow caution signs and kept the speedometer at a steady fifty-five miles, the posted speed limit.

He waved at a couple of oncoming cars with out-of-state plates. They waved back and he smiled. How fortunate they were to have seen the pristine beauty and electrified gambling action of Lake Tahoe before it was gone forever.

Rick pulled into a picnic area that was little more than a wide spot in the road. It could accommodate no more than two or three cars safely, so the RV took up most of the space. He stood, stretched as much as the space would allow and walked toward the bathroom. A quick touch of flame to the cigar brought it to life and he puffed until a cloud billowed around him.

The cramped interior of the bathroom contained a toilet stool and a combination tub and shower that held a very frightened old couple from Goshen, Indiana.

Eichner had struck up a conversation with them in an RV park along the American River, near the base. It was easy to get inside by asking directions to a town on the other side of Lake Tahoe. They consulted their road atlas and turned to find themselves facing a gun.

A few minutes later, and with the aid of a few yards of duct tape, they were bound, gagged and placed in the tub. They had been in the process of leaving when Rick came upon them, so all he had to do was retrieve the keys from the old man's pocket and drive away.

Rick spoke to the frightened old couple in the tub as he finished urinating, even though they couldn't reply, "The trailer behind your RV looks plain, yet has enough firepower in it to level San Francisco and Sacramento combined. Four nuclear warheads and the gear I need to turn Lake Tahoe into an empty hole in the ground for a thousand years.

"This fifth one is bungee-corded to your bed...My idea of nuclear security. Get it? Nuclear security." He didn't bother checking to see if the old couple was laughing. The sixth device had been left in a storage locker in Rancho Cordova to be used later.

"A quick stop at the lake to do a little gambling...plant one of the devices and boom…biggest diversion in modern history! You'll have front-row seats and I'll be long gone."

He leaned against the kitchen counter and thought about his upcoming stay at the ranch. "I can wait out the uproar, unlike you Americans with your frenzied lives…Yuri Petronovich has patience to wait for your incompetent authorities to tire of the search. Then I'll be on my way to a life of glory!"

Another quick touch of flame to the cigar produced an even bigger cloud of smoke. His escape plan was in place after months of careful thought and planning. A storage yard in South Shore, Lake Tahoe offered twenty-four hour access through a keypad controlled gate. He had stashed a pickup truck and camper there under a false name. The rig held everything he needed to exist with no outside contact for at least two months.

It also had almost five hundred thousand dollars stashed in a hidden compartment. The three hundred thousand he stole from his gambling buddies was hidden in a secret compartment in the truck. The rest had been siphoned from secret offshore banking accounts. Bureaucrats in Moscow who deposited the money during the Cold War would never have guessed it would be used for an operation like this.

The small-minded politicians who now ran his beloved Russia made him want to vomit. Citizens with no idea how weak a so-called democracy could be elected them and stumbled down the capitalist road to mediocrity. They needed a lesson. He was going to be their teacher and the hero of the new revolution.

He started the engine and pulled onto the main roadway. A driver of a car going in the same direction slammed on his brakes in an attempt to avoid the slow-moving RV. His brakes locked up and the car slid sideways into oncoming traffic, striking the front of a pickup. The driver of the car was killed instantly and a passenger in the truck was ejected through the windshield onto the hood of the car.

Rick surveyed the result of his carelessness for only a second and continued, glad that both vehicles had missed his rig. "Oh well, guess it just wasn't their day." He accelerated steadily to the speed limit.

MANHOLE UNDER THE BLACK JACK BOMBER

The crater that was once a manhole was swarming with rescue crews. The twisted steel framework for the jury-rigged lifting system had been cut away to allow access to the tunnel. Halogen work lights illuminated a pit at the bottom. Three security policemen were digging frantically with small trenching tools and even their bare hands. They had uncovered the head, shoulders and one arm of a middle-aged man.

Bart joined them in the pit. The dust and blood covered man grasped his arm in a surprisingly strong grip. He was fighting for every breath and trying desperately to communicate.

"It's okay, pardner," Bart said as he knelt next to him. "We'll get you out of here fast as we can." His eyes adjusted to the bright lights and dusty air and he looked closer at the bloodied face. He couldn't be sure, but the victim looked a lot like a retired security policeman who now worked as a DOD policeman on base. "Bill...Bill Johnson, is that you?"

The man groaned, looked away and replied, "Yeah, Colonel, it's my sorry ass...Others make it out okay?"

"Others?" Bart queried "We searched the entire drainage tunnel and you're the only one we found."

He gasped for breath. "Not in the drainage tunnel...Underneath me....dug up from...an old gold mine shaft...Used ore-car tracks...moved the warheads out."

"We thought that might be how y'all pulled it off."

"Waited 'til the last minute to dig up to the drainage tunnel...to not set off sensors...Smooth as a Swiss watch...Took over the Alert Pad...Got the nukes into the tunnel."

"So they're buried under you?" Bart's eyes narrowed.

Bill coughed. "No...Rick said you might...set them off...by accident...Moved 'em to a truck...Came back to get the comm gear...Rick went bat-shit crazy...Said we was plotting...Shot Jason in the face...Told us...get up into the drainage tunnel. Blew up before we got all the way there."

"So, there were others?"

"Yes, I'm saying...probably all dead...except for that asshole...Only one could've made it out...Lying son of a bitch...Had a remote...surprise for you...Turned out it was for us...biggest fools on the planet."

"Some surprise." Bart shook his head. "Then the timer setup was fake?"

"Yeah. Jack said it was a light show…not connected to anything…Used to pressure you."

"Who's Rick?"

"Eichner, local guy, like the rest of us." Bill squirmed and looked around. Two medics stood by to take him to the base hospital once his legs were freed. "I know things…don't look too good, Colonel…I'm not a bad guy…in a jam…flat-out desperate. Think you could help me out, here?"

"Probably too late for that…With fatalities and all …"

"No! Can't be…Nobody was supposed to be hurt…agreed on that…Thought we were the only ones…" Bill was visibly shaken and had a tell-me-it-ain't-so look.

Bart shook his head. "You've been around the Alert Pad long enough to know cops will die defending it. Think they'd let you waltz in without a fight?"

"No…that was the beauty of the plan. Rick got us long-range Tasers…shocked 'em 'til they passed out…had mortar shells with knockout gas…Put 'em in the back of the semi. Supposed to come to in twelve hours or so…Not supposed to die…"

"Well, four of 'em did…refused to give up. Somebody's gotta pay."

"Guess the bull's-eye's on me…Damn it, Colonel, would you tell them…I cooperated?"

"Sure, but you're gonna have to give up a whole lot more about the plan and who's involved."

"Tell me…what you need."

Bart joined the others in digging with his bare hands to free the trapped man and motioned for a young security policeman to move closer. "Airman Barrett, write down whatever he says…And why are they here?" He pointed to Agents Johansen and Benson.

"Colonel Jackson told me to bring them," he stammered. "Said give them access to whatever they want…Should I get him on the radio?"

"No, I'll call him." Bart stepped away from the work crew and switched his radio to a private frequency. "J.J., Bart, over."

The reply was immediate, "Calling about the NSA agents, right?"

"Roger that."

"Give them unrestricted access and help…Understood?"

"You're the boss…Mind if I ask why?"

"Not open for discussion…Way over our pay grades. We'll talk about it later."

"You're driving this trolley."

"Thanks…you know I appreciate it." Jackson signed off.

Bart walked back to the crater. "Take those two wherever they want to go…Anybody questions it, tell 'em to talk to me."

"Yes, sir!" The young airman snapped to attention and rendered a salute. Bart returned it and got back to work, helping to dig.

Airman Barrett rejoined the NSA agents. "Don't know who you are, but you can go wherever you want…Must know somebody."

The two black-suited figures offered no reply as they picked up their briefcases and followed the young airman toward the rear hatch of the B-52. They had work to do.

BASE COMMANDERS' OFFICE
323rd ABG HEADQUARTERS

A half-dozen key personnel were seated at a conference table that formed a "T" with the base commander's desk. Another half-dozen stood along the walls. The smell of stale cigarette smoke clinging to a few of the uniforms hung in the air. An occasional whiff of strong coffee reached Jake Thomas and the two NSA agents as they faded into a back corner.

Bart stood at the opposite end of the table from Colonel Jackson delivering a progress briefing. "Other end of the tunnel was hidden by brush in old mine tailings a quarter mile down river. OSI is going over every bit of the evidence we've collected so far. Looks like a heavy truck and trailer were used to get the weapons out and an older model sedan leased to Eichner's construction company was abandoned there."

"It's a start," J.J. commented. "What else turned up?"

"A profile of this Eichner character is starting to emerge. No family we can find…Mainly socialized with the core of his attack team. Has other contacts…mostly clients of his construction company. Shows a track record the last few years of heavy gambling and womanizing."

"What about ties to terrorist organizations?"

"Nothing obvious…Few short calls to Russian consular offices…Might could be an attempt to get a working relationship going. Could be a merc…But that raises more questions than answers…Like, where'd he get his training and what are his motives?…Seems to have popped up out of nowhere…My money is on long-term deep cover op."

"You'd know better than anybody," Jackson noted. "What about this Bill Johnson…He going to make it?"

"Don't know.…Looked pretty banged up when we dug him out. He's in the base hospital now, under guard. Gave us a lot of inside dope on the intruders."

"JAG will be putting together a case on him."

"We'll work with them."

J.J addressed everyone in the room, "Lot of good work in a short time. It'll reflect in your performance reports…indirectly, of course, since it's classified. There will be individual decorations…also classified. On a personal note, I want to thank every person who was involved. Now, I know you need to get back to your work centers, so unless you have something else, that's it."

Heads nodded and the group began to file out. Colonel Jackson motioned to Winfield. "Would you and Sergeant Thomas stay behind? I'd also like to talk with Agents Benson and Johansen."

Bart nodded toward the NSA agents. "Together?"

"Yes, together…I have a follow-up project for the four of you."

Bart sat down and motioned for Jake to join him. Benson and Johansen sat on the other side as the door to the conference room was closed by the last of the departing group.

J.J. clasped his hands on his desk and cleared his throat.

"Let me begin by saying that everything I am about to tell you is highly classified and will not be discussed with others unless I give my specific approval...clear?"

The four nodded and he continued, "Sergeant, I believe you know Agents Benson and Johansen from working with them a few years ago, correct?"

Jake squirmed in his seat. "Respectfully, sir, I don't know if I'm at liberty..."

"I'm not asking you to divulge any classified information, Sergeant...Just letting you know I've been told about it."

"Yes, sir. Although this is the first time I've seen them in person. They were Mission Controllers for a TDY I did in the Philippines."

"Good...Bart, were you aware of his past work with the NSA?"

"Not the exact nature...I thought he was training anti-insurgent forces."

"And that's what we want the records to show," Agent Benson said as she leaned forward. "He was actually working for us on missions to recover equipment from downed aircraft in rebel-held territory.

"Our people were stretched thin and Sergeant Thomas proved to be a very valuable asset...Performed to our highest expectations. Good to be working with him in person."

Bart chuckled and turned to Jake. "Damn, son, you're an even bigger badass than I thought!"

"Just doing my job, sir."

"You were good at not giving anything away."

Jackson clapped his hands together. "Now that we've broken the ice, let's see what needs to be done to bring this to a conclusion. Bart, I want you to take operational control of the recovery mission...be my personal representative in the field. You'll have all base resources at your disposal."

"With all due respect, sir...spooks are probably better suited for this job."

"I want an Air Force officer with a take-charge attitude and from your past work you aren't afraid to think outside the box."

"Got me into hot water with my bosses more than once."

"True, but it's also why you command respect above and below you in the chain...Not trying to put you on the spot, but I think you're the best man for the job."

"Again, sir...I'm just a base cop. But since you want me to continue with the pursuit, I'm more than happy to. We have a pretty good idea Eichner's headed to Lake Tahoe, so we'll start by going there. What about the locals, though? Shouldn't they be in charge?"

"Under normal cirumstances...But higher-ups want military people front and center. We'll let them know you're coming, but not what your status is...Let them assume you're NSA. Benson and Johansen will go with you...Should keep questions to a minimum. I want this under our control, since those nukes belong to us...Won't sleep 'til they're back on base. Take whatever you need and go get this bastard!" He slammed his fist down on the desk.

"Yes, sir. Bill Johnson says Eichner wants to turn the tables on the mob...I feel like that means he's planning on setting off one of the nukes. We put a BOLO out to law enforcement…Told them to observe and report, not to approach…Rounded up a list of vehicles from his construction company and included them."

"Good. Who do you want on your team?"

"Thomas, Agents Benson and Johansen and Airman First Class Joanna Davies."

"Davies? One who killed the intruder with just a knife?

"That's her. I like her skill set and it'll look like we're on vacation together…Won't stir up as many questions."

"Sounds like a plan. I checked and Tahoe airport's socked in with fog…Guess you'll be driving…CHP says they'll give you an escort."

"Not a good idea, sir…draw too much attention. Besides, you can't go fast anyway with all the curves and drop-offs on Highway 50."

"Your call, Bart…just get my nukes back."

Colonel Jackson wet his lips and spoke in measured terms, "This comes from the highest level…Try and capture Eichner alive. But if he tries to detonate one those nukes…take him out hard, clear?"

"Crystal."

"Good. Take sat phones…Call as soon as you locate him…I want my weapons back ASAP!"

***

CHAPTER 14

CONSORTIUM HEADQUARTERS

"You are sure she is going to Lake Tahoe?"

"Yes…positive."

"And the ID has been confirmed?"

"As you ordered."

"What about the agent known as Tupelo…Have you identified him yet?"

"No, Commissioner…I am still working on that."

"Do not only work at it…Get it done!"

"Yes, sir. My inquiries are proceeding as fast as prudently possible. I should have the information in a day or two, at the very most."

"Excellent…Goodbye."

The Commissioner pressed the intercom button and spoke, "Conrad, would you come in with your notepad."

The door opened a minute later and his assistant took a seat in front of the desk, pen in hand.

The Commissioner picked up his coffee cup took a sip and sat it back down. "A situation has developed in the Northern California project that offers the chance to resolve some old issues...I want a strike team there immediately. Draw from available personnel in the area, including the smuggling group in Seawind Bay. I should think six men will be adequate. This will be a clandestine operation with full combat gear, including body armor, gas masks and night-vision...Our Sacramento safe-house has them."

"Should I inform them of the nature of the mission, sir?"

"They will be destroying a CIA safe-house and taking a female operative hostage. I will give them further details by secure video when they arrive in Sacramento."

"Anything else, sir?"

The Commissioner glanced at his Rolex. "Tell them I want them there in no more than three hours...and they can look forward to a sizable bonus."

Conrad closed the door behind him and the Commissioner spun his chair around to the floor-to-ceiling windows. He hoped the opportunity had finally come to avenge the broken London operation years ago and the death of five of his best agents. Could this be his chance to kill Tupelo and his agent-wife?

CALIFORNIA HIGHWAY 50
EAST OF RANCHO CORDOVA, CA

Joanna Davies squirmed in the middle seat of the custom van. The plush seats should have made her feel comfortable, but she wasn't. Sitting next to Sergeant Thomas should make her feel good, but it didn't. She hadn't felt right since the takeover of the Alert Pad and felt somehow responsible for the breach of security. Telling herself there was nothing more she could have done brought no comfort. Joanna stared out the side window at the towering pine trees that lined the road.

A woman who was introduced to her as an NSA agent was stretched out on the back-seat of the van. Joanna knew little about the NSA, and most of that came from spy novels. She assumed ninety-nine percent of what they did was classified so far above her level she probably shouldn't ask them the time of day and that was okay with her. Some things were so secretive she was probably better off not knowing.

Still, if the rumpled woman behind her was a representative of the most highly-trained, clandestine organization in the intelligence community, it raised a number of questions.

Mary Benson was tossing, turning and snoring loudly enough to be heard in the noisy van. Joanna smelled a pungent, acrid body odor when Benson brushed past her in the van wearing a dusty and wrinkled dark blue business suit. A wide run in her dark panty hose revealed a pale leg that looked none too fit.

She glanced down at her pressed jeans and crisp white top

and was sure she projected a professional image, even in casual clothes.

The van braked hard to avoid a deer bounding across the road and she turned back toward the front.

Lieutenant Colonel Winfield was driving, since it was his van, with Jay Johansen in the passenger seat. Jake Thomas sat next to her in the middle. *How did a lowly senior airman end up here?* Somebody higher up wanted her to be along on this mission.

"You okay?" Jake asked.

"Guess so…why?"

"You were kinda half-smiling and all of a sudden your face went dark."

"Thinking about the dead intruder."

"Did what you had to do…that's all there is to it."

"I get all that…but killing someone takes a little getting used to. You ever had to?"

"Yes."

"Did it bother you?"

"No more than necessary…just doing my job. Later on, I was angry."

"At them? They came out on the short end of the stick, didn't they?"

"Don't get me wrong…Glad they ended up dead and not me. I resented the fact they forced me to make the choice. They threatened me or somebody else…brought it upon themselves. End of story."

"Still think about it?

"Every time I strap on a weapon…And I'll do it again if I have to."

"There's a saying in the South that some people just need killing…We call it draining the gene pool."

"True…Don't stop doing your job."

"Just don't want to get too used to killing anybody."

He was dressed in casual civilian clothes. The skintight black knit shirt looked like a golf shirt until she noticed the martial arts logo embroidered above the pocket.

The knit bands on the sleeves were stretched by his bulging biceps and a hint of dark chest hair peeked through the V-neck. It was obvious he worked out and wasn't afraid to show it.

She thought of her fiancé and the few times she mentioned hitting the gym. John begged off, saying it would reduce his studying time.

Jake glanced at her and she blushed when she realized she had been caught staring.

She recovered quickly. "Noticed the martial arts logo…That the style you study?"

"It is…Hakkoryu Jujitsu," he replied.

"Black belt?"

"For quite awhile."

"Is it a good style?" She realized how dumb the words sounded and could feel her face redden again.

He either didn't notice or was being kind. "Studied it for over ten years…ideal for our line of work. Takes into account size and strength limitations…lets you use your opponent's force against them, similar to Aikido. Ever watch a Steven

Seagall movie?"

"A lot…I loved *Under Siege.*" It was the most she ever heard him say at one time that wasn't connected to police work. "So you take it because you're small!"

His smile faded and she choked on her words.

"Didn't realize size meant so much to you." He saw her reaction. "Sorry…sounded defensive, didn't it? But yes, it's one of the reasons. I'm only five-eight…Gives me an edge…Just don't like talking about myself…"

He shifted the focus back to her. "You train?"

"I do…Dad made me take karate classes when I was young so I could defend myself. Plus, I've studied at each base I've been assigned to…Taking Kuk Sul Won from Master Yang."

"Good instructor…Kuk Sul is very close to what I teach."

"Really," she replied. "Maybe I should take your class, too."

"No formal class…Just a few friends who work out together. Besides, sounds like what you're learning works just fine." He saw a lot of himself in her eagerness to be a good cop. "Maybe we could work out together."

He hoped she would say yes—and martial arts wasn't the only reason. She had a quick mind, easygoing disposition and was pleasant on the eyes.

"Sounds like a great idea," she offered. "What do you think's gonna happen when we find this guy?"

"No way of knowing…Figure he has revenge in mind or maybe some kind of political statement…Could be he's going to plant the bomb and demand a ransom. He'd have a bonus on top of what the government paid."

"Could be…It's been done before."

OFFICE OF THE DIRECTOR, NSA WASHINGTON, DC

Justin Todd, Executive Assistant to the Director, pressed the intercom, "John Banner is on Line 3, sir."

The Director had been anticipating the status call from one of the brightest members of his agency and head of the NSA's West Coast Division. "John, what's happening at Mather?"

"Getting more worrisome by the minute, Director. Classified communications from SAF's office indicate one or more of the perpetrators escaped and are on the run…with nukes in hand."

"I can confirm that…Sat in on an NSC briefing an hour ago…everyone's scratching their heads. We gave them all they asked for and still ended up on the short end of the stick…Do we know how they got away?"

"A clever strategy involving an abandoned mine tunnel and some serious treachery…still piecing it together. Glad we have Benson and Johansen on site…I'll send you their report."

"That was quick thinking…Reminds me why I made you Division Chief."

"Thanks, but afraid I have more bad news…"

"Worse news?"

"They also got away with a BlackStar unit."

"God, no!…Worst news I've heard in a long time. What are we doing about it?"

"Benson and Johansen are combining with three Air Force

people, including our occasional asset, Tupelo, to track them down. Right now there's no clear indication where the criminals are headed or how many of them there are…"

"Who's leading the team?"

"Tupelo…figured that was best, given his background. He's got a hunch Eichner may be heading to Lake Tahoe."

"His hunches have paid off before…don't see why we shouldn't go along with them now."

"Agreed, sir."

"Good. While I have you on the line, have you thought any more about the multi-service Black Star investigative team we talked about?"

"It's a good idea, provided it's structured to give us double-checks and safeguards."

"Noted, John…But I don't want them spying on each other…Breeds mistrust."

"How would you monitor their performance?"

"Still kicking that around…Call me if you come up with any thing. See you in two weeks, anyway…We'll talk more in depth then."

"Yes, sir. I'll call you tomorrow morning with an update."

"Call me at home this evening…I'm a little wary of my office line."

"Really?"

"Yes. There have been a couple of untraceable leaks."

"We're the NSA…How could that happen?"

"Who knows?…May be one of my section chiefs or electronic surveillance…Hard to tell."

"I'll keep my head on a swivel."

"I can always count on you…Talk to you later."

The line stayed open a second after the call ended.

Justin hung up the phone and returned to the work on his desk.

MAJESTIC CASINO HOTEL PARKING LOT
SOUTH SHORE, LAKE TAHOE, NEVADA

Rick marveled at how easy it was to get temporary help. A quick call to a local moving and storage company and he had two men and a bobtail truck at his disposal. He asked for men who were familiar with deliveries to the Majestic Casino and was pleasantly surprised to learn that both had been there numerous times.

They knew the people who handled incoming freight for the casino and belonged to the same union. A few well-placed twenty dollar bills would expedite the delivery even more.

He watched while they used hand trucks and a winch-driven lifting device to transfer one of the nuclear weapons, safely ensconced in a wooden shipping crate, from the trailer behind the RV to their truck. In minutes, they were ready for the most significant delivery the casino would ever receive.

"So, what is this thing, anyway?" One of them asked.

"Piece of experimental theater equipment used to put on a light show." Which was partially true…A light show that would be seen fifty miles away. *They'll have a front row seat.*

"Never seen nothing like it before…Too bad we won't get

to see it work."

"Who knows? Maybe you will."

"Ain't likely, mister…Can't afford hundred–dollar–a–seat tickets."

"Do this job right and maybe you'll be able to."

Forty minutes later they had delivered the crates to the Majestic and were back at the stolen RV. Rick supervised the transfer of the remaining devices from the trailer, as well as the smaller item from the RV.

They were now safely installed in his getaway rig and ready to go. He motioned the two men over and signed the invoice that would be paid with his construction company credit card. It was one of the last transactions that would ever appear on the card and presented a dead-end for any investigation.

"I really appreciate the good work you guys did and, like I said earlier, maybe you'll be able to afford those theater seats."

He handed each of them two hundred dollars in cash.

"Uh, thanks, mister, but that's a lot of money…I mean, we was just doing our job."

"You never got a tip before?"

"Sure, but usually twenty bucks or something…not like this."

"Consider this your lucky day. I'm in a good mood and besides, it's tax deductible for my company…Enjoy it." *Won't feel quite as guilty when you're vaporized.*

"Sure will."

They grinned at each other.

They left and Rick grabbed a satchel from the pickup. It was time to do a little gambling and then start his journey to the ranch in Montana. He whistled a happy tune as he strolled across the parking lot.

BART'S VAN
CALIFORNIA HIGHWAY 50

"Been done before?...You serious?" Jake asked.

"As a heart attack," Joanna answered. "When I was a kid, a guy sneaked a bomb disguised as a copy machine into one of the casinos...Demanded ten million bucks."

"Did it work?"

"Nope...Other casino owners offered to cover any damage from the blast. Sounds extreme, but they wanted to discourage other criminals from trying to extort them.'

"What happened?"

"They evacuated the entire casino hotel, all nine floors...It went off as promised...blew a whole floor right out of the building! I remember seeing pictures of the mountains taken right through the fifth floor. Everything gone except the concrete pillars...Blown away!"

"Now we're talking about a bomb that could return the whole Lake Tahoe area to a big glassy crater...Like it was during the last Ice Age! Hey, Colonel, won't this thing go any faster?"

"Only if it had wings and a jet engine, son." Bart replied in his slow, southern drawl. "Be there in less than an hour...Catch a few winks if you can...We'll need everybody at a hundred percent."

Jake settled back in the seat and closed his eyes. *Sleep...Right.* He opened them just enough to notice Joanna surreptitiously watching him. They had talked more about personal things in the last hour than in her entire training time.

He folded his arms across his chest, sighed, and did his best to catch a quick nap as they drew closer to one of the most beautiful mountain lakes in the world.

The gray mist swirled around him like it always did in the dream, but this time it was different. It usually started with him standing in the middle of an intersection, trying to decide which way to go. He had already moved down the street toward the curve at the end. He heard faint rustling noises in the mist and detected the scent of unwashed bodies.

They were still after him, but the guy-wire taut tension was subdued and the premonition of impending doom was weaker.

He became aware, as usual, that he was not alone. The figure standing next to him was not hooded though, and did not produce a sense of anxiety.

He turned his head to identify his ally when the van hit a bump in the road and he awoke with a start.

"You okay?" asked Joanna

"Yeah, "Guess I was dreaming."

"Must have been a nightmare...Your heart is pounding!"

She was holding his hand to comfort him. It felt good and he waited a moment before he let his hand fall away.

"No big deal...recurring nightmare...Guess the tension

brought it out."

"It's okay...Like my mama always says, daylight chases away demons of the night."

"I like that." He closed his eyes and tried to sleep, but was startled again when Bart went around a curve and braked hard.

SOUTH SHORE LODGE
LAKE TAHOE, CALIFORNIA

Nora stopped at the office long enough to let the clerk confirm her identity, then drove half a mile along a road that was a game trail for deer that wandered through the resort.

She parked in front of a cabin that was perfectly designed to hide its clandestine features. It looked like the other dozen or so structures hidden in the towering pines, but was actually a virtual fortress. A stone path that led to the front door had sensors to detect any approaching person. Hidden security cameras constantly scanned the area and the front stoop was hinged to drop offending visitors into a dungeon-like pit.

The scent of evergreen mixed with the musty smell of pine needles that covered the ground around the cabin greeted her like an old friend as she strolled to the door.

Three quick knocks, followed by four more elicited movement from inside. A gray-haired man in his early sixties opened the door just wide enough to peer out and ask, "What can I do for you?"

"John here?"

"Guess you didn't hear...He fell on a hiking path and broke

216

his leg…Had to return to the Bay Area."

"Thought he broke both legs and went to his mother's house in Fresno…"

The man swung the door open, revealing a MAC-10 pistol in his right hand. "Come on in, we were expecting you. I'm Ken Sobiniak, head of the security detail."

"Guess you already know who I am."

"Yes, indeed, Agent Delta, but I heard you retired some time ago."

"I did, but you know this business…agents never completely retire. Been doing background research for the Agency on a freelance basis."

"And I run this place…Don't take active missions anymore."

"Me neither, except when it's critical. You worked in the Far East when I was active, didn't you?"

"Suppose that's why we never ran into each other in person. Let's get you settled in…Had dinner?"

"No…rushed up here as soon as I could. Any other guests?"

"Just me and three guards…You can come out now, guys."

Two men stopped out from behind partially closed bedroom doors and walked toward her with hands extended. The taller of the two reached her first and grinned as he spoke, "It's an honor to meet you, Delta!."

"An honor?"

"You're a legend in the Agency…Some of your missions are used in the academy."

"Didn't know that…"

"Indeed they are," the other agent chimed in. "Your solution to the Borgenson Exercise was brilliant."

"That old paper? I'm surprised they still include it in the curriculum. I thought there were three of you…"

A paneled section of the living room wall held a mirror with a rough-pine frame. The four-foot section swung back to reveal a passageway beyond, and a swarthy young man stepped out holding a short, drum-fed street-sweeper automatic 12 ga. shotgun. His voice was deep and softer than she would have expected.

"Please to meet you, ma'am, I'm Denny Palumbo."

"Ma'am? Boy, do I feel old…"

"No offense intended…Actually, after all the stories I've heard…you're a lot younger than I thought you'd be."

"Well, thank you…You redeemed yourself, lucky you… Back to the business at hand…I'm not being chased and don't think I was followed. Just looking for a place to hang out until my husband gets here."

"He also an agent?" Asked Jack, the tall one.

"Not exactly…Lieutenant Colonel in the Air Force…On some business over at the casinos."

"Casinos? Strange place for a military guy to be doing business." The comment came from Toby, the smaller agent.

"Not really…"

"How about we get Delta's luggage for her?" Sobiniak interrupted. It was a command, not a request.

"This one piece is all I have, Ken," she replied. "Only be here for a day or two."

"Wish I could get my wife to pack that light," Denny

commented. "Almost takes a trailer to hold all her stuff, even for a weekend."

"In her defense, this was a last-minute thing...didn't have time to plan ahead," Nora noted. "Now, I haven't been here in years, but I seem to remember a couple of bedrooms down that corridor." She pointed to the hidden tunnel from which Denny had emerged.

"Three, actually," Denny corrected. "One is for two guards, the other two are for subjects...er, guests...Don't have windows and they share a bathroom."

"Fine with me. I don't need to see out and Bart will take the other guest room, if that's okay." She directed the question to Ken.

"Don't see why not," he answered. "Have a subject coming in four days...Clear until then."

"That will work out fine." Nora smiled. "Now, if you don't mind...Think I'll go to my room and call my husband."

"Have to make the call out here." Ken looked at the radio she was carrying. "Guest rooms are built into the hillside...don't get signals and we don't put phones in them. That's a secure line."

He pointed to a multi-line phone on an end-table next to a wooden couch with plaid cushions. "We'll go into the kitchen while you make your call." The others followed him out of the room.

***

CHAPTER 15

CONCORDIA CASINO
STATELINE, NEVADA

Bart Winfield was no stranger to casinos. He had been in half a dozen around the world and they all had the same nerve jangling, sweaty smell of desperation scented with stale cigarette smoke. He walked down two steps and found himself in the middle of the one-armed bandits. A right turn and forty-foot walk through rows of slot machines gave him a clear view of the craps and blackjack tables.

"Eichner seems to prefer table games," he said to Jay Johansen as he walked beside him. "Spotted by security here and two other casinos from faxed copies of his driver's license and a sketched image Bill Johnson described to a police artist…Triggered memories of a man who spent way too much time scoping out security arrangements."

"Yeah, saw stills from the security footage," Jay replied. "Nondescript comes to mind…Average height, weight, build…Brown hair…brown eyes. Would've slipped by unnoticed except for that habit of studying security…Was warned about not taking pictures…That put him on a citywide alert list."

Dealers remembered him asking about blackjack table procedures, like the schedule for swapping out deck shoes. They alerted their pit bosses who let ceiling security know. Pictures were taken of Eichner for future reference and a file was opened.

Once he caught the attention of the security pros, information was traded with other casinos through an unofficial network that cooperated like antibodies attempting to rid a body of infection.

In seeking to protect their businesses, they provided information that would have taken weeks to uncover using conventional police techniques.

Jay worked to keep up with Bart's long strides as he moved into the middle of the gaming action. Jake and Joanna were checking out another casino with Benson. Bart's earpiece crackled. "Sergeant Thomas to Colonel Winfield, over."

"Like I said, call me Bart while we're on this assignment."

"Yes, sir. Airman…I mean, Joanna and I've been through most of the Majestic…Not a trace. Coming out of the elevator at the eleventh floor high-roller casino, over."

"Roger that…We're in the Concordia. Meet you at Harrah's if we don't find him here…Don't see how he could've gotten too far though, over."

"Wait a minute, sir…Think I spotted him in an enclosed room at the back…Can't be sure…window reflections blocking my view."

They walked a little further and Jake keyed the mike again. "Ninety-nine percent sure it's him. He can see us, but can't hear what we're saying."

"Stay back as far as you can without losing contact," Bart replied. "Don't want to spook him…May've planted a bomb and have a remote trigger…Bless his little heart, wouldn't want to kill him for looking at us the wrong way, now would we?"

"Ain't that the truth…" Joanna added in a southern accent.

Bart continued, "Besides, we want a chance to ask him some questions. I'll contact the brass at your location…let them know what's going on. Any other way out of there?"

There was a pause while Jake talked to somebody. "Security guy says a side door to an auxiliary grill, but they have a couple of men covering it from inside the kitchen. He's in the process of notifying their people on the overhead catwalk. I told them to be discrete. Damn it! Three more just got off the elevator. They're sending in too many people all at once…Eichner will make them for sure. What do you want us to do?"

"All right, just stay calm…Take it slow and easy…Try to contain the situation before he sees what's going on."

"Too late…Eichner's staring right past me toward the elevator and knows it's not routine…Not half-a-dozen guys in suits showing up at the same time. We need you here ASAP!"

"On my way, son, over."

"We'll wait right here," was all Jake could think of to say. "And hope this doesn't blow up in our faces. Subject's looking spooked…"

"Again, keep it under control, hear?"

"Do my best, sir…over and out."

The quiet hum of the fifth floor casino turned to complete bedlam in less than a minute. Eichner saw security gathering in the elevator lobby and tried to leave through the kitchen door.

He turned away when he saw two casino security men in the kitchen through a small window in the door. A quick glance toward the main entrance showed Jake, Joanna and the other security people moving from the elevator toward the glass doors that led into the private card lounge.

The realization he was trapped brought a frenzied look of desperation to his face. He pulled a pistol out of his waistband and fired a shot into the ceiling. At the same time, he reached into his back pocket and pulled out a device that looked like a radio.

"Nobody move!" he shouted. "This is a remote control for the mother of all bombs! Move any closer and I'll vaporize everything for five miles!"

Every person in the room froze where they stood. Only their eyes moved, darting from Eichner's rage-distorted face to the device he held and then to each other. Cigar butts dropped from mouths that hung open and drinks fell to the plush carpet as frightened patrons lost their grip on drink glasses.

The waiter stood like a statue with a tray held above his head. A palpable sense of fear clung to every surface and person in the room.

Eichner moved backward to the windows that lined the outside wall of the casino.

"Get somebody in here to negotiate with me!" he yelled at nobody in particular.

Nobody moved. A middle-aged gambler mumbled, "Whadda ya want us to do, man?…We're only tourists."

Finally, the waiter, who stood the closest to Eichner, spoke, "Can I get you anything, sir?"

"What?" Rick looked at the waiter like he was insane. "What the hell do you mean, can you get me anything?"

CIA SAFE HOUSE AT SOUTH SHORE LODGE

Nora picked up the phone, dialed her coded ID and was connected to a communications center in San Francisco."

"Confirm ID," a voice at the other end demanded.

"Delta ID 416233 Whiskey, Foxtrot, Alpha requesting a radio link."

"Confirmed…say the frequency and encryption key."

She gave them the necessary information and a few minutes later heard the background hiss of a satellite radio signal.

The satellite phone in Bart's pocket buzzed and he answered, "Colonel Winstead."

A couple of clicks later, Nora's voice came through with the alien quality of an encrypted call.

"Baby, can you hear me?"

"Scrambled a little, but yes."

"I'm at the South Shore Lodge under my old code name."

"As Delta?"

"I said I'd be here the last time…"

"You already got here?"

"You said to get out of town, so I grabbed my go bag and boogied."

"Right…Sorry…got a lot on my mind right now. This isn't good…You need to turn around and go back home."

"Okay, now I'm thoroughly confused. First you want me to leave town…now you want me to go back. What's going on?"

"Can't say…even on a secure line. Trust me, you don't want to be here."

"But I am and I'm too tired to drive back. It's safe here and I have a nice warm bed waiting for you when you're done."

"Don't know when that'll be and if something goes wrong… might be over in a flash."

"Doesn't change what I said before…I want to be with you no matter what."

"Can't talk you out of staying?"

"Not likely…Think of it as incentive. Save the world and I'll be waiting with open arms. Anything I can do to help?"

"No…Rather have you there. You staying in the guest room?"

"Yes…I like the idea of the cave behind it."

"Could come in handy, depending on what happens. Matter of fact…might want to stay back there as much as you can…Just as comfortable and it might be safer in the mountain."

"I'll keep the news on.…Go finish what you're doing and get over here."

"Roger that, little darlin'…love you."

PREFERRED PLAYERS LOUNGE
MAJESTIC CASINO

"What I meant, sir, was can I get you a drink or something?"

"No, you idiot!" was Eichner's terse reply. "What I want is whoever is in charge of this dump!"

The waiter shrunk back. "Sorry, dude…Just trying to make things a little easier…"

Eichner eyed him a little closer. "Wait…Somebody who's cooperating. That's more like it. Tell you what, Champ…Go lock those doors. Shove everybody out who's standing near them and make sure those three don't come in."

He pointed toward Jake, Joanna and Mary Benson. "They look like trouble…Get those security thugs out of here, too. Make everybody else sit down and get them something to drink…But only one. Don't want some drunken wannabe hero dying and screwing things up…And get me a telephone!"

The waiter set the tray down on a table and stepped in one direction, then another. He finally settled on moving toward the door and gestured at the group standing near it.

He assumed the haughty air of a maître d', which is what he hoped to be someday. "All right, you heard the man…Move outside the doors…Come on now…hurry, hurry… hurry."

The group standing near the door had no choice. They slowly stepped back far enough to allow him to close the double glass doors in their face. Eichner bellowed a muffled command and the waiter turned the lock on the door.

Joanna leaned close to Jake. "Okay, now what?"

Jake keyed his radio mike. "Thomas to Winfield, over."

"This is Bart, over."

"It just went down the toilet...Eichner's taken hostages and cleared the room of all security, including us. We're in the elevator lobby. What's your twenty, over?"

"Just came through the front door of the casino headin' toward the elevator. On the way up, but don't wait. I want you on the catwalk in the ceiling...assuming there is one."

"Roger that...Davies and Benson will brief you.

He turned to one of the hotel security men. "Excuse me, is there a ceiling catwalk in there?"

The security man nodded.

"Okay, great," Jake said. "I need to be above him as soon as possible."

The security man pulled a radio out of his casino blazer and less than a minute later said, "Follow me, please."

Jake glanced over his shoulder through the glass doors. Eichner was pacing back and forth. His forehead glistened with sweat and he clutched the remote control with white knuckles.

He looked up in time to lock eyes with Jake and snarled at him.

It wasn't a good idea to taunt Eichner, but he couldn't help raising his hand and pointing at the madman with his thumb up, like he was holding a gun.

He mouthed the words, "I'm coming for you!"

Eichner slapped his chest with the pistol and yelled back, "Bring it on!"

Jake turned away and followed the casino security man.

"Soon," he mumbled.

A few minutes later Jake carefully slid a ceiling tile aside far enough to see Eichner below, sitting in one of the plush arm chairs. His eyes were still adjusting to the semi-darkness and the air smelled like a musty attic. He knelt on the catwalk and got as close to the opening as he could.

Two security men crouched behind him on the platform.

One of them leaned toward Jake. "What's the plan?"

"Your guess is as good as mine," he replied. "Ask the guys in the control room what's happening down there."

"They say he tipped over some of the tables to form a barricade…Sitting with his back to the windows watching the main doors."

"Where's the remote?"

"In his lap."

Jake slowly backed up the catwalk, forcing the security men to duck walk behind him. They backed through the fire wall door and quietly closed it.

He keyed his mike. "Colonel, this is Jake. I was above Eichner a minute ago, over."

"What did you see?"

"He's sitting in front of the outside windows with the

curtains closed."

"What are our options?" Bart asked.

"Couple of possibilities. First is an explosive entry through the windows behind Eichner…But, he'd have too much time to react and press the button on that remote. Sniper shot from a chopper outside the windows is a no go…Heavy curtains mean no visual. No infrared either, since there are others near him. Final option is a drop out of the ceiling."

"Roger that," Bart replied. "Timing would have to be perfect, though…We'd have to get hold of the remote before he could press the button. Real chancy…could turn into a disaster in a flash, if you'll pardon the bad pun."

"Reminds me of training exercises where you start out with an easy sweep of a building," Jake commented. "Then add a bunch of variables…like throwing in a sympathetic hostage or a snarling dog to complicate things until it's totally out of control."

"Really love chaos, don't you?" Bart replied.

"I do love a challenge…Look forward to everything going to pieces. *That's when I feel most alive.*

"Well, son, I'd say we're almost there…Some of the most pristine real estate in the country and a few hundred thousand folks vaporized raises the stakes to an unheard of level…Should pump your adrenaline off the chart."

"Not about the rush, sir…It's the precision. Plan so that, no matter what, it all comes out as close to perfect as you can get…Right down to the smallest detail."

"Always wondered what made you tick."

"A job well-done…That's all I need."

"Wish that's all there was to it. Assuming we get out of this mess, we're still gonna have a dozen agencies crawlin' up our butts with flashlights. We don't make it, they'll be Monday-morning-quarterbacking us for the next fifty years. Won't matter, though, since we won't be around to hear it…"

"What'll it be, Colonel?"

"Continue to analyze…Choose the solution that looks best. Love to let higher-ups make the decision, but they're not here. Don't know how much stress this jerk can take, but I'm gonna go in and talk to him about givin' up that remote."

"Think he'll go for it?"

"Won't matter…I'll maneuver him under you while I'm distracting him with talk. When I say, listen, Rick, I'm just trying to make this come out okay, you drop down on him. Between the two of us, we should be able to get the remote away."

"Sounds like a plan, sir."

"Joe Anthony, head of security, is here. We agree the bomb has to be in reach of the remote's signal…probably no more than a thousand feet or so, especially through concrete. His staff is searching the casino from top to bottom.

"Casino security says Eichner's wound up tighter than a two-dollar watch. First, he jumped out of the chair and paced up and down. Now, he's sitting there tapping his foot and muttering to himself. A technician is working on the audio. Says we should have it in a sec."

Sounds from the card room suddenly got louder. Eichner

was shouting at some of the hostages to line up in front of the windows, facing out.

Bart mumbled. "Sounds like he's close to goin' over the edge…Talking to himself and he's ordered hostages to form a cordon in front of the table barricade."

"Why's it quiet all of a sudden? What's happening?" Asked Jake.

"Not much…He sat back down," Bart answered. "Staring at the floor with his head in his hands. One minute he's agitated…Next thing he's quieter than a mouse peeing on cotton."

"What about the control?"

"Don't see it…Probably still in his lap."

"Getting back into position," Jake whispered.

"Good idea. Say a prayer for both of us…Winfield, over and out."

Jake passed through the fire wall door and moved silently down the catwalk until he was crouching near the partially opened ceiling tile. He could see the top of Eichner's head. Jake carefully slid the ceiling tile back an inch at a time.

A few bits of acoustic tile drifted down and clung to Eichner's hair and shoulders. He sat up and looked around. Jake moved away from the opening and froze, barely breathing.

Eichner stood up with the control in his left hand and began gesturing emphatically with it. Jake couldn't make out all that was being said, but it was obvious that Eichner's blood pressure continued to go up.

He eventually calmed down and sat back down in the chair

with the remote on one arm and the pistol on the other. He began mumbling to himself again.

Jake clicked his mike once, paused and keyed it two more times to indicate he was in position.

Bart Winfield's whisper came through, "He told us we have five minutes to get a negotiator in there...Guess I'll take Johansen and go in. Hopefully, the asshole will decide I'm the figure of authority he's been asking for."

Jake whispered. "Took the FBI Negotiations and Tactics Leader Course, didn't you?"

"Couple years ago...But how do you train for something like this? The tiniest thing can spell disaster...And it all depends on a suspect who's becoming unhinged. Not exactly the scene you want to drop in on..."

"Roger that, sir...Ready to save the day?"

"Settle for saving our butts! Remember, the goal is to go home when the shift's over."

"Good point, sir." He focused his attention on the sliver-like view of the suspect sixteen feet below and slowed his breathing to calm himself. "Hope I don't break a leg landing on him, sir." *Distance and angle...Go for the remote and the gun...Subdue Eichner.*

"Don't worry, son, we'll tape an aspirin on it."

Jake considered the possibilities over and over as he crouched above the most dangerous man in the world and waited for the cue from below...

"Waiter, what's your name?" Eichner asked the eager young

man.

"Gregory, sir."

"Gregory...not Greg?"

"Greg is my father."

"Okay, Gregory it is. I like your take charge attitude...as long as you realize who's in charge."

"Yes, sir." The tall, thin waiter stood still, waiting for more directions.

"Looks like they found somebody for me to talk to. Let's hope he cooperates as well as you...let him in."

CONSORTIUM SAFE HOUSE
SACRAMENTO, CA

"In bed with this really nice redhead chick when the phone rings," Chance, the newest member of the strike team, lamented. "How long you think this'll take?"

His question was directed to Jim—no last name, another member of the six-man team, who looked like he could be a high school teacher or bank clerk. Unassuming in every way, he could easily fade into a crowd at any shopping mall or movie theater. "Could be a day, maybe a week...depends on how things unfold and what kind of orders we get. Best to plan on a couple weeks...That way, you don't get all tied up in knots."

Part of Jim's assignment was the indoctrination and field training of the latest recruit to their team. He knew a little of Chance's background—most of which was biographical in nature and might be false. He was supposedly reared in a middle class family in Thousand Oaks, California and dropped out of community college after the third semester to join the Marine Corps, despite the protests of his parents. He served six years, including two overseas tours. "You were Recon, right?"

"Yeah," was the terse reply.

"They always tell you how long a mission would last?"

"Wouldn't know...Injured on my first real one...Couldn't requalify, so they stuck me in the office. Got tired of listening to war stories from guys on the team. Beat up one who ribbed me about how capturing a desk was my only real accomplishment...Put him in sick bay for a couple weeks. CO busted me to Private and transferred me to supply. Got old in a hurry...didn't re-up."

"You get here the usual way?"

"Don't know...What's usual?"

"Bar or martial arts class...sometimes a gym. Our recruiters keep an eye out for the right kind.

"They can tell by looking if you're right?"

"Not always...Although people we're looking for do have a certain way of carrying themselves. Usually, there's an incident that points them in the right direction...Something as simple as two guys bumping into each other. They watch for a reaction. On rare occasion, they see an actual fight and pick out a possibility."

"Bingo!"

"Huh?"

"Throwing iron around at a local gym when this big dude tells me he needs to use the squat rack I'm working on. Told him I'd be done in a minute…Walked over to the lat machine. His buds teased him…Said he should teach me a lesson."

"Then what?"

"Came over and said I should apologize for being in the way. His friends kept egging him on. I didn't say anything, so he shoved me, trying to get my goat, I guess. Warned him not to put his hands on me again…But, of course, he did. Took him down…choked him out. Then went after his buds."

"What'd they do?"

"The usual…nothing. They were all smaller than him. Guess they figured I could probably take them just as easy. They split in a hurry…Left Billy Bob Badass laying on the floor."

"What did you do?"

"Revived him…Didn't want to face charges if the asshole died on me. Told him to stay away from the gym when I was there. Then I left."

"End of story?"

He chuckled. "Not exactly…Shit-For-Brains followed me to the parking lot with a knife. Took it away from him and buried it in his leg. Stupid is forever…figured he needed a reminder. Thought that'd keep him away from the gym for awhile.

"That's when Dave came up to me and asked if I worked in law enforcement or something. Told him no… I was in between jobs. Bought my lunch…Then offered me a job."

"Who'd you think you'd be working for?"

"Close security firm specializing in protecting high-dollar assets…people and facilities. Didn't matter…Pay sounded good and I was bored out of my mind."

"Long as you understand the stakes…Doesn't take a whole lot of screw-ups and you're gone…And I don't mean fired."

"Got that part right off the bat," Chance replied. "Don't intend to make a lot. If I do, whatever happens is righteous."

"Sounds like you got a handle on it. Not being nosey, but where did you get the burn scars on your neck?"

"Happened when I was a teen…Bad car wreck. Don't remember anything 'til after I woke up in a rehab hospital…not even my parents. Told me they were killed in the wreck… Ended up in foster care…No relatives, other than a grandmother who's in a nursing home with Alzheimer's. Lawyer says my father was a gambler who was deeply in debt…Everything went to pay off loans. Joined the Corps soon as I could…Sort of like a family."

"Sorry about your parents."

"Shit happens. You get over it or die."

"True. Let's go back to the equipment room and get the gear we'll need. What's your favorite sidearm?"

"Brought my own." Chance patted the pistol under his left arm. "1911A with extended mag."

"Somebody should have told you…no personal firearms. Leave it in a locker and use a company piece. It's untraceable…Throw it out the window if you're pulled over."

"What about sighting it in?"

"Armorer does that…But if you feel you must, there's an indoor range in the second subbasement. Also a crate of 1911s to choose from. Laser sights if you want…flashlights, too, including infrared. There's a pretty good selection of other weapons on-hand…Everything from S&W 59 or 559s to MAC-10 and 11s, UZIs, H&K MP-5s. Don't see what you want, tell an armorer and they'll get it for you. They'll also make sure your favorites are stocked at all other safe houses…And you can take one of each home with you after the op."

"Seriously? I like that…What about ammo?"

"We stock a wide assortment for various mission types…Pistol loads of different kinds, including Glazer…Shotgun shells, including, double and triple-ought, and slugs, of course. Door-breachers, armor-piercing, flash-bangs, terminators, flechettes and even flares."

"Couldn't ask for more."

"We aim to please…We'll also suit you up with a SWAT uniform…Personal body armor, holsters and rigs…Extra mags and ammo. Comm gear with earpiece radios, sat phones and company cell phones. Flash bangs and concussion grenades, along with whatever police or martial arts gear you feel you need. Again, anything else…tell the armorer."

"Think I'm gonna like it here."

"Hope so." Jim smiled. His earpiece beeped. "Call coming in from one of the big guys. Let's go see what he wants."

***

CHAPTER 16

PREFERRED PLAYERS LOUNGE
MAJESTIC CASINO

Gregory carefully turned the lock on the double door, slowly poked his head out and looked up and down the hallway. Bart and Jay had separated from the group of security people huddled in the elevator lobby and moved toward the card room.

"You the negotiator he's waiting for?"

"I am," Bart replied.

Gregory watched the elevator doors, expecting them to burst open and disgorge a horde of black-suited, helmeted goons who would shoot everyone in sight, including him. "Alone?"

"Just me and him." Bart pointed to Johansen and they slipped through the partially opened doors.

Once Gregory was satisfied the cavalry wasn't coming, he faded back into the room, locked the door and let go a deep sigh of relief.

Bart approached the table barricade and spoke to Eichner. "Howdy, Bart Winfield's the name...with security." He extended a handshake, which was ignored. "Okay, pardner, you wanted to talk to somebody...Guess I've been elected."

Eichner flew out of the chair in a rage, once again waving the remote in his fist. "What the hell's going on here? First of all, I'm not your *pardner*...I'm the one who's in charge, so get that straight...And this isn't a democracy, nobody elected you. I want a negotiator, not some Mickey Mouse rent-a-cop!...And who's that?" He pointed to Johansen. "Some other third-rate flunky? I ought to blow the shit out of this place just to prove a point!"

"Whoa, there...how about we slow things down a bit? Johansen's here as a witness...to make sure we get everything straight. And as far as that goes, since I'm here anyway...Can't we just chew the fat for a while...Make my bosses think I'm earning my pay?"

"Chew the fat? Where you from anyway, hayseed?" Eichner went on before Bart could answer, "Doesn't matter...Yeah, I guess...At least until somebody with real power gets here."

He pointed to Johansen and then to a corner of the room where hostages were huddled. "He stays over there, got it?"

"You got it, amigo."

"Hey, asshole, I'm not your friend!...I thought that was clear. So, try anything and I'll end this in a flash." He held his

239

finger over a large red button in the center of the remote.

Johansen moved toward the corner of the room while Bart climbed over the tables. "Got it. Now, tell me what you need to make everything hunky dory."

Eichner laughed.

Bart gave him a puzzled look. "What did I say?"

"You must really be some kind of hillbilly...Don't know if I've ever heard a real person say hunky dory."

It was Bart's turn to smile. "Haven't heard the word hillbilly in a long time, either...I'm river bottom...Tunica, Mississippi. Where you from, son?"

"Long way from here." Eichner's face darkened. "Let's cut the small talk and get down to business."

"Sure 'nough, son, just tell me what you want."

"Don't call me son!"

"Okay, then...mind if I call you Rick?"

"How do you know my name?"

"Does it matter? Look, I don't want to be here any more'n you do...Rather be out in my bass boat terrorizing the local fish population."

"And I'd rather be playing cards...All right, you can tell them what I want...Some food, since the kitchen's apparently closed...And a bulletproof vest for me."

"Sure 'nough, Rick...no hill for a stepper. What kind of food?"

"Sandwiches are fine...and something to drink."

Bart used the radio to convey the order to Joanna. He ended with a code phrase for Jake. "Get that done in a heartbeat...you hear, darlin'?"

They would have held off a little longer if he had ended it with sweetie. Instead, Jake slowly slid the tile back until the space was wide enough for him to drop through.

He grabbed onto an overhead pipe and waited for Bart to maneuver Eichner under him. It didn't take long. Eichner stepped backward as Bart moved toward him. *Couple more steps...*

The crouched position on the catwalk was awkward and he longed to stretch out his legs to restore normal blood flow. The control in Eichner's left hand was tantalizingly close. Still, the sixteen-foot distance seemed like a yawning chasm.

Eichner stepped slowly backward as he talked with Bart and stopped directly below the breach in the ceiling. Jake could hear the conversation between them.

Bart was cajoling Eichner with soothing words that a skilled negotiator would use. He ended a sentence with, "Listen, Rick, I'm just trying to make this come out okay..."

Jake thought of his martial arts instructors teaching him to blend into the environment and to move with confidence. Endless repetitions had trained his body to act in fluid motions that delivered devastating blows with pinpoint accuracy. He concentrated on the shoulder of the arm that held the control and released his grip on the pipe.

Eichner looked up to see Jake dropping toward him. He instinctively turned away from the falling body and the heavy combat boot glanced off his shoulder as they fell to the floor. The impact was strong enough to dislodge the remote from his grip. It bounced once and Bart scooped it up.

His fingers had barely wrapped around the control when something hit the floor behind him with a thud as an acrid cloud of yellow smoke began billowing all around them. He could see Johansen through the haze as he prepared to pull the pin on a second grenade.

The hostages scattered and surged toward the exit in a blind panic. The locked glass doors stalled their progress and they pushed frantically against them until they finally burst open. The unruly crowd spilled out into the rest of the casino and moved toward the elevator lobby.

"What the hell are you doing?" Bart yelled in anger at the NSA agent.

Jay froze in place. "Distracting him…"

Jake jumped up from the floor, spun around and yelled, "Hey, where did Eichner go?"

They searched through the blossoming smoke, but he was nowhere to be seen. The nose-stinging fog blanketed the room and obscured the view. It took precious moments for them to search the card lounge.

It was soon obvious he was gone. Casino security had tried to screen everyone who left the room through the glass doors and he did not appear to be among them.

Gregory stumbled out of the smoke and yelled, "He got out through the kitchen!"

Bart started to move in that direction when Jake grabbed his arm. "Wait a second, sir…I gave him a pretty good shot and casino security is in there. Besides, he doesn't have the remote control anymore…Speaking of…look!"

Bart stared down at a built-in timer on the remote that read 43 minutes and 22 seconds as it steadily counted down. "Damn, son…Not red numbers again! Looks like we have a bomb to locate in less than an hour."

He looked down at the descending digits. "A lot of innocent people are counting on us…Anybody got any idea where he might have hidden it?"

Joanna and casino security pushed their way into the room through the departing hostages. "I have one, Colonel!"

"Let's hear it, but be quick."

"Question keeps popping up…Why bring the bombs to this casino? Can't just be revenge…One bomb will waste everything in a five-mile radius. Eichner was a contractor…He do any work here?"

Bart posed the question to Joe Anthony, who had joined them from the elevator lobby. The answer came back after a quick radio exchange. "Seems that a company called EichCon did some remodeling in the lobby about a year ago…Also built some supply rooms in the basement about six months ago."

"Can you show us? Bart replied. "My gut says it won't be the lobby…too much traffic. Let's hit the basement first."

He grabbed the security director by the arm and half-dragged him toward the elevator. "Come on, Joe, we're probably gonna need your help."

Jake, Joanna, and the NSA agents dashed into the elevator with them and Jake pressed the button for the sub-basement.

Johansen pressed himself as far as possible into the corner

of the elevator car, hung his head and stared dejectedly at the floor.

The group stared back and forth at each other and watched the lighted buttons display the downward progress. A Barry Manilow tune filled the confined space, but Bart barely heard it above the sound of blood roaring in his ears.

He leaned over toward Johansen and spoke in a voice barely above a whisper, "Look, son, I don't know what your problem is…but smoke grenades weren't part of the plan. Maybe your mama gave you too many toys to play with when you were a kid…Don't know and it doesn't matter…Only gonna say this once, so listen up…Pull another stunt like you did back there and I'll shoot you myself! Understood?"

Johansen wisely said nothing, nodded and cowered even more. The elevator crawled slowly toward the basement.

CONSORTIUM SAFE HOUSE
SACRAMENTO, CA

The Commissioner finished laying out plans for the raid on the CIA Safe House at Lake Tahoe over the video conference call. "I know this is not the typical mission…"

"None of them ever are," Sparks, one of the team members whispered.

"Do you forget this is a two-way feed, Mister Sparks?" the Commissioner queried with an icy tone.

"No sir…sorry."

"Your apology is accepted. Now, where was I?…The risks

are obviously higher for this work…therefore, the reward will be commensurately bigger. Standard fee for this sort of operation is fifty thousand dollars. I am doubling that and it will be deposited in your equity account…Should you fail to safely return, it will be given to your beneficiary.

"Furthermore, we have decided to add a mission bonus of six hundred thousand for successful completion. That will be divided among survivors. Medical expenses will be covered, as well as paid recovery time. Any questions?"

"What about recovered items?" The question came from Steptoe, a recent addition to the team.

"We are not pirates, sir…we do not allow booty. However, if a recovered item, as you phrase it, has intelligence value, you will be rewarded. Get approval from your team leader before confiscating it. Now, unless you have something else, I have another meeting in three minutes. Goodbye."

The screen went dark.

"Glad we didn't have any other questions," Chance whispered to Jim.

"Shouldn't," was the terse reply. "We all know our jobs…Steptoe is our weapons man, Skullcracker is the explosives expert, Trucker is in charge of transportation and Sparks runs comm."

"What do yo do?"

"Backup for all of them…and babysit you."

Chance bristled at the last comment. "Babysit? I can do any of the other jobs…"

"Not until you're certified by me…So be my shadow and

help when you can…or if I tell you to."

"Yes, suh, massa…"

"And work on getting rid of that smart ass attitude…It'll only get you in trouble," Jim admonished him.

"Yeah, right…I'll work on it."

NICK BORETTI'S OFFICE

Nick Boretti sat in an overstuffed armchair in front of his desk and sipped a glass of twenty year old scotch. "Don't know about you, but I'm getting real tired of old men telling us what to do."

Antonio Lemonica was his boss and sat behind Boretti's desk out of deference and habit. Tony, as only his closest confidantes referred to him, thought for a second before asking, "Guys in Chicago or guys in Europe?"

"Europe. I know we're supposed to work with them 'cause of our things in Macao and Hong Kong…But tell me why we shoud let them stick their greaseball noses into our thing here?"

"Asked Provencano the same thing this morning." Guido Provencano was head of the syndicate for Nevada and lived in Las Vegas. "Alls he would say is, it is what it is…Which don't say nothing, but you know how he is."

"Yeah, that's how he is…What are you gonna do?"

"Ain't sure…What brung it up was the guys in the ceiling spotting this Eichner mook playing cards in Majestic's upstairs lounge…Sent Toby and Craig to grab him…It don't happen. Joe Anthony and his people got the whole friggin' floor sealed off…Won't say why…Somethin' about national security or some bullshit. Then, all of a sudden, wham! Toby says one of his buddies works for Anthony...Tells him Eichner's gone...Bam!...Right out from under their noses."

"Guy's gotta have connections..."

"Maybe...Got away by killing a coupla Anthony's men... Meaner'n a junk yard dog...Should work for us."

"We should be so lucky, but what are you gonna do?" This time it was a rhetorical question asked with a shrug of the shoulders.

"Ain't sure...Got every guy on the street looking for him...Don't care what nobody in the old country says. Too many questions keep popping up about this wise guy. Maybe we'll find him first...Get some answers."

MAJESTIC CASINO

Scarlet numbers on the timer showed 41 minutes and 13 seconds when the doors finally slid open and the entire group tried to squeeze out of the elevator at once. They followed Joe Anthony down a hall lined with food carts, boxes and crates of kitchen produce. Stray spinach leaves poked out from one and a squashed tomato made the floor slippery. The smell of rotting vegetables was something buffet patrons would not smell.

Mary Benson waved a Geiger counter as she passed the objects. "Normal levels here," she announced. None of them looked large enough to contain the nuclear device.

A scan of both sides of the hallway showed no irregularities until Bart reached a door marked with a yellow sign in big black letters that read Electrical Room-Authorized Personnel Only. He turned to Anthony. "Why does this door have a different lock set than the others?"

Joe shrugged his shoulders. "No idea...Let me check something." He spoke into his radio and the answer came back in less than a minute. "Got a problem here...According to our blueprints, B117A doesn't even exist and you're right... not one of our locks. None of my master keys'll fit..."

Bart interrupted, "What do you mean, doesn't exist?"

"Just that...doesn't show up on any of our floor plans. New supply rooms next door are exactly where they're supposed to be. This room, on the other hand, shouldn't be here Looks like a little was taken off of the supply rooms to make it."

Jake knelt down and examined the area around the door.

"Door's been opened recently...Notice the scrape marks?"

"Can you pick it?" Bart asked.

"Looks like a tough one...might be better to break in, since we're pressed for time."

"Are there any tools around here?" Bart directed the question to Anthony. "You know, like a pry bar or ax... something like that?"

Two armed security guards stepped out of the elevator and Joe shouted, "Snell, get a pry bar or a tire iron...Something to open this door."

The guard acknowledged with a wave and ran out an exit door that led to the underground parking garage.

Bart turned to Jake and Joanna. "This door may be booby-trapped...Move everybody back at least fifty feet. Jake, you got your mini-scope?"

Jake grinned and pulled the flexible tube from a side pocket of his cargo pants. "I don't leave home without it."

He handed it to Bart, who knelt down and pushed it under the door while swinging it from side to side. "Too dark to see much...There's a little light coming through a vent from the room next door. Can't see what's inside for sure...Shapes that look like supply cabinets. Good news is it doesn't look like any wires on the door. What do y'all think?"

"We're running low on time," Joanna offered. "Might be best to go ahead..."

Conversation stopped when the security guard burst through the parking garage door carrying a four-foot steel crow bar extended at arm's length like it was made of gold. "Had this in my truck."

"Thanks, pard," said Bart. "Guess that settles it...We'll prize it open. Everybody else, please move down the hall."

Joe Anthony and the two guards herded a curious kitchen staff to what they felt was a safe distance. That left the team from Mather and the two NSA agents huddled around the door.

Bart nodded to Benson and Johansen. "Y'all can move down there with the rest if you want to...Might be safer."

"From the short time I've worked with you, Colonel, I trust your judgment...so have at it."

Bart shrugged his shoulders and inserted the bar between the door and frame. He and Jake grunted and applied as much force as they could. The door creaked, groaned and popped open a few inches. The group breathed a collective sigh of relief at the absence of an explosion.

Bart ran the beam from his flashlight around the door frame. He found nothing and directed the light into the room. There were no obvious trip wires or explosive devices showing. The light switch showed no obvious signs of tampering, so he pushed the door open all the way.

A flip of the switch brought fluorescent lights slowly to life and revealed a room about the size of a large bathroom. Shelves along one wall held survival food packs and boxes of ammunition, as well as camping gear. Five-gallon bottles of drinking water lined the other wall. Two rifles and a shotgun were propped in the far corner in front of a large utility cabinet. Its doors were opened enough to reveal an empty pistol case. A hiking pack leaned against the wall, just inside the door.

Jake surveyed the room, stepped back and looked at Bart. "I don't get it, sir…Where's the bomb?"

Bart rubbed the back of his neck. "No idea…Looks like nothing more than escape gear…May have left them here to pick up later."

"Sure put a lot of thought and planning into this," Joanna observed. "Somebody trained him well."

Jake carefully opened the cabinet doors. The shelves held more supplies, including boxes of ammunition, one of which was empty.

They began searching for any clues to where Eichner might be headed.

Bart let out an exasperated sigh after a few minutes. "Stop…that's enough…Let's step back…Put our heads together and try to figure out what he did with the bombs."

They stood in the cramped storeroom staring at each other until Joanna face-palmed herself. "Wait! He'd want the bomb to be up higher in elevation, wouldn't he? You know, for maximum blast effect. How could he sneak it up higher in the building without raising suspicion or having it discovered during a search?"

Jake jumped in, "I know where you're headed with that…She reminded me of an incident years ago…Guy threatened to blow up a casino if the owner didn't pay. Other casino owners were afraid there'd be future extortion attempts…Offered to help cover any damages if he told the bad guy to go to hell…"

Bart broke in with an exasperated sigh, "Look, son…hate to cut this short, but we're on a timer…How 'bout the Reader's Digest version?"

Jake frowned. "Long story short…he refused to pay. They cleared the building and waited…Bomb blew out the entire fifth floor."

"Damn, son!" Bart's jaw dropped. "Blew it out?"

Benson spoke up, "I remember seeing it on the evening news…Rest of the hotel was fine, but that middle floor was totally gone. You could see mountains on the other side of the lake right through the building…Nothing but concrete pillars."

"Wait, you're telling me the building didn't collapse?" asked Johansen. "A little hard to believe."

"Well, believe it," she replied. "Of course, they built them a lot stronger back then…concrete pillars stood in place."

"Guess I missed that one," Bart commented. "Overseas at the time…What's the connection?"

"Bad guy got it past security by disguising it as an ordinary copy machine," Jake answered.

Bart yelled down the hall to the director of security, "Hey, Joe, y'all had any large deliveries in the past few days?…Be at least the size of a copy machine or bigger."

"Let me see." There was a pause. "Hang on a second, they're checking the delivery logs."

It took less than a minute for the security control center to come back with an answer. "Besides the usual food and drink deliveries, there was some lighting and sound gear that came in this morning…For a concert next weekend…although, that soes seems a little early. Could that be it?"

"Maybe…Where's the theater?"

"Top floor."

"Then that could be it. Joe, would you be kind enough to show us the way?"

"No problem, Colonel…Follow me."

They headed toward the elevator with Anthony and his men in tow. The elevator seemed even slower as it crawled upward and the music seemed more oppressive. The timer displayed 27 minutes and 19 seconds with a ruby red glow.

The music changed to a light rock version of Steppenwolf's "Born To Be Wild." Joe Anthony was subconsciously mouthing the words, "Fire all of your guns at once and explode into space…"

They all stared at him.

He grinned and shrugged his shoulders. "Hope it doesn't happen here…"

After what seemed like ages, the gentle *ting* of a bell announced their arrival at the fourteenth floor.

CIA SAFE HOUSE AT SOUTH SHORE LODGE

"Man, I can't believe the missions you went on during the Cold War," exclaimed Toby. "Lot more exciting than now."

"I suppose it would look that way to someone who's just starting their career." Nora realized that her son would have been about his age, if not for the fiery accident that took him. Her heart ached and she continued to avoid tears. "We felt like we were doing our jobs the best we could, even if there were times when nobody seemed to have a clue…especially our bosses."

"That's one thing that hasn't changed," Jack interjected. He stumbled over his words. "What I meant to say…What I meant was…it's still a confusing world, even today. Hard to know who our friends are…"

Ken saved the young man from further embarrassment. "What our young colleague is trying to say is there's a certain amount of ambiguity at the upper echelons. Nobody's sure where they stand with the guys at Langley…Who, in turn, aren't sure where they stand with the career bureaucrats on Capitol Hill."

"You're right…nothing's changed." Nora chuckled. "About

the only thing any of us can do is run as fast as we can to keep the wheel turning."

"Speaking of...About time for Jack and Toby to make their rounds of the perimeter. We have trip wires and sensors, but I still think the human element is the best guard...Gentlemen, we'll see you back in twenty minutes. Denny and I'll do the dishes."

The agents would have preferred to stay and listen to more of Nora's stories, but duty called. They checked their weapons and headed for the door. Denny excused himself to go to the bathroom and Ken began clearing the table. She joined him in the kitchen where he was scraping plates into a trash bin.

"Gosh, they make me feel so old!" She smiled.

"Try being around them twenty-four seven," he replied. "Glad I only have three years till retirement. Still, they're a good crew and I appreciate their enthusiasm...most of the time."

She spoke softly, "Hope they never have to go through what we did. I pray the end of the Cold War has brought us some lasting semblance of peace."

"Me too...Problem is there are still people out there who want to change the world order to their advantage."

"Oh, don't get me wrong," she shot back. "I'm too much of a pragmatist to think our country can ever let its guard down...even for a second. You and I both know it can blow up in our collective faces any time...anywhere."

"Isn't that the truth...Now, do you want to wash or dry?" He extended a sponge in one hand and a dish towel in the other.

He looked over her shoulder at a red light mounted over the

door that was blinking. "Problem in the office. Strange, though…I thought everybody we expected had already clocked in…Better go check."

He patted the MAC-10 under his arm as he started to the door. "Might want to wait in the cave."

Nora detected an undercurrent of urgency in his outwardly calm manner. She dropped the dish towel on the counter and headed for the secret passage off the living room. Being cautious had saved her life many times in the past…

***

CHAPTER 17

MAJESTIC CASINO THEATER

A bewildered stagehand watched as the ragtag group of law enforcement people ran across the stage at him, led by a tall lanky guy who showed by his stride and demeanor he was in charge.

"Show us the shipment that came in this morning," Bart demanded.

The theater employee stared at Bart. *Who the hell does he think he is, barking orders at me?* He started to give him a piece of his mind when he saw Joe Anthony. "Right over there, sir!"

He pointed to a couple of crates sitting at the side of the stage. "Delivery guys said it was delicate electronics stuff...not to mess around with it. In fact, the head guy was darn near nasty about it…treated me like I was some kinda redhead stepchild that don't know no English!"

"Thanks, pardner." Bart reached the crates first and took note of the rubber-coated cable that led from one to another. It was thick and appeared to be either a power or control cable, or both. The crates were of a simple wooden design, similar to those used to ship cargo, except the top and sides were held together with screws instead of nails.

The shipping labels appeared to be genuine, although cleaner than he would have expected if the crates had been trucked in. There were markings on all sides that said Fragile, Handle With Extreme Care!

"We need a Phillips!"

Jake unzipped a side pants pocket, extracted a tool kit and opened it to show a variety of hand tools, including a ratcheting screwdriver that held an assortment of tips of various sizes. He selected a Phillips-head that looked like it would fit and handed it to Bart, who went to work on the first crate.

Jake pulled a Swiss Army knife out of still another pocket, selected the larger of two Phillips-heads and started to undo the screws on the lid of the other crate.

The others set to work assisting in whatever way they could. Johansen used a sat phone to update Colonel Jackson on the progress of the search while Benson quietly questioned the stagehand about the description of the man who delivered the crate. He positively identified Eichner from a casino surveillance photo.

"You men secure the area," Joe yelled to his men. *No idea*

257

what's in these things…Highly classified…Could be explosive.

The owner of the casino had directed him to provide any support that was needed and that was all he needed to know. Besides, it was a matter of national security and he knew that most questions would go unanswered.

His men quickly secured the theater and turned the lighting up to allow Bart and Jake to work on the crates. The radio in Joe's pocket crackled with an urgent message. "Hey, Colonel, finally got some good news!"

"About time, Joe. Could use some grins and giggles…"

"Gambler leaving the back parking lot reported a suspicious RV…Somebody banging on the inside. My guys found an old couple bound and gagged in the bathroom…Shaken up and bruised a little, but otherwise okay. Showed them a picture of that Eichner guy…They say he's the one who kidnapped them and drove their RV here."

"Great news…Glad they weren't hurt. They know anything about some equipment Eichner might've had with him?"

"That's where it gets a little crazy…Said he kept mumbling stuff about nuclear warheads and turning Tahoe into a big hole in the ground…Sounds like they're in shock to me…There's an empty cargo trailer he hooked to the back of their RV…Big enough to carry a number of crates like this."

"Looks like he's given us the slip…Anyway, can't worry about that right now…Need to deactivate this bad boy sooner instead of later."

Bart bent back over the crate and resumed his task. The theater was colder than he usually preferred, but that didn't stop beads of sweat from running into his eyes. He wiped them away with his sleeve and worked feverishly to gain access to whatever was inside.

He was the first to release the top on his crate—Jake was only a few seconds behind him. Bart stood up. "Wait, just a dadgum minute! We're not EOD...This could blow up in our faces!"

Anthony flinched at EOD. "A bomb? I thought this was top-secret comm gear that might interfere with the casino's computer systems." He wondered if he should contact Mister DePasquale, the casino manager. "Excuse me, Colonel, should we evacuate the building?"

Bart sighed heavily and shook his head. "Wouldn't do a bit of good...No car's fast enough to outrun this if it goes off. You've done all you can...except maybe pray."

Anthony's knees went weak. *Is it nuclear?* He wondered if he should call his wife, but knew she was only minutes away and could not outrun it either. "Do you have any idea about when..."

He was interrupted by Jay Johansen, "Hate to sound nervous...You looked at the remote lately?"

Bart did and replied, "Eighteen minutes, fifty-two seconds left...What's your point?"

"Might be a good idea to get back to it...The technicians say they've never worked with a version of this device that's been tampered with...May need all the wiggle room we can get."

CIA SAFE HOUSE OFFICE
SOUTH SHORE LODGE

The night clerk/agent tried desperately to stretch out his arm, hoping to avoid another blow from the pistol butt. His fingers fluttered and he couldn't hold his hand more than a foot off the floor.

The other hand held an ink pen, as if he was ready to check them in. He sat propped against the back wall behind the counter of the ersatz motel office. Blood from a sucking chest wound ran down the center of his body and formed a puddle between his legs. "I can't help you…"

His words were weak and the two figures in SWAT team gear crouched on either side of him leaned in closer to hear.

He waited until they were mere inches from him. "Your luck's run out, shit heads." He pressed the button on the ink pen and two ounces of C-4 were ignited by the piezoelectric spark. —not enough to bring the walls down, but more than enough to mortally wound anybody within six feet of the blast.

The counter was blown over and the explosion ignited two of the smoke grenades carried on the bulletproof vests of the Consortium hit-men. Within seconds the small office was filled with a choking fog that carried the stench of sulfur and lent a yellow color to the cloud.

Another figure tried to push his way through the twisted door and realized his two team-members were beyond assistance. He spun around to check the area for other operatives and came face-to-face with Ken Sobinak. He was raising his weapon, but stopped when he felt the barrel of a firearm prod him under the chin.

The owner spoke in low tones that were barely audible, "Twitch an eyelid and I'll paint the ceiling with your brains...clear?"

"You got the gun...you're the boss."

"Glad you understand that," said Ken. "How many on your team?"

"Team...What team?"

Ken rolled his eyes. "Five...four..."

"No, wait! Six...including the two in there." He nodded toward the demolished office.

"Who sent you?"

"Don't know..."

"Three...two..."

"I'm not lying. We get our orders from Peters...Don't tell us who's paying."

Sobiniak kept the pistol under the henchman's chin and eased back a little. "You know you're going to give me answers...The question is how painful it'll be."

A look of genuine fear showed on his face. "Gimme a break, okay?...I do what I'm told...Don't ask...they don't tell...Easier all around. Get my drift?"

Ken lowered the suppressed machine pistol and shot the now cowering figure in the leg. He shoved a forearm into the injured man's mouth to mute the forming scream.

A copious stream of blood immediately began to flow. "Look, Einstein, you need to remember who's holding the weapon. The bullet severed your femoral artery…You're going to bleed out in a few short minutes, pal. Tell me what I need to know and I'll put a tourniquet on it. Otherwise…kiss your ass goodbye."

The wounded man's eyes went wide and his muffled words indicated he was willing to cooperate. Ken slowly moved his arm away. "Now, who sent you and what were they after?"

The reply was squeezed through pain-clenched teeth, "Some dude called the Commissioner…"

"What's the mission objective?"

"Kidnap some female op…Picture in my vest pocket."

Ken carefully lifted the pocket flap, removed the photo and turned it over. He stared at a decade-old blurry image of a women in a business suit. He wasn't positive, but it looked like Delta.

The realization she was the target changed his priorities in a flash. He released the other man and turned to leave.

"Hey, we had a deal," the wounded man said. "You know, tourniquet…"

"You've got a belt…Do it yourself."

"What if I can't get it tight enough?"

"You die."

MAJESTIC CASINO THEATER

Bart and Jake crouched down and lifted the tops from the crate just enough to check for wires or sensors.

"Don't see any obvious booby traps," Bart noted as he

moved his penlight around the slight opening. "Let's slide the tops off...Damn, son, wires and precision parts all over the place...Looks like I got the grand prize."

"And I got the consolation prize," Jake countered. "Some sort of power supply setup...Now what?"

"Beats me all to hell." Bart rubbed the back of his neck. "Maybe the spooks can help." He pointed to Benson and Johansen and motioned for them to move closer.

Mary turned to the stagehand. "Please wait in the lobby, if you don't mind."

Jay finished his call and joined the group. "The eggheads say there are only a couple of ways Eichner could've rigged the bomb. Since they don't know exactly what he did...They say we need to cut power to the timer only."

"What if they're wrong? Thought they were supposed to be the experts...They know what they're talking about? "

"No clue...I'm just passing along what they said," Jay shot back. "Won't have to worry about it for very long...The clock is ticking."

"True on both points," Bart responded in a calm voice. "Since we don't know how to cut power to just the timer, seems to me we have three options. We can do nothing and the bomb goes off. We cut the cable and if we're wrong...the bomb goes off. Last, and hopefully best, we cut the cable...Bomb doesn't go off.

"Two out of three ways, the whole lake and half the mountains around here disappear in a blinding flash...Odds seem to be in favor of cutting the cable."

He moved closer to the crate and was greeted with 5 minutes and 12 seconds. "You're definitely right about one thing, though...running out of time. Anybody got a better idea?"

They stood mute, so Bart continued, "Guess we cut the cable...So how in God's name do we do it? Puppy's almost as thick as my arm...Sure won't do it with a pocketknife."

The cable was as thick as a flashlight, and covered with a tough-looking rubber coating. Bart doubted that even his razor sharp combat knife could cut through it fast enough to prevent a stray signal from reaching the bomb. "Doesn't look like armored cable, which is good...Do we have anything big enough to cut it?"

They looked frantically at each other, as if one of them might pull bolt cutters out of their back pocket.

Joanna Davies threw her hands out in front of her. "Wait! I know...a fire ax...If there's one around."

"Found one!" Benson yelled from behind the stage curtain moments after a frantic search ensued. She rolled her suit jacket around her elbow, smashed the glass front, grabbed the ax and ran over to the crates.

Bart looked around. "Guess it won't do any good to tell everybody to clear the area."

He swung the ax in a high arc over his head and brought it down as hard as he could on the cable, which parted with a flash. Winfield staggered back from the stench of ozone and burnt rubber and waved the smoke away from his face...

BLACKSTAR BOMBER

COMMISSIONER'S OFFICE
CONSORTIUM HEADQUARTERS

"What do you mean, the mission is falling apart? Explain!" the Commissioner roared into the phone.

Bernard Bergstrom, Acting Director of North American Operations for the Consortium was sweating profusely, in spite of the air conditioning in his office in Toronto.

It felt like the Commissioner could reach through the phone and choke him. He pushed the image from his mind and stuttered a reply, "I am in communication with Sparks…He says two of his team members have been killed and he is severely wounded."

"What about the other half of the team?"

"He doesn't know."

"Tell the team leader to terminate Sparks, per protocol and have him call me directly with an assessment of the situation."

"That's not possible, sir…Sparks says Jim Guidot is dead…A wounded CIA agent set off an explosive device and killed two of the team."

"Guidot was one of our best…What manner of incompetent fools did you send with him?" It was an indictment, not a question.

"One recent trainee," BB replied. "The rest were well-seasoned operatives…"

"We'll discuss it later. In the meantime, what are you doing to salvage the operation?

"I've ordered the backup team to get there as soon as possible. Weather conditions have cleared in the area and they will be able to helicopter in. They're thirty minutes away."

"Good...You may redeem yourself yet," the Commissioner replied in a sarcastic tone. I expect hourly updates and, for your sake, hope the backup team can complete what I thought was a simple abduction."

"But, sir," Bergstrom haltingly replied, "It is, after all, a CIA Safe House with a trained crew of operatives. You, yourself expected casualties..."

"One death, perhaps, and some minor injuries...Not a dead team leader and two other operatives unavailable. The thought of only two team members and a trainee left to secure the safe house is unsettling."

"I understand...but unfortunate occurrences can happen in a hastily assembled op...Surely, you must know that."

"What I *know* is you have not performed to expectations. I may need to consider a demotion...or worse, if this operation fails."

"That won't be necessary, Commissioner," BB pleaded. "I have been a faithful member..."

"That will be a factor in my decision," the Commissioner noted. "I have other missions to monitor...Call me in an hour with good news."

MAJESTIC CASINO THEATER

They stood frozen in place. Bart looked down into the crate. The numbers on the timer had dimmed considerably, but the count continued down through 4 minutes and 14 seconds. "It's still going! Jay, ask your so-called experts what the hell's going on!"

Jay spoke frantically into the phone while they anxiously waited.

"Tell 'em to get a move on…"

"Can't tell them anything…They're arguing with each other, trying to figure out why it's still ticking."

Bart rubbed his hands through his hair and let out an exasperated sigh. "Power's coming from somewhere, like a battery, maybe."

They leaned over the crate and concentrated on the contents. A smoothly polished cylinder dominated the device, with control wires running from it to the molded box at the other end that contained the timer.

The steady march of numbers passed down through 3 minutes and 15 seconds and the smell of desperation hung heavily in the theater.

Bart was so absorbed with the timer itself he had not paid much attention to the small black box attached to the back of the timer. "Hey, Jake, does that look like one of the batteries we use in our field radios?"

"Sure does," Jake's face lit up. "Red and black wires lead over to the timer…Gotta be the back-up. Let's cut them!"

"Whoa, there, son…Might not be the best way to go. Let's wait and see what the so-called experts come up with. Although, Nora has her own definition of an expert…She says an "ex" is a has-been and a "spurt" is a drip under pressure."

The joke brought only a wan smile from the others. "Tough crowd," Bart commented.

A few of them laughed at that and Joanna spoke up, "This close to being vaporized tends to dampen your sense of humor, sir. I'm not worried, though…If anybody can figure this out, Colonel, I'd put my money on you."

"I'll second that," Jake chimed in.

"Me, too," Mary added.

"Thanks for the vote of confidence," Bart answered. "Jay, what's the word?"

Jay shrugged his shoulders and pointed to the phone. His expression said it all.

"This isn't getting us anywhere," Jake finally said. "Let's cut the wires…Worked before…ought to work again."

"Again, let's not be hasty," Bart answered. "We're all frustrated, but maybe we need to step back…Shouldn't take another big chance 'til we at least hear from them."

He leaned over the crate and the numbers faintly marked 2 minutes and 49 seconds before detonation.

They froze in position and waited for a cue. Tension in the room seemed to lend a yellow haze to everything and the seconds ticked by like hours.

Johansen finished the conversation with a perplexed look. "Can't seem to agree with each other. First, they tell me to disconnect any battery we find…Then they say that might release the control rods and set the thing off. Don't seem to have a clue…Think we're pretty much on our own."

"Of course we are," Mary Benson added sarcastically.

"They're a thousand miles away and will probably wake up in the morning without a mushroom cloud hanging over them. Almost out of time and looks like a coin toss is the best chance we've got!"

"Truer words were never spoken," said Bart. "One way or the other, we're gonna have to do something...Timer says 2 minutes and 31 seconds. What's it gonna be, y'all?...Red wire or black?"

Joe walked up behind the group. "Why not both?"

"Cut them together..." Bart replied. "...could get a tiny surge that'd reset the timer to zero...Probably has capacitors built in that store enough energy to trigger the bomb after the power's cut. Cut one wire...lets those capacitors discharge harmlessly."

"Wow, Colonel," Joanna commented, "You sure do know an awful lot about nuclear weapons!"

"Not really..." Bart grinned. "Saw it in a movie."

"I'm no rocket scientist or expert, for that matter," Jake said. "But if it's like a car...Red wire is hot and black is ground. Cut the black wire first...It might have enough power to detonate."

"You sure?"

Jake stammered slightly, "No...but if it was up to me, I'd cut the red one."

Bart looked around the stage. "Any better idea?"

Nobody spoke.

"Then I'm gonna cut the red one...Soon as my hand stops shaking."

"Want me to do it?" Jake offered.

"No thanks, son…It's on my shoulders…That's why I get paid the big bucks."

Bart wiped sweat away from his forehead with his sleeve. The now-pinkish glow from the timer showed 1 minute and 21 seconds. He opened the stainless steel fingernail clippers on his Swiss Army knife, looked up and muttered under his breath, "Dear Lord, guide my hand."

"Didn't realize you were religious," Jake commented.

Bart started to snap back a terse reply, but answered instead, "At a time like this everybody gets religion…Besides, asking for divine intervention can't hurt, can it?"

His hand moved toward the red wire as the timer blinked 57 seconds. "Let's make the big leap," he mumbled as he snipped the wire…

LOVE'S TRUCK STOP
FERNLEY, NV

"I asked for you, Bergstrom, not one of your flunkies. Don't ever shuffle me off to them again, understood?" Rick Eichner kept his voice as low as he could while suppressing his anger.

He stood at a pay telephone in the Trucker's Lounge. Dressed in faded jeans, dusty cowboy boots and a long sleeve plaid cotton shirt, he looked like any of the long-haul truckers watching TV or reading magazines that mostly featured big rigs on the cover.

The room had the smell of a high school locker room from men and woman who were waiting to use the showers. He took the yellow Cat Diesel cap off, slapped it against his leg and put it back on his head. His next words were chosen for effect.

"You have one minute to get the information or I call your boss!"

"Be right back...Don't go away," Bernard pleaded.

"One minute..." Eichner hummed to himself while he waited.

One of the three other pay phones was in use and the third was out of order, so it was not surprising that another trucker stepped in front of him. "You done?" he demanded with a growl. "I gotta a load to check on."

"Tough shit," Eichner hissed back. "Go take a shower so I don't have to smell you."

The trucker moved in close enough to smell the hot dog he had for lunch and poked Rick in the chest with his forefinger. "Who the hell you think you're talking to, asshole?" Each word was punctuated with enough force to knock most men off balance.

Rick used the knuckles of his right hand to deliver a lightning fast, powerful blow to the driver's throat. The man gasped for breath and sank red-faced to his knees. It happened so fast that only a few of the other drivers in the lounge noticed. They continued watching an old episode of *Walker, Texas Ranger* on the wall-mounted television.

Bergstrom chose that moment to return to the phone and Eichner turned his attention back to the call.

"I'm afraid I don't have all the information you requested, Mister Eichner. We haven't finished our research..."

271

T.C. Miller

"Give me what you have…I'll call for the rest later."

"Certainly, sir…We confirmed that Benson and Johansen work for the NSA in a highly classified special assignment. There is little information on two of the Air Force people, Thomas and Davies…We think they are what they appear to be…active duty enlisted people who work in the security field…"

"You mean, intel work?"

"No…Security Police…base-level cops."

"Why would they be involved?"

"Don't know…perhaps because of your actions at Mather Air Force Base?"

"What about that Lieutenant Colonel, Winfield?"

"Gets interesting there. According to our source, there is a seven year gap in his military history. He was ostensibly assigned to a plans office at the Pentagon…which would make sense at that point in his career. There was even a lease executed on a townhouse in Rockville, Maryland, which would be normal. We found anomalies in other areas, however."

"Like what?"

"He was never issued a parking permit for any of the Pentagon parking lots…Should have had one, even though 0-5s are fairly common there."

"Maybe he used the subway…"

"If so, he paid cash…no Metro Pass purchases. Furthermore, a check of his credit card records shows only occasional purchases in the DC area…I doubt he actually lived there."

"Then where was he?"

272

"Still trying to pin that down…I asked the Commissioner to use his high-level sources, but haven't heard back."

"What about Winfield's wife?"

"Started checking her out and ran into a dead end…"

"Dead end?"

"Yes. We know they married before the Pentagon assignment and she was in OSI, the Air Force division that includes intelligence gathering. It appears, however, that she left the military shortly after they married."

"Not unusual, if he didn't want her working outside the home."

"That's what we thought, until we found her name on a classified visitor's log at CIA headquarters."

"Maybe visiting an old friend…"

"Not likely…she signed into Human Resources for new employee indoctrination."

"Hmm, that changes everything…Where is she now?"

"At a CIA safe house in Tahoe…"

"Why didn't you say that in the beginning? Give me the address."

"The Commissioner will have to authorize the release of that…"

"Then I'll call him."

Rick hung up the phone and started to dial the Commissioner when he realized half a dozen men were gathered around the prone trucker. They had revived him and he sat up against a row of plastic chairs, unable to talk. He pointed to Rick, who returned the gesture with an icy stare.

T.C. Miller

"Be glad you're still alive," he said as he strolled casually out of the room. Nobody followed.

COMMISSIONER'S OFFICE
CONSORTIUM HEADQUARTERS

"I thought you would want to know that Eichner called me…"

"Yes, Bergstrom," the Commissioner answered. "Did you give him the information he requested?"

"Not entirely…Considering the sensitivity and our gentlemen's agreement with the Agency, I told him to contact you…"

"This is why you will never become the permanent director…Eichner is paying a small fortune in fees to us. You should have considered that and given him the address."

"I was only trying to protect…"

"You were trying to protect yourself and angered a client in the process. An abundance of caution is not reason for dismissal from our organization. However, it can place roadblocks in your career path."

"But, sir…"

"I have no time for this, Bergstrom. I will wait for Mister Eichner's call…We both need to get back to our jobs."

The line went dead.

***

CHAPTER 18

CIA SAFE HOUSE SECURITY CENTER
SOUTH SHORE LODGE

Nora/Delta looked around the cave and wondered how it got its name—no rocks or dirt were visible. It was a series of connected rooms behind the false wall in the living room that included a guards room, communal bathroom, two guest rooms with a private bath between them and the security room where she sat at an alarm console with built-in monitors.

Surveillance through twenty-one cameras in and around the safe house gave her an unimpeded view of almost every square foot of the property. Hidden microphones let her listen to sounds from inside and out. She could direct cameras with a joystick control to zoom in and out and adjust focus.

The door between the main part of the house and the cave was securely locked with a multiple pin system similar to a bank vault door. It was made of inch and a half thick titanium steel that could only be penetrated with explosives and, even then, with some difficulty.

She had her venerable Walther PPK on the console, along with four magazines loaded with .380 Glazer ammo. A specially modified M16 with a short barrel and suppresser sat next to it, as well as four magazines of .556 ammo. It came from a walk-in closet-sized gun safe in the corner.

Her attention at the moment was directed to one of the monitors that showed a dark-suited figure lurking among trees at the edge of the parking area. No identification was possible, even when she shifted the camera to night-vision mode.

He wore a balaclava mask to conceal his facial features and there were no identifying name tags or patches on his SWAT team uniform.

She keyed the radio mike. "Delta to SH-1, what is your twenty?"

"Can't say...bogeys in the area may be monitoring us," came the reply from Ken Sobiniak.

Nora doubted the possibility, since the radios were encrypted and thought maybe the CIA had become a little paranoid. "Be advised, I have one just outside the house in the line of trees on the west side of the parking area."

"What's he doing?"

"Nothing...which seems strange. He's geared up for covert work, but just standing there. Could be a lookout, I suppose."

"Who knows?...Thanks for the heads-up. I'll secure the office area and check him out on the way back. ETA in fifteen minutes.

Nora's attention was drawn to another monitor which showed two figures in the same style clothing approaching the front entrance in duck-and-cover movements. She flipped a cover off the switch on the console that controlled the trapdoor built into the front entry concrete pad. The camera above the door should give her a nice view of the surprised look on their faces when the bottom dropped out. She patiently waited for them to step onto the porch .

Instead, when they were only a couple of strides away they split up and went to a window on either side of the stoop, attached small shaped-charges to the window frames and stepped to the side. A quick push of the button on a detonator and the metal bars and window were gone in a puff of smoke and a flash of yellow light.

The intruders crawled through the openings and Nora switched to another camera that showed the living room area. The invaders went straight to the panel in the wall that concealed the passageway to the cave...

MAJESTIC CASINO THEATER

They waited for the brilliant white flash that never came. There was a slight whine from the crate that wound down to a gentle whirring and stopped after a few seconds. The group leaned over the edge and stared at the darkened timer. Cheering and cries of joy broke out as they jumped up and down. Jake found himself hugging Joanna and it felt good. It went on longer than it should have and they finally broke off the embrace, stepped back and high-fived each other.

Bart exhaled heavily and sat down on the edge of the crate. "Whew, that was closer than stink on a skunk!"

The theater echoed with laughter. Jay told the scientists at the other end of the line the bomb had been deactivated. He rolled his eyes and shrugged. "They said to have a drink on them."

"Sounds like the only good idea they've come up with today," Bart replied. "Come on, y'all, let's go put down a few."

He yelled across the stage at Anthony, who was giving directions to some of his staff, "Hey, Joe, wouldn't happen to know where a body could get a cold one, now would you?"

"As a matter of fact, I would," he answered with a big grin. "And your money's no good here...Drinks are on the house! Mister DePasquale, the manager, says you're his guests...He also said to forget about driving back to Sacramento tonight. You're staying in high-roller suites for as long as you want."

"Awfully nice of him," Bart said.

"He appreciates it when someone keeps his casino from becoming nothing but a big hole in the ground."

"I believe we'll take ya'll up on that offer, at least for one night."

Bart lowered his voice and turned back to the team, "Need to call Colonel Jackson when we get downstairs and tell him to get a Nuclear Emergency Security Team up here to retrieve the bomb and secure the area. We'll take turns guarding the weapons until the NEST arrives. Who wants the first four-hour shift?"

Mary Benson raised her hand. "Johansen and I'll take the first shift, if you don't mind...We need to make some calls, anyway."

"Suits me. By the way, I'm impressed with the way you and Johansen worked with us...smoke grenade thing aside. Bless your hearts, ya'll can come work with me anytime you want."

Mary returned a tight smile and Jay nodded his head. "Appreciate that, Colonel...We don't often get thanks from people outside our agency, since they don't even know we exist...It's been a pleasure working with you and your team."

Bart turned the phrase, "your team" over in his mind. It felt right. "Feels like I've been born again, y'all!" He guided them toward the exit as he leaned in close to Jake and Joanna. "Good job...This will reflect most favorably in your performance reports."

Jake suddenly exclaimed, "Wait, what about Eichner!...We forgot all about him!"

Bart stopped in mid-stride. "Well, slap Aunt Gussie in the face, you're right! Been so busy trying to keep it in one piece, that jasper slipped my mind entirely. Hey, Joe, your people know what happened to him?"

"No idea...Asked the local police to put a BOLO out...probably in the wind. Didn't want to distract you while you were working on the bomb...Found two of my men dead in the kitchen. Eichner apparently got the drop on them and escaped down a service elevator...."

"Sorry to hear about your men," said Bart. "May have gotten away...but hopefully empty-handed...right? We'll have to let civilian law catch 'im."

Joe gave Bart a puzzled look. "Thought Colonel was a nickname...You mean you're a real colonel?"

"Didn't say that..."

Joe dropped the subject. "Well, hell, what difference does it make? We're alive...right? That's all that matters."

The rest of the group mumbled in agreement. Benson and Johansen stayed behind with two casino security men to guard the inactive weapon.

"Eichner's somebody else's problem now," Bart noted.

He thought he heard Benson mumble something like, "Wouldn't be so sure of that." At least that's what it sounded like. The excited voices of other people were so loud, she may have said something else. *Don't matter...Probably never see them again.* They were in an entirely different business...one that could consume a person if you let it.

"Y'all stay awake and we'll be back up in four hours to spell you," Bart said over his shoulder. "We'll do paperwork back at the base tomorrow. Last one to the elevator is it."

He took a few steps when the sat phone beeped. "Must be Colonel Jackson," he mumbled as he pressed the receive button. "J.J. do I have some good news..."

"Bart, it's Nora. We need your help...now!"

"Where are you, baby?...What's goin' on?"

"An assault team is attacking the safe house...I'm hiding in the cave, but it's only a matter of time til they break through the hidden door."

"They know about the cave? Stay put…I'll be there fast as I can. Joe, do you have access to a chopper?"

"Mister Lemonica's private bird is on the roof above us…"

"Need to borrow it."

Joe was already on the radio, "Says it's okay with him, but his pilot has the day off."

"I can fly it," Bart said.

"Then follow me, I'll help you prep it."

CONSORTIUM EMERGENCY RECOVERY TEAM HELICOPTER

"Best landing site is either on the beach or in the parking area in front of the safe house," the copilot of the of the Aerospatiale SA 330L Puma, informed the pilot. "Although, clearance in front of the target might be a little tight, due to trees."

The flight from Sacramento had been uneventful as the two 1,575 hp roof-mounted turboshaft engines effortlessly powered the four-bladed main rotor up from near sea level to the 6224 foot level of Lake Tahoe.

The medium-duty helicopter was ideal for this sort of operation. A six-man team of operatives lounged comfortably in a cabin that could hold up to 16 passengers. The starboard side-door contained a hoist that could be used to retrieve equipment or the occasional casualty.

"How far is it from the beach to the objective?"

"About a hundred meters," answered the copilot.

"I've flown into some crazy-ass tight spots, especially in Europe…prefer to avoid them whenever possible."

"Heard that," the copilot answered. "Guess it'll be the beach…right?"

"Unless we see something on approach that indicates a problem…Tell the team we're twenty minutes out."

"Roger that."

The copilot turned around and entered the main cabin, nudging the six men as he moved around the folding seats. "Wake up, Sunshine," he said to nobody in particular. "Twenty minutes 'til play time."

A tense encounter years before taught him to avoid engaging individual operatives unless absolutely necessary. Most of them used travel time to psyche themselves up for a mission and had personal routines they followed.

Some went through mental exercises designed to sharpen their observational skills. Others relived past missions and a tiny minority prayed, although most knew their occupation separated them from any real chance at redemption.

A crew member who served as both flight engineer and loadmaster moved over to the sliding cargo door.

Satisfied they all got the message, the copilot returned to his seat and stared out at the beautiful pine forests that led up to the largest alpine lake in North America.

APPROACH TO SOUTH SHORE LODGE
CIA SAFE HOUSE

"Man, you fly this thing like it's part of you," Jake noted from the copilot seat of the Bell Long Ranger helicopter.

It had taken less than ten minutes to untie and prep the bird for flight and another six minutes to get to the South Shore Lodge.

"Done a few trips in similar ones," Bart replied. "Gonna set down in that meadow across the road from the front of the lodge…Be a five minute hike to the safe house…Tell everybody to gear up."

It was an unnecessary command. They had been ready since leaving the roof of the Majestic Casino.

"Never been in a luxury chopper before," Joanna commented. "Actually, never been on a helicopter at all, unless you count the ones in front of the Piggly Wiggly that you put quarters in."

Her remarks brought smiles to the other members of the team.

Bart had decided to let casino security guard the weapons he and Jake disarmed and left Joe Anthony in charge.

Benson, Johansen, Davies, Thomas and Bart, along with the CIA resident staff should be enough to handle the small crew that was attacking the safe house. Nora had told him that Ken Sobiniak thought there were probably a half dozen or so intruders.

Bart wasn't concerned about the numbers so much as the timing. The attack was well under way and appeared to be backed with solid intelligence.

Their biggest asset might turn out to be the facility.

Surveillance equipment, sensors and counter-personnel measures were extensive and supplied a first-line of defense.

He switched on the intercom. "This is not going to be a cavalry charge to the safe house. We'll move in as two teams...Benson and I will go down the main road. Thomas will lead Davies and Johansen down the back service road.

"Suppressed weapons will give us a slight advantage, but when you can, use your hands or your knife to take them out. Just remember, they're trained and experienced...Questions?"

Silence was the only answer as the helicopter touched down in the unlit meadow and the rotors spooled to a stop. Bart was out and opened the door to the passenger cabin so the others could pile out.

They crossed the road and moved past the blast-damaged office as the smell of burnt flesh and wood wafted toward them. A split in the road led either toward the front of the cabins or to the rear service road.

Jake touched Bart on the shoulder as they reached the fork. "Sounds like a chopper coming in over the lake," he whispered.

"Got it...Take the back road. I'll leave Benson near the front of the safe house while I check out the beach."

Bart could see a figure about fifty feet in front of them moving covertly down the dirt road using the pine needle-coated surface to mask his movement. He also used the numerous pine trees lining the road as concealment.

Winfield waited until he was close enough to control the situation and whispered, "Freeze...One wrong move and I'll cut you down."

The figure responded in a low voice that brought memories of joint operations with the Agency, "I'm a federal agent…Identify yourself."

"Winfield, who are you?"

"Bart…that you? Ken…Ken Sobiniak." He slowly turned around. "Don't know of too many people who could get the drop on me. Nora's in the safe house security center."

"I know…she called. Got here fast as I could." He motioned for Benson to move up to them.

The sound of a helicopter flying low came over the lake reached them as a muffled wump-wump-wump. "You wanna take the house or the chopper?"

Ken didn't hesitate. "Don't have time to give you the passcodes…"

"I'll take Benson to cover me and give the chopper a hot welcome…Join you soon as I can."

Bart and Mary headed for the lake.

REAR OF THE SAFE HOUSE

Jake motioned for Johansen to cover the back of the building to make sure none of the attack team caught them by surprise. Jay took cover behind a dumpster and scanned the area for enemy operatives.

Joanna sneaked up to the kitchen door while Jake covered her and found it locked. She froze at the sound of an unfamiliar voice.

"You better hope you're with Winfield," a deep male voice

murmured.

"I am," she answered.

"What's his first name and his wife's name?"

"Colonel…I mean, Bart…and Nora."

"I'm Ken…"

Jake placed the barrel of his weapon squarely in the stranger's back. "Ken who?"

"Sobiniak…Bart sent me to help…Damn, that's twice tonight."

"That's Joanna…I'm Jake…Where's the Colonel?"

"Taking care of another problem down at the beach. Now that we've all been introduced, how 'bout we take back the safe house?"

Ken flipped over a six-inch long section of the back porch railing to reveal a hidden lighted key pad. He quickly entered an eight digit code. The door opened smoothly with a barely perceptible click and they slipped carefully into the kitchen, weapons at the ready. The smell of fried chicken greeted them and Jake felt his stomach growl. It was way past supper time.

Joanna carefully closed the door and locked it to prevent anybody from catching them by surprise. She followed a few steps behind them.

They paused at the doorway leading into the living room. Two figures dressed all in black were crouched in front of a section of the wall. They were placing det-cord and appeared to have almost completed the task of encircling the panel that hid the security room door.

Jake moved into the room just as one of them turned around.

They froze in place and the ninja-like figure reached for the pistol on his belt…

SAFE HOUSE BEACH AREA

The Consortium Puma came in low over the lake as it approached the beach near the safe house. The pilot waited until it was a few yards from land and executed a sharp ninety degree turn to place it parallel to the shore line. It hovered six feet above the water as he crabbed sideways until he was just over dry land.

"Don't see anybody…You? he asked the copilot.

They had both scanned the trees in back of the beach with night vision and infrared.

"Nothing bigger than a chipmunk," he answered.

"Guess we're okay…Open the cargo door."

Hans gave the sliding door a powerful pull and as it slid open he saw a figure step out from behind a tree and run full speed toward the chopper. "Uh, what the…"

His words were unintelligible to the flight crew and they continued to hover.

The running figure pulled the pin from an M15 white phosphorus grenade and tossed it at the open door.

Hans recognized the familiar gray grenade, known as a Willy Pete, by the yellow band of color around it and desperately tried to slam the door shut.

The incendiary device hit the edge of the door, ricocheted into the cabin, bounced off the bulkhead behind the co-pilot's seat and landed in the lap of one of the team members.

"Oh, God, Oh, God, Oh, God!"

The fuse ignited fifteen ounces of phosphorus and the surprised team member instantly had a five-thousand degree inferno between his legs.

His shrill scream was almost inhuman. He instinctively grabbed the device, burning his fingers to the bone in an instant as he tried to fling it out the now closed door.

The sizzling grenade careened and fell between the pilot and copilot as it blossomed into a full burn.

Smoke rapidly filled the interior and blinded everyone. The stench of burning flesh permeated the air.

The Puma rocked back and forth and tilted crazily one way and then another as the pilot reflexively moved it away from the landing zone and any further threat. It traveled about fifty yards offshore before the raging inferno reached the fuel tanks.

The massive yellow and orange fireball flared out in all directions as the flaming craft dropped into the water with a thud and a splash.

Bart ran to the edge of the beach in time to see the ball of white fire slowly sink into the 1,645 foot depths of the lake.

The phosphorus continued to burn brightly underwater, consuming the craft and its occupants as they disappeared into the inky depths.

Bart turned and headed back toward the safe house with Benson trailing him. He approached quietly from the side and spotted the figure Nora had mentioned crouching in the underbrush. The smell of pine needles wafted up as he moved up behind the man dressed all in black. Bart placed a combat knife against the man's throat.

"Move a muscle and it'll be the last thing you ever do," he hissed. "Hold your weapon to the side and drop it."

He complied. "Now, kneel down and cross your legs... Good. Put your hands behind your back..."

The enemy agent started to whirl around. Bart slammed the pommel of the knife against his head and watched him fall helplessly to the ground.

He used zip ties on the prone figure's hands and ankles and left him curled up on the ground in a fetal position.

Bart whistled quietly for Benson. She joined him from the lookout position where she had taken cover. They moved up to the gaping holes where the front windows had been and peered cautiously in.

The two Consortium men inside were almost finished rigging the det cord. One was twisting wires together and connecting them to a detonator while the other gathered up tools. The operative who was collecting tools suddenly stopped and turned toward the kitchen as he started to pull a weapon from his belt.

Bart leaned in the window with the MAC-10 and commanded, "Drop what you're holding and raise your hands."

At the same time, Jake barked, "Move and you die."

The befuddled man looked back and forth at Bart and then Jake. "Don't shoot...I'll tell you anything you want to know..."

The other enemy agent began to lower his right hand toward a leg holster.

"Not a smart move…One second to make a choice…live or die…Choose wisely," Bart offered.

The Consortium agent raised his hands and his accomplice followed suit. "Ain't gettin' paid to die."

"Smart man," Bart replied. "Hands behind your head, lock your fingers."

The two men started to comply when the one who had been rigging the charges reached down into his collar and extracted a wicked looking knife with a six-inch double-sided blade. He plunged it hilt-deep into his partner's heart and turned it around to throw at Bart.

Bart fired a quick burst that stitched him across the chest. Blood gushed out of his mouth as he dropped to the floor like a wet newspaper—dead before he got there.

"So much for questions," Bart commented.

Jake and Joanna joined Bart, Mary and Ken them in the living room.

Winfield leaned back and looked up in the direction of the hidden camera. "Hey darlin'…Mind lettin' us in?"

Nora closed the cover on the dungeon drop actuator and flicked a switch to release the electronic lock. She ran to the security room safe door and twirled the wheels that unlocked it. The last bolt released and she tugged the door open.

Bart swept Nora up in his arms. "My sweet baby," he whispered in her ear.

"My knight in shining armor," she whispered back. Her arms were wrapped tightly around his neck as they held each other in a tight embrace.

Ken searched the dead agents for any useful information and found a frequent-user reward card from a Sacramento strip club. It was the only clue to their identities. "Guess, this is all we get...Everything else is a dead-end."

"Wouldn't be so sure," Benson said. "We're beginning to establish a pattern of weaponry and clothing from a number of cases over the last five years."

"Who are they?" Bart asked.

"Don't know...still gathering intel."

"They're outfitted like a real TAC team," Nora observed. "Whoever's backing them doesn't mind spending a boatload of cash."

"Sure don't," Ken agreed. "If it was still the Cold War, I'd say the Soviets...But since they're more or less off the playing field...who knows?"

Bart interrupted their speculation, "Whoa, almost forgot, we have a prisoner...Maybe we can get something out of him."

The group gathered around the still-prone figure in black in front of the safe house and shined their flashlights on him. He was bleeding around the wrists where he had tried to free himself.

Bart was the first to speak, "Struggling is useless, pilgrim...Calm down and answer my questions."

He yanked the black balaclava mask from the captives head and lit his face with the flashlight. "Who are you...and who sent you?"

A sullen stare was the only reply. The Colonel studied the

young man's face and a feeling of deja vu swept over him like a wave. Something about this captive was familiar. He leaned in closer and looked into the root-beer brown eyes. "Do you recognize him?"

Nora had been standing in back of the rest of the group and stepped forward to get a better look. She crouched down and moved closer.

The look of shock on the captive's face grew with each heartbeat. He cleared his throat and spoke in a wavering voice, "Mom?"

***

EPILOGUE

NSA WEST COAST HEADQUARTERS
SOUTH SAN FRANCISCO BAY

They gathered in a secure conference room in a nondescript building across the street from a bay side trucking terminal. No signs identified the sole tenant of the four-story structure and mirrored glass prevented any view of the interior.

Entry to the facility was made through a double gate by contacting a security guard on an intercom system. The unseen guard opened it only after he checked a list of authorized visitors and ID was verified by an encrypted, closed-circuit television system.

A security post next to the elevator lobby allowed visitors to finally put a face to the guard through green-tinted, six-inch thick glass that could withstand the explosive force of a rocket-propelled grenade.

The elevator car was also hardened and could be sealed off with the flip of a switch to become a holding cell.

Each meeting attendee went through careful searches and was swept for recording and transmitting devices before entering the executive conference room. Security was tight because the most coveted secrets of the nation were discussed openly in the room.

The Director sat at the head of the table and rarely spoke, although clearly in charge. Visibly nervous agents directed their briefings to him. They seldom had an opportunity for face-to-face time with the old man—a legend in their line of work and knew that a few words from him could make or break a career.

He listened intently to elaborate slide presentations while an aide asked an occasional question or two. Finally, he turned to address the dozen people gathered around the conference table. "Thank you all for your valuable input. I don't think this affair could have been handled any better and I want to especially single out agents Benson and Johansen for their quick thinking and creative fieldwork."

The two agents tried to appear nonchalant, but still sat a little higher in their chairs. Praise was doled out sparingly and usually through an interoffice memo. Hearing it in person made it so much sweeter.

They knew the door to future promotions had opened a crack and were eager to wedge it open wider. The same door, however, could just as easily slam shut if mistakes were made.

The Director continued, "As you know, this case is far from closed, at least for our agency. This Eichner character is still on the loose with nuclear material…including a BlackStar system. That cannot be allowed to continue.

"The public version we released says Eichner died in a highway accident on a two-lane blacktop road in the Sierra Nevada mountains. It took local rescue teams a day to reach the wreckage and recover a mangled body that was burned beyond recognition. A clandestine switch of fingerprint and dental records ensured the body was identified as Eichner by the local coroner. The complete lack of family members means the body will be stored in a secure walk-in cooler from which it will eventually disappear.

"A cover story was created to leave the impression of a disgruntled, degenerate gambler who was trying to extort money from the casino. Their management was happy to go along with the tale, since it painted them in a favorable light.

"The device in the casino theater was labeled a bomb only after it was replaced by a credible mockup of something a knowledgeable person could build with readily available plans."

He took a slow drink of water and continued, "Joe Anthony was publicly credited for disarming the device and no mention was made of either our NSA team or their companion agents from Mather Air Force Base. I appreciate the discretion that has been shown up to this point and here's how I want this wrapped up."

The Director swiveled his chair to address Benson and

Johansen, "You will head the effort to recover the two missing devices and be given a number where I can be reached directly. I want a report every twenty-four hours...or sooner, if you encounter an emergency.

"Try to capture him without harm...Which means alive and in one piece. We need to interrogate him about many things, not just this incident. I have a feeling he'll prove valuable in uncovering other Soviet moles, as well as giving us more information about the operation of other foreign intelligence organizations...Remember, even the smallest detail can complete the puzzle."

It was a favorite saying of the director and was constantly emphasized at the Agency's training centers.

He leaned back in his chair. "I talked with the Secretary of Defense today. He wants their materiel, as he refers to the weapons, back in military hands as soon as possible. He also demanded that Air Force personnel be involved in the secret search for Eichner."

The Director sighed heavily. "My first inclination was to forcefully decline their assistance, but then I thought about the people from Mather and reconsidered. They worked well with you and their desire to avoid public exposure was admirable. I want you back here in two hours with plans to track and capture Eichner with their assistance...Questions?"

"No, sir."

"Good...Do your research and get back here ASAP."

Benson grabbed her notes and headed for the door with Johansen closely behind her.

The Director addressed the section chiefs, "I want one hundred percent of our assets available to them, since this is a major event in the agency's history…I won't tolerate even the smallest of screw-ups. Anyone who doesn't feel up to the task should have their resignation on my desk within the hour…Understood?"

Heads nodded, and the director turned to his assistant to discuss his appointment calendar for the rest of the day.

Benson pushed the elevator button.

Jay leaned toward her and said in a near-whisper, "Tell me again, why we're including the Air Force people?"

"The Director said to."

"I know…But why is he insisting?"

"Because he can…You heard what I heard. I just don't feel like being a wet-nurse to some junior spy wannabes."

"Understood, but they did a pretty good job in Tahoe, you know, considering their lack of experience…"

"Didn't call them inexperienced," she replied. "We know Thomas' background and the Colonel handled the bomb like a pro…strong, steady and confident.

"What have you dug up on him?"

"Not a whole lot…In fact, I pretty much hit a brick wall…"

"Brick wall? We should be able to access any file at any level…We're the freakin' NSA!"

"Not when it's "Eyes Only."

"By which agency?"

"POTUS."

He turned toward her with eyebrows raised. "The President put a lock on his file?"

"That's right…at least for a good chunk of this guy's Air Force career. Not even redacted…Simply doesn't exist. Like he was dead at certain times."

"How does his Air Force record account for those times?"

"Says he was on special assignment to the Secretary of the Air Force. Except when I checked SAF's files there wasn't anything to see."

"Why would POTUS pull him into his circle and classify it so high?"

"No idea…Apparently more than one occupant of the White House has done it. We're talking about work spread out over seventeen years…Ops files that are locked up tight on a need-to-know basis."

"Who is this guy, anyway?"

"Who knows? I get the feeling the Director does…Maybe that's why he told us to read the Colonel in on some of our most sensitive info…He'll crucify us if we don't."

"True…Look what happened to Brennan and Davis."

"Got what they deserved…You don't take a weekend off in Jamaica in the middle of an op and then try to cover it up."

"Think he'll ever let them work in the field again.?"

"Not likely."

The elevator chimed and they stepped in. Thankfully, there was no music playing. Benson touched the button for the fourth floor. "Would be nice to have a weekend off now and then…Guess that's not going to happen."

"Probably not," Jay replied. "What do you think about working with the Air Force people?"

"Doesn't really matter, does it?…Got no choice."

"Can they keep up?"

"After Tahoe, I'd say yes…Seem pretty sharp. Actually, truth be told, I'll look forward to working with them…Might take some of the pressure off us."

"Losing your drive?"

"No…Stronger than ever…Just like to have a day or two off every once and a while."

"Would be a nice change…and you never know…Might pick up a new perspective from them…different set of eyes and all that."

"Could be…stranger things have happened…"

CONSORTIUM HEADQUARTERS
CENTRAL EUROPE

"Must I remind you the Commission is not accustomed to failure?" The question was mostly rhetorical in nature.

"No, Herr Commissioner, of course not," replied Dieter Manheim, Deputy Commissioner of Operations. "We are seeking a more detailed examination of the failed mission…It appears that a team of intelligence agents headed by the American agent Tupelo…"

A look of scorn came over the Commissioner's face. "Tupelo dropped out of sight years ago…The identification must be flawed. Redouble your efforts."

"But sir, we examined surveillance recordings from the casino where the bomb was planted. There are over two thousand people on it and we excluded all but a handful."

He handed the Commissioner a still photograph taken from the casino recording. "This man seems to be the most likely candidate. It is not as clear as I would like and he may have undergone reconstructive surgery…"

"A logical assumption," the Commissioner interrupted as he examined the photo. *It does look like Tupelo.* "Do we have any corroborating evidence?"

"Our technicians managed to isolate his voice and compare it to a telephone conversation you had during the incident in London some years ago…It seems to be a close match according to our algorithms."

"But not exact?"

"Given the conditions under which the conversations were recorded and the subsequent elapse of time…I would not expect it to be perfect…It was, however, close enough to be worrisome."

The Commissioner rose from his chair and turned his back on Dieter to stare out the window. He spoke after a lengthy pause, "I do not worry excessively about one man. If Tupelo has resurfaced, he would be part of the overall equation, but not the ultimate threat."

Dieter noted the dismissive tone. "How do you want the matter concluded, sir?"

"Look further into the incident, but do it quietly. I do not want our veracity to be questioned and it might eventually prove to be a case of mistaken identity. I doubt that Tupelo knew I was observing him in Vienna. It seems unlikely he would surface after years of inactive service…and why now?"

"I do not have the answers. However, I have dispatched an agent masquerading as a member of the Nevada Gambling Commission to make inquiries at the casino. Perhaps we can backtrack through his current cover story to gain some insight into his true identity."

"Good thinking, as usual…If it was indeed Tupelo, it might change the nature of a select number of our operations. In fact, the first impact would be on Eichner's mission and how deeply it may have been compromised…Speaking of him, where was he headed after the debacle at the casino?"

"We have not been in touch with him since the incident. Our Mafia clients are profoundly worried the attack came so close to succeeding and are making inquiries about Eichner and his background. I suppose they might somehow discover his connection to the Consortium. How do you wish to handle that aspect?"

"It is possible they may find clues to his relationship with us, but no matter. I will call DePasquale and explain that Eichner requested our assistance in an operation he was planning without divulging the nature…or to whom it was directed. I can not, of course, discuss other clients, or even potential clients with him, but may intimate that we were involved in disarming the device. That should placate him…In fact, he may feel grateful."

"And if he makes further inquiries?"

"Of whom? Both the NSA and US military will deny any involvement in the disarming of the bomb…which should lead DePasquale to conclude it was our intervention that saved his business. He has no credible sources within either organization to uncover the truth and we do…That is why he pays us handsomely for information. Instruct our operatives to be alert for any questions from organized crime people, but I do not think it will be a problem."

"As usual, Herr Commissioner, you have given the situation considerable thought and produced a remarkably insightful commentary."

"Yes, I have. How do the Americans phrase it?" He chuckled. "That is why I am paid big bucks."

"Indeed, sir. Will there be anything else?"

"Unfortunately, yes. I am dissatisfied with Bernard Bergstrom's performance as Acting Director. Therefore, I am removing him from the post and replacing him with Arthur Magnuson."

"Is Bergstrom returning to the position of Director of Operations?"

"No."

International News Service (INS)

BREAKING NEWS BREAKING NEWS BREAKI
Toronto, Canada (**INS**)

November 14, 1989

A local businessman with international ties was killed in what is being termed a freak accident outside the building that housed the operation he headed, Consortium Business Associates.

Police report that Bernard Bergstrom, Acting Director for North American Operations, was leaving work for the day when the vehicle he was driving jumped a curb and ran over a natural gas line that served the building. The resulting explosion extensively damaged the building. Witnesses reported the blast could be felt and heard three blocks away and shattered windows in nearby buildings.

The fireball caused by the incident reached heights of sixty to seventy meters. Toronto Fire Service Captain Willis Hargis informed INS that his crews were on scene in less than ten minutes and were able to extinguish the blaze minutes after cutting off the gas supply.

Hargis speculated that Bergstrom may have suffered a sudden medical emergency. "It is my professional opinion the crash was an unfortunate accident. Arson investigators will conduct a routine investigation into the incident."

People departing the building moments before the accident said the driver was slumped over the wheel as the vehicle plowed through a landscaped garden and sheared off a meter attached to the gas line.

George Martin, an employee of the firm Bergstrom headed was quoted as saying, "My boss seemed to be unconscious and unaware of the fire, thank God. He'll be sorely missed."

He went on to note that Bernard was a confirmed life-long bachelor who is survived only by his mother, believed to be a resident of a nursing home in Ottawa."

Fire officials expect a final report to be released early next year.

****

BONUS PREVIEW

of

BLACK STAR BAY

Volume 2 in the

Black Star Ops Group Series

CHAPTER 1

CANNERY
NEAR SEAWIND BAY, CALIFORNIA

"Who's there?" she croaked through a dust-dry throat as the squeaking sound of rusty bedsprings pierced the darkness.

"Joanna...that you, Nora?"

"Yeah."

"You okay?"

"Think so...you?"

"Tasered...Shot me up with something. Where are we?"

"Some old building, from the musty smell.

"That other smell what I think it is?"

"You mean rat droppings and pee?"

"I hate rats!"

"Me, too. See the guys that got you?"

"No, we waited at the diner for a couple hours. Went to look for you...Got us in the parking lot...Real pros."

"Didn't see them?"

"Like I said, real pros...hit us from the side. Got a pretty good lick in on one...then they zapped me...Heard a sizzling sound before that...Guess they got Jake first. Woke up and heard snoring...thought you were one of them."

"That's okay...thought you were a rat." She laughed.

"Thanks a lot...Like I said, I hate rats!"

"It was the smell, and skittering around."

"Oh, don't say skittering...I'll come undone!"

She smiled at the indignant reply. "Gotta be honest, I'm scared. Was it them? What happens now?"

"Hard to say...Guess we need a plan...Any ideas?"

"Uh, uh, still coming to. Sure help if I could see."

"Yeah, adds new meaning to being in the dark, can't even see my own hand! Wait, think I see a crack of light under a door."

"Where?"

"Over there...other side of the room...Least I think it's a door...Can you get free?"

"Not sure. They did a pretty good search...gun's gone, knife's gone. Had a fingernail file in my back pocket, sure hope they missed it. Thank you, Jesus! Still there...if I can just get it..."

"Hurry, before they come back!"

"If I was going any faster, you'd see nothing but a blur."

"Can't see anything, anyway."

"Oh, sure, excuses."

"Best I got right now."

"All right…got a strand cut!"

"Way to go…Now hurry up!"

"Hold your horses, little missy." *She seems more like a daughter than anything.*

"Can't stand being tied up…Feel so damned helpless!"

"Yeah, it's the worst part…Okay, hands are free. Give me a minute, have my feet loose…there!" She carefully swung her feet over the edge of the bed and felt her shoes touch a hard, irregular surface. "Rough concrete."

"Okay, over here."

"Feeling with my foot…seems clear."

"Your voice…getting closer."

"Roger tha…ow! Hit a corner…like a box, maybe a footlocker…now a I feel a metal railing."

"The bed moved."

She felt like screaming with joy when their outstretched hands met, but remembered the situation, and remained silent. She felt the other woman tugging at the fingernail file. "No, don't," she whispered. "Let me get you loose…You're younger, and a better fighter."

"Why, thank you!"

"Welcome." *I'd rather be in this mess with her, than most people I know.* It didn't take as long as she thought to saw through the ropes that bound the other woman's legs to the bed. It took a little longer to free her hands, but her fellow team member soon stood on shaky legs. After a quick hug they turned and started moving slowly toward the sliver of light across the room.

They went carefully, searching for anything that might serve as a weapon. She felt like doing a happy dance when she nudged a piece of metal pipe on the floor that was as long as her arm. Finally, she reached out and touched the area above the sliver of light—it was a door. She turned around and whispered, "How do we get them in here?" Joanna shrugged her shoulders in an unseen reply.

"Can't bang on the door...They'd know we're free. Can't scream and yell...They'll know we've come to."

"What if I say you can't breathe?"

"They'll know we're awake."

Despair covered them like a wet blanket. Nora felt like sitting down on the floor and crying like a little girl. *Not giving up that easily...should ask her to slap me back to my senses.* Instead, she took a deep breath and slowly let it out.

Joanna sensed her frustration and whispered, "Time to put on big-girl panties and deal with it! We're warriors, right?"

"Hoo-rah!" she whispered back. "What would warriors do?"

"For a start, don't panic."

"How about a medical emergency?"

"Like they'd care...Prob'bly just feed us to the fishes...May be their plan, anyway."

"I think..."

Her sentence was interrupted by the metallic sounds of a padlock being opened on the other side of the door. *Dammit, eyes haven't adjusted.* The door began to swing open as the sliver of light became an ever-growing triangle that spread across the floor.

Joanna slipped behind the opening door as Nora stood frozen with indecision. A well-worn work boot stepped into the widening fan of light as the barrel of an automatic rifle was thrust cautiously ahead of the figure. The smell of body odor and tobacco breath wafted into the room. Nora faded back into the darkness and waited, her shoulder-length brunette hair offering some camouflage in the darkness. A sense of calm settled over her, as training and instinct took over. Adrenaline began to pump through her arteries and events seemed to play-out in slow motion.

Their captor was halfway through the door when she raised both hands and charged with all of her strength. *Take that, sucker.* The guard saw the movement and turned toward her just in time to have the edge of the door strike him from his groin to his forehead. He seemed to be divided in two with a look of shock frozen on the right half of his face.

Joanna gave the door a powerful kick, and the added force robbed the guard of consciousness. His eyes rolled up in his head and he slumped to the floor like a chocolate bunny left in the summer sun. The rifle fell away from him and Nora scooped it up, recognizing the AK-47 design in an instant. She pulled back the bolt to chamber a round and flicked the safety off. Her finger rested along the trigger guard—ready to release a spray of deadly fire on anybody unlucky enough to be in the hall.

A quick pull on the door revealed an empty corridor running thirty feet to a cavernous area that appeared to be part of a warehouse or factory. The hallway was lit by ceiling-mounted bulbs that cast an anemic yellow glow every ten feet or so. She returned to the room and grabbed a radio from the belt of the unconscious guard.

"Looks clear," she whispered to Joanna. "Smell the salt air? Must be close to the water." They moved carefully into the hallway. The younger woman pulled the door shut and replaced the lock. "Left the keys in his pocket...They'll have to find the spare. Let's see what's out here." They moved slowly down the hallway.

CANNERY
SEAWIND BAY, CALIFORNIA

Bart and Jake stood stock-still when they heard footsteps outside the partially-opened door. One of the kidnappers had come back to close the door, and was reaching for it when he looked Jake in the eye. He froze, trying to decide whether to reach down for the rifle he had leaned against the wall or continue to close the door—indecision cost him his life.

A throwing knife seemed to leap out of Jake's cargo pants pocket with a mind of its own and fly straight to the guard. It embedded itself almost fully in his chest and pierced the heart. A shocked look and one last gasp were the final conscious actions of his wasted life. He fell face-first to the stone floor. A few spasmodic jerks followed and a trickle of blood colored his lips. A final breath was squeezed from his body with a quiet sigh and he went limp.

"Nice throw…Glad we're on the same team." Bart patted him on the shoulder.

"Part of the job, sir." There was no emotion in his voice.

"Serious training, no doubt. Let's move on…see what we're facing."

Jake led the way to make sure that none of the guard's coworkers were waiting in ambush. The larger room was clear, and he motioned for his teammate to follow—which he did, slamming the door shut with a resounding clang.

"They'll think he's doing his job," Bart whispered.

Jake nodded from the center of a room that was half the size of a basketball court. Wooden shipping crates and cardboard boxes covered most of the floor. "Lot of stuff must've moved through here over the years."

"Intel said smuggling booze during prohibition was big bucks…the building was good cover."

"And the Russians are taking full advantage of it."

"Sure are…So what's behind door number two?" He pointed to the opposite wall and the only other exit from the crypt-like, brick-walled room. Surprisingly the hinges were well-oiled and opened silently.

Jake pulled a telescoping mirror out of his shirt pocket. Similar to what dentists use, it allowed him to see around corners without exposing himself to direct fire. He crouched down, stretched the mirror out, and peered around the door frame.

A hallway led only to the right and terminated at a door that had a window in the top half. It revealed a cavernous room on the other side that looked like the inside of a factory. An open-rafter ceiling held pipes and conveyor belt supports hung in a random pattern. Long strips of florescent lighting were covered with metal grills that protected the room below if a bulb should break. Dust mites floated in the flickering light. Age and a lack of cleaning lent a hazy-yellow hue to the window and obscured part of the view of the larger room.

They moved carefully up to the door. "Nobody in sight, want me to poke around?"

"No...since it's just two of us, we go in together...Duck and cover 'til we find something...We get separated, meet back here...Sound good?"

"You're the man with the plan...I'm ready anytime."

The door made a scraping sound as it opened far enough for them to pass through. Bart used his height advantage to peer over Jake's five-foot, eight-inch silhouette. They paused to see if there was a response, then slipped into the larger room. It was a secondary canning line for specialty items and mostly empty. A sliding door on the other side was propped open and gave a glimpse of the main part of the cannery.

They moved toward it in sequence—first one, and then the other—until they were within ten feet of the larger room. Each took a side of the door and peered into the larger room. Faint voices came through large double-doors on the other side of the main room that opened to a wharf. The smell of salt air and fish found its way under the door. The sun would set over the Pacific Ocean within the hour and automatic security lights were coming on. Their golden glow illuminated a fishing trawler and the gangplank that led to it.

Jake was about to move into the main room, when Bart put a hand across his chest to stop him. "Somebody's coming."

Excited murmuring emanated from the back wall of the main room where corridors branched off to other areas of the building. Two men were talking in one of the corridors, but Bart's Russian was rusty and he only picked up a word or two. He keyed his mike. "They're upset about something."

"Yeah...none too happy."

Two burly figures dressed in black tactical gear burst out of the far corridor at a near-run and headed toward the door that led to the wharf. One stepped out and yelled something in a Slavic language to a guard on the trawler. In less than a minute, two figures came out of the pilot house and ran down the gangplank. They entered a yellow pool of light as they stepped on to the wharf and Bart was able to identify them.

"They're both here."

Jake started to move, until he was once again restrained. "Whoa, there...let's not get hasty."

His expression turned in a flash from one of annoyance at being restrained to a question. "What?"

"Don't know if the women are here or on the trawler. We force those two back on the boat, they might leave...Helluva lot harder to stop them on the water...Let's search the building."

"Good point. Two hallways...Each take one?"

"Negative…Stick together and cover our sixes…I'll take point."

"Right behind you, boss."

"Hallways look the same…take the first."

Two doors on the right and one further down on the left lined the thirty-foot hallway. Bart's senses were hyperactive, and he moved slowly to avoid detection. Still, even the gentle rustling of his tactical rip-stop pants was magnified to a point that seemed to deafen him. He reached for the first door and eased it open. It appeared to be nothing more than a storage area with work tables and shelves.

He gently pulled the door shut and signaled for Jake to follow him to the next room. The beam of his flashlight swept the room until he realized that it was the guard's quarters. A strong smell of body odor and whiskey assaulted his nostrils. Two bunks were occupied by what were probably sentries who had just gotten to sleep. An irritated voice mumbled something in Russian and Bart replied with a "sorry"—in Russian.

They backed out of the room and gently closed the door. Jake pulled a double-tube of super epoxy out of a pouch on his belt and ran a bead down the closing edge of the door. He squirted a little into the latch and the lock and stepped back to avoid inhaling the fumes. Within seconds, the door was secured as tightly as if they had nailed it shut. "Hold 'em for awhile…Have to kick their way out." He grinned.

"Good work…Move to the last door."

"Padlocked."

"Got your picks?"

"Always." The lock clicked open in no time, but the door would not budge. "Blocked." He pulled the telescoping mirror from his pocket and extended it underneath. "Almost dark...Whoa, looks like a body."

"Push."

The combined force of the two men gradually moved the door open wide enough for them to squeeze into the room. Bart found a light switch high on the wall and wavering florescent lights flickered slowly to life.

"Damn, this bad boy took a beating." Jake followed up his words by putting a finger on the prone figure's neck and shaking his head from side to side. "Dead."

"Must've taken a while...Scratches on the door...You'd think he'd have a radio."

"Empty bracket on his belt...radio's gone."

Bart pointed to the other side of the room. "Two prisoners were here...I swear I can smell Nora's perfume. So where are they?"

"Trawler's my guess."

"Maybe, but why all the commotion? Might could be they escaped."

"Not down this hallway...would've seen them."

"Maybe got out earlier."

"Could be..."

"Look out!"

Bart's warning was a second too late. Jake was kneeling next to the body when he was bowled over by the door being pushed open further. The impact sent him sprawling over the body as two dark-suited figures forced their way into the room. He drew a suppressed pistol from a holster on his vest and shot the first guard twice in the face at close range. The dying body pitched forward and trapped him.

The second guard stood still—eyes opened wide—with his partner's brains splattered all over him. He wiped his eyes with a sleeve as Bart snapped off a round. It went wide and caused an explosion of splinters that sprayed the guard in the face. He raised his arm again to protect his eyes and a second shot hit him below the chin. He dropped his hands to his throat as blood spurted between his fingers. The impact of a third shot thrust him backward and halfway into the hallway.

Jake squirmed his way out from under the body of the first guard, pulled the second guard in from the hallway with Bart's help and closed the door. "Thanks, Boss, think anybody heard?"

"Won't matter…They got three men missing…Won't take 'em long to figure out it's not a smoke break…Better get moving."

The radio on the dead guard's belt squawked, followed by a voice in Russian.

"What'd they say?"

"Not sure…Sounds like they're pissed, though…Let's move."

"Roger that," Jake cautiously opened the door and waited while his teammate stepped through. He closed the door and replaced the padlock—after pulling a few pieces of wire out of a pouch and stuffing them into the lock. Even the original key couldn't open it now. "Slow 'em down a bit…Shame there was no time to set a trap."

Bart grinned. "Not as much time as I'd like...But I popped the pin on a grenade...wedged it under one of the bodies...Old Viet Cong trick." He looked around. "We're a little out in the open...slip in there." Motioning for him to follow, he moved into the storage room they searched earlier and closed the door behind them.

Jake sat down on a work table and relaxed as much as anyone ever could in combat. "Month ago, could you imagine yourself here?"

"Not on your life, son...Not on your life."

***

TIMBER CREEK PRESS